BETTER OFF UNDEAD

CYNTHIA EDEN

Published by Cynthia Eden.

Cover art and design by: Sweet 'N Spicy Designs

Proof-reading by: J. R. T. Editing

Print 5-1

CHAPTER ONE

Monsters were real, and she was the one who had to deal with their drama on a daily basis. Detective Mary Jane "*Just Jane – Only Jane*" Hart was well and truly tired of their paranormal bullshit.

Hunting human killers was hard enough. But hunting paranormal murderers? That was a whole new level of dangerous.

Jane eased out a long breath as she stared down at the victim before her. Another night, another body. She was starting to think this unfortunate trend was the new story of her life. Carefully, not wanting to contaminate the scene but needing to get closer, Jane crept toward the body.

A male, fit, looked to be in his early twenties. Handsome, at least, he *had* been. Before some *thing* with very sharp claws had gotten hold of the guy. Now the poor vic had deep slash marks all over his face and body. The left side of his face showed four long, bloody slashes. The right was a mirror image. The fellow's throat had been ripped open and his body was bloody — his clothes torn. *More slashes.*

This hadn't been some easy death. The victim had been tortured before he'd finally been put out of his misery.

Someone had been playing with his prey.

"A cemetery," the nervous mutter came from behind her. "Poor guy was m-murdered out here?"

Jane schooled her features before she glanced back at the uniformed cop who was practically shaking in his standard issue shoes. Mason Mitchell was a good cop. Sure, he was still green on the job, and that was just one of the many reasons he appeared to be on the verge of either vomiting or passing out, but he was *solid.* He did the right thing, and the fellow genuinely wanted to help others.

Too bad he was playing way out of his league with this particular murder.

Mason had been the one to find the body. The one to put in the call to the station. The one to get Jane out there. Because certain cases were always referred to her these nights…any case that so much as hinted at being the work of a monster.

No way a human left those slash marks on the victim. Too deep. Too long. Too much like the marks that would be made from claws.

Her gaze darted to the ground. She didn't see any footprints, but it was damn dark. She'd need a crime scene team out there, ASAP. She would also need to get the medical examiner, Dr. Bob Heider, on the case immediately. Like her, Dr. Bob knew the score and he would —

"*Jane…*"

The whisper of her name was so low that, for a moment, she thought that she'd imagined it. But —

"*Jane…*" Low, but definitely real. She spun around, her gaze trekking over the cemetery. It was night, too freaking dark out there, and the heavy stone crypts and mausoleums seemed to surround her.

In New Orleans, people weren't buried in the ground. The dead were put in the above-ground crypts and mausoleums for protection, and well — now the tourists sure loved to come to the "Cities of the Dead" to walk around and hunt for ghosts.

And vampires.

Be careful what you look for…you just might find what you seek.

"Detective Hart?" Mason called nervously. "Is everything all right?"

Her hand had dropped to her holster. She wasn't packing normal bullets in her gun, not these days. After her last big case, when she'd learned the truth about monsters, Jane had made it a point to always be prepared. *A smart woman keeps silver bullets and a stake at the ready.* "Did you hear someone calling me?"

"Um, yeah, I was calling—"

"*Jane...Hart...*" That rasping voice said her name again, only it was louder this time.

Mason shut up.

Jane tensed. Okay, so someone was hiding in the dark, calling her name, and watching as she stood over a dead body. Not suspicious at all.

Right.

Jane yanked out her weapon. "Stay with the body," she ordered Mason. Because a body disappearing in this town? Oh, yeah, that happened. Far too often for her liking.

She rushed forward, heading into the deeper shadows of the cemetery. That voice had sounded as if it came from up ahead, to the right. If the killer was hanging out up there, thinking he could jerk her around, then the guy needed to think the hell again. Her right hand gripped the gun while her left held a small flash light, a light that she positioned directly over her weapon.

I will take you down. No one gets away with murdering humans on my watch.

And, for the moment, anyway, Jane was assuming the dead man was a human.

She passed the broken statue of an angel— one of its wings had fallen to the ground. Jane hurried past the angel, slid between two tall crypts and—

"Put your hands up," Jane snarled to the shadow she saw there. "I don't know who you are or what you *think* is happening—"

A woman screamed. High pitched. Terrified. The shadow burst apart, and Jane realized she was staring at *two* people, not one. Her light hit the couple—young, maybe teens. The girl was wearing heavy Goth make-up while the boy looked like some kind of surfer, only when the surfer opened his mouth—

Fangs. He has fangs. "I will shoot you right now," Jane snarled at him. "If you have so much as *bruised* her, I will—"

"Relax, Jane, he's not a vampire."

The surfer's body swayed, as if he was close to passing out.

The girl with him screamed again.

And Jane—she risked a quick glance over her shoulder. Because that deep, dark, *familiar* voice had come from right behind her.

She couldn't see the speaker clearly in the shadows, but then, she didn't need to see him. She recognized Aidan Locke's voice instantly. Not surprising, really, considering that just hours before, she'd been in bed with the guy. "*Aidan.*"

"He's not a vampire. Just some punk kid." Aidan's voice was mild as he stepped closer to her. "And I think you're about to scare the piss out of him, sweetheart."

Hell. Jane focused on the couple once more. "A man has been murdered here tonight."

The girl screamed again. Jane winced. That chick had some powerful lungs. Jane tried to sound soothing as she said, "I need you both to come with me." Because maybe they'd seen something that night. Maybe they knew something about the killer.

They inched closer to her. There was no blood on their clothes. They were shaking, their fear obvious. Did they have any idea just how dangerous this place was? "Are you here for some weird make-out crap?" Jane demanded. "Because tourists have *got* to stop playing around at this place." Before more people ended up dead.

Real monsters didn't like it when humans came to their playground. And this particular cemetery? *St. Louis Cemetery, Number 1.* It was a paranormal mecca.

"S-Steve said it would be fun," the girl squeaked.

Jane rolled her eyes. God save her from boys with stupid make out ideas. "You're not supposed to be here unless you're with a damn tour group." High rates of vandalism — and the fact that the paranormals had claimed this cemetery — meant that access had been strictly limited lately. Or it *should* have been limited.

"Maybe you should lower the gun," Aidan advised Jane softly.

So she was still aiming her gun. Jane wasn't sure she trusted the kids. Actually, she didn't trust anyone. With her past, how could she?

Jane's right side seemed to burn as she stood there. An old reminder. As if she needed reminding.

"Jane..."

Fine. She lowered the gun. "I need to keep searching the cemetery. If the killer is here —"

"I'll search," he assured her.

"No, Aidan, I —"

But he was gone. And the guy was no doubt moving at that supernatural speed of his. As an alpha werewolf, there was very little the guy *couldn't* do.

A good thing...and a bad thing.

Jane heaved out a long breath as she stared at the terrified couple. "Did either of you see anyone else at the cemetery tonight? Did you *hear* anything?" *Like a dying man's screams?*

They just stood there, shaking.

The victim had been tortured. There was no way he'd gone down easily. Or quietly. "How long have you been here?" Jane demanded.

"A-about ten minutes," the girl confessed. "We...we were gonna get here sooner, but I had to wait until my parents went to sleep before I could —" She broke off.

But Jane knew how that sentence would have ended. "Before you could slip out." Jane huffed out a hard breath. "Trust me on this one, you owe your parents. I think their late night just saved your life."

There was a rustle behind her. Jane turned around, her fingers still tight on her gun —

"No one else is here," Aidan said. "The place is clear."

But...

But I heard someone calling to me. Just a few moments ago. I heard a man's voice. Only that voice *hadn't* belonged to her lover.

Had it belonged to the killer?

"Jane?" Aidan pressed. "What is it?"

"I..." A siren screamed in the distance. More cops, maybe even the ME, coming to the rescue. "They may have seen your super speed thing," she whispered to Aidan. "You...going to take care of that?" She hated asking because it felt so wrong.

*Take care of that...*Careful phrasing for a task that scared the crap out of her. Aidan Locke wasn't just a werewolf. He was *the* werewolf, the alpha in town. And being an alpha meant that he had certain powers and strengths that normal werewolves didn't possess. One of those powers was the ability to control humans — what they thought. What they *remembered.* She didn't like that control because the idea of it scared her.

Sometimes, Aidan scared her, too.

She hated it when he used his power to control humans. No one should be able to influence someone else's thoughts. "Let's talk to them first, okay? If they didn't see anything, you don't have to mess with their minds. You don't have to do it." *Because it's wrong and I hate it.*

"I'll talk to them," Aidan promised her. "But I don't think anyone saw. I'm more careful than you realize." His blue eyes gleamed in the darkness. "You go handle the dead."

Right. That was how they did things, wasn't it? Part of their new, twisted partnership?

Aidan was the paranormal law in New Orleans. He made sure the monsters toed the line and if they didn't…if they crossed the line and hurt humans…

Then I'm supposed to help him take the beasts down.

Aidan's hand rose. His fingers slid over her cheek. Such a gentle touch. He was always very careful with her. But, when the mood hit him, Aidan could change. In the blink of an eye, he could transform from a man into the form of a wolf.

A wolf with very, very big claws.

Claws big enough to slash a man to death in seconds.

"Jane?" His hand fell away from her cheek. "Is something wrong?"

Only my life. Only this nightmare that is starting all over again.

A new dead body, a new night…

What would happen next?

She shivered as she hurried back toward her victim. Right then, the dead man could be her only focus. It was her job to give justice to the dead.

And she'd give him that justice, no matter the cost.

***

Aidan Locke watched from the shadows as the cemetery became a full-on crime scene. Blue lights were flashing and the young couple that had been trembling in such fear before the sight of Jane and her drawn gun—they were now in the back of a cop car. Crying.

They didn't know anything. When Jane had gone back to the dead victim, Aidan had questioned the two humans. Demanded the truth. They wouldn't have been able to resist his control. After all, they weren't like Jane.

No one else was quite like Jane.

Almost helplessly, his gaze slid back to her. She was pacing in front of the cemetery's entrance. Her movements were tight, angry, but, every few moments, she glanced into the cemetery's yawning gate, her stare almost…nervous. As if she were looking for something.

Or someone.

His head cocked as he studied her. His Jane was certainly an enigma. He'd never expected her. Never expected to find a woman he wanted so completely.

And a woman who could wreck him so thoroughly.

He and Jane weren't supposed to be together, but he'd fought his pack for her. Just as he would fight anyone or anything who ever came between him and the woman he needed more than he needed air to breathe.

Jane was—

The wind shifted and the scent hit him. Strong. Powerful. Overwhelming.

Blood and death.

A primitive instinct stirred within him at that scent because he *knew* a vampire was close by. And when a werewolf caught a vampire's scent, there was only one possible response—attack.

Vampires and werewolves were natural enemies for a reason. They really fucking hated each other.

Aidan could feel his canines lengthening. He had to clench his fists because his claws wanted to spring from his fingertips. The last thing he needed to do was transform right there, with cops swarming around—he would have to erase too many memories later. Far better to just stay in control. To slip away. *Then* he could hunt down the vampire bastard and *end* him.

He whirled away from the blue lights and the crowd of cops and onlookers. Humans — they'd come out to see what fresh hell had been wrecked in the city. In his experience, humans liked to watch danger from a safe distance.

Don't get too close. Don't let it hurt you. Just watch the pain of others.

Most humans had no clue just what sort of real danger stalked near them every day.

Aidan quickened his steps as his nostrils flared. The vampire was close. It sure took some cocky bastard to come into *his* city this way. Especially after the way he'd ended the last vamp who'd dared to challenge him.

Aidan turned away from the main road. He slipped between two buildings. Walked onto a dark street, one that — at first glance — appeared completely empty.

His claws were out now, long and thick and ready to attack. He could feel his beast pushing inside of him. *Kill. Destroy.* When a vampire was this close, the wolf always reacted with the primitive instinct to battle.

The shadows to the left moved as the vampire just fucking boldly strode right toward him. "So I get to meet the alpha on my first night here," the vamp's voice rang out, loud and clear and not the least bit frightened. Dumb bastard. "I'm honored."

Every muscle in Aidan's body quivered with the urge to attack. "What you are..." Aidan gritted out, "is dead."

The vampire laughed. "Actually, I think the technical term is *undead*. But hey, I'm not here to argue—"

"I'm here to kick your ass," Aidan snapped. He leapt toward the vampire, moving at a speed so fast humans would have seen him as a blur. He locked one hand around the vampire's throat and shoved the guy against the nearest brick wall—the wall of the building on the right. When the vampire hit the wall, there was a hard, thudding impact, and dust seemed to shoot from the bricks behind him.

Aidan lifted his right hand, claws extended, ready to take that vamp's head—

"*Jane,*" the vamp gasped out.

The bastard dared to say her name?

"You must want to suffer," Aidan whispered to him. "A long, painful death instead of the quick kill I had planned."

"Not...here...for war..." Each word was croaked out, probably because Aidan was squeezing the guy's throat so tightly that speech was nearly impossible. "Here...to...talk...peace first."

Aidan laughed. "Since when do vampires believe in peace? We both know all you live for is blood and death."

But this vampire...he wasn't fighting Aidan. He *could* fight. Vamps were far stronger than humans. Yet this guy had just been waiting for him. And even as Aidan's claws came closer to his head, the fellow just...watched him. *Kept waiting.*

What kind of game was the vamp playing?

Aidan freed the guy and stepped back, but he made sure to keep his claws at the ready.

The vampire sucked in a sharp breath. Yes, vamps still breathed. Their hearts still beat. They didn't become walking corpses, no matter what the movies said. They were just fucking strong. Fucking deadly. And, in his experience, fucking evil.

"So..." the vamp finally muttered. "The stories are...true. You don't kill...without reason."

"I'm the paranormal law in this city. I keep the city safe, for the humans and the monsters. *That's* what I do." His gaze sharpened as he studied the vampire.

Even though it was dark, Aidan could see perfectly. Another nice, werewolf bonus. The vamp was tall, nearly Aidan's own height. His dark hair was swept back from his forehead, and the guy's eyes were narrowed as he stared up at Aidan.

"I'm not here to start a war with you," the vampire said. "I'm actually...I'm not really here for you at all."

"Why were you near that cemetery? Did you kill that poor bastard in there?"

"No." The vampire gave one negative shake of his head.

Like I'm supposed to believe you? Vamps lie. "Then it sure is one hell of a coincidence that you were close when the guy was slaughtered."

"I could say the same about you," the vamp murmured. "One hell of a coincidence that *you* were so close when the man died."

"I'll just kill you now," Aidan decided abruptly. "Make things easier —"

"I'm here for Jane."

Aidan's vision seemed to go red. "You have a death wish, huh? Thought as much."

"I'm trying to do this right. I waited to talk with *you* first as a sign of respect. I know what you are to this city. And I don't want a war with you." The vamp's words were said flatly, with no emotion.

"Smart decision." Aidan could feel his beast, moving just beneath his skin. The wolf wanted out. The vampire had dared to tell him that he wanted Jane? Oh, the hell, no. No one else would ever have her.

Jane is mine. Just as I am hers. Always.

"My name is Vincent Connor. And despite what you think about vampires, we aren't the enemy."

Aidan gave a grating laugh. "Tell that to the last vamp bastard I ended. Tell that to the victims who were left dead and broken in his wake."

Vincent looked away. "Are all werewolves *good*?" His voice had thickened. "Or are some of them murdering bastards that *you* have to end, too?"

Sonofabitch. All Aidan could do right then was growl. Because the vamp was right. Werewolves did go rogue, too, and when they did, Aidan was the one who had to stop their killing sprees.

"I am not the enemy," the vamp said doggedly. "I am here to help Jane. I came to you because I am trying to do all of this *right*. I know what she is. Hell, you think you could keep her a secret? Word travels in paranormal circles, and it travels fast."

Aidan lunged for Vincent.

But this time—the vamp fought back. In an instant, he yanked a gun from beneath his coat and pressed it to Aidan's chest. "Silver bullets," he said softly.

"Those supposed to scare me?" The gun was pointed right over his heart, but Aidan just laughed. "I've been shot plenty of times. If you

fire, you'd better hope I don't move too fast and
mess up your shot…" Which he would. "You'd
better hope you get enough silver in my heart to
put me down because I will make you suffer so —
"

"I don't want to fire. I want you to *listen*."
The vamp looked down at the gun, then back up
at Aidan. "I am not the enemy," he said again.

Bullshit. "Every vamp is my enemy."

Vincent sighed. "Will you still say that when
Jane becomes a vamp?"

The wolf clawed at Aidan's insides. "Are you
threatening her?" The bastard dared? He *dared?*

"I want to help her. I want to help you both."
Smart vamp — he'd come packing more than just
supernatural strength. "You and I both know
this…situation with Jane can't last forever."

"Yes, it can." And Aidan caught her scent in
the air. Lavender and apples. Sweet, sensual
woman. Jane. She was rushing toward him, and
the last thing he wanted was for her to see the
vampire.

The vampire's head had jerked and his
nostrils had flared. Vincent had obviously caught
her scent, too. His face had gone slack with
surprise and —

Yearning? *Forget that shit.* "She's taken,"
Aidan growled. "Now get the fuck…" Still, his
words were barely more than a growl as he
ordered, "Get the fuck out of my city…or die."

Even a silver bullet to the chest wouldn't stop him if this guy thought he'd get his hands on Jane.

"Aidan?" Jane's voice reached him. Worried. Desperate. "Aidan, what's happening?"

Before he could speak, the vampire shoved him back—shoved him so hard that Aidan flew a good ten feet into the air. *Someone is stronger than he let me believe.* Aidan hit the side of a dumpster, and the metal groaned beneath him. He shot to his feet—

The vampire was racing toward Jane.

She'd pulled out her gun. She was aiming at Vincent. Silver bullets or wooden ones? What was she packing that night? If she fired with silver, it would barely slow down the vamp. "*Jane!*" Aidan roared. If that vamp tried to hurt her—

He pushed himself faster, harder, desperate to get to her. His claws reached out, ready to swipe at that vampire's back.

Jane lifted her gun and fired.

And the vampire—

He just vanished. Fucking vanished. The bullet that Jane had shot went through the air and slammed into Aidan's shoulder. He grunted at the impact, but kept rushing toward her. He yanked her into his arms and held her tight.

She was shaking. "He...disappeared."

Shit, shit, shit.

"Aidan, what in the hell just happened?"

He just held her tighter as he glanced around the area. *My worst fucking nightmare, that's what.* Because a normal vamp couldn't vanish that way. Even a powerful, born vampire couldn't do that crap.

His gaze scanned the darkness as he kept Jane locked within his arms. If that vamp came back...*You'll have to go through me before you can ever get to her.*

And that was a promise he'd take to his grave.

CHAPTER TWO

"I didn't mean to shoot you." Jane winced as she glanced at Aidan's shoulder. They were at his bar, Hell's Gate, and guilt had her stomach twisted in knots.

They'd come in the back door of the place, missing the crowds on Bourbon Street, and they'd hurriedly slipped upstairs to his office. The guy's office was huge—and complete with its own bathroom.

They were currently standing in that bathroom and Aidan had yanked off his blood-stained shirt. Well, yanked, ripped it apart...same thing.

"I need to get the bullet out," Jane said, biting her lip. "I wanted to get it out at the scene, but you were intent on us hauling ass away from there."

"Because I wasn't letting the vampire get near you." His voice was gravel rough. Before she could say anything else, the guy shoved his claws into his shoulder and pulled out the bullet. Blood gushed.

"Jesus, Aidan! Stop! You know I hate it when you do that!"

But it was too late. With a tendril of smoke rising from the wound — and another tendril coming from his fingers — Aidan dropped the bloody silver bullet into his sink.

The legend about werewolves and silver was actually true. Silver hurt werewolves, it burned them, and the longer the silver stayed in their bodies, the weaker they became. Not that she'd ever seen Aidan in any particularly weak form but...

"At least let me wash the blood away." She wanted to take care of him. Was that so wrong? They were in a relationship, after all. Twisted and strange, but they were together. And she'd *shot* him. That guilt was not going away anytime soon. She reached around him, turned on the faucet and had warm water spraying down in seconds. She grabbed a cloth, wet it, and began to wipe away the blood.

Aidan stood statue-still beneath her touch. Jane risked a quick glance up at him from beneath her lashes. His face was set in stone. Such a hard, dangerous face. Not handsome, but rougher. Sexier.

She generally found far too many things about Aidan Locke to be sexy. A smart woman would have run the instant she found out that the guy was an alpha werewolf. But instead of fleeing from him…

I always run to Aidan.

Her touch was light as she cleaned his wound, a wound that was already healing. His werewolf blood was pretty amazing. Only an alpha's blood held that healing power.

She stepped away from him and put the cloth in the sink. Rinsed away the blood. Then watched the blood wash down the drain.

"The wound doesn't matter." His words were a rumble from behind her. His hand closed around her shoulder and she looked up, staring at their reflections in the mirror. He was so big, around six foot two, maybe six foot three, with wide, powerful shoulders. His hair was dark, thick, and his eyes were a bright blue. She always felt a little lost when she looked into his eyes.

She was so much smaller than him. Jane had always wished she were taller, but she knew that she looked like some kind of ballet dancer. Fragile, delicate — that was her build. She had to work twice as hard to be taken seriously at the police station, but she did it — she'd do anything for her job.

Keeping others safe had been her mission for years. Her goal, ever since she'd been eleven years old and her life had been ripped apart.

I won't let the same thing happen to others.

But the deaths kept coming. And the monsters weren't stopping.

Once more, her gaze fell to the sink. *And the blood keeps flowing.*

"He wanted you."

She stiffened.

"The vamp in the alley was there because the asshole wanted *you*." Aidan turned her to face him, caging Jane between him and the sink. "I'm not going to let him get his hands on you."

Jane focused on keeping her breathing steady. Her heartbeat was racing in her chest and fear had tightened her muscles. "Another vamp after me, huh? Guess it must be a day that ends in Y."

"Jane…" He growled her name. And normally, she found that growl of his crazy sexy.

"It won't stop, we both know it." Her voice was rough. Hard. Very close to her own growl. "The paranormals out there — they know what I am. *You* know. And as much as we both want to pretend things are fine, they aren't." They couldn't be.

Because Jane wasn't just a human, some mortal who'd fallen in love with a werewolf and was trying to make that weird relationship work.

According to Aidan, according to the nightmare that was her new life…she was something…more.

A vamp-in-waiting. A born vampire. If she died a violent death, then some sort of insane adrenaline burst was supposed to ignite in her blood during those last precious moments before her heart stopped beating. She would die, but only for a short time. She'd wake as a vampire — one of the strongest immortals ever.

Born vampires were exceedingly rare.

And…incredibly powerful.

Evil. Let's not forget the evil part. She didn't want to go from being a protector to being the monster in the dark who preyed on humans.

She didn't want to become just like the monster that had killed her own family.

"Jane."

Her chin lifted. "Do you think that vamp killed the man in the cemetery? Is there about to be another blood bath in the city?"

His jaw had locked. "I…don't know. He said he didn't."

Her laughter was bitter. "And you believe a vampire?"

He didn't answer. She supposed that was answer enough. Aidan generally hated all vamps. She knew he had some primal instinct to attack vamps — all werewolves did — but Aidan was able to hold himself in check better than the others. Alpha advantage in self-control and all that jazz. Curious, she asked, "How close were you to killing him?"

"Not close enough…"

Her breathing wasn't slow. It was too fast. Fear blossomed in her chest. She hadn't even realized a vamp had been close, not when she'd gone hunting for Aidan.

"Don't be afraid. I won't let him get to you."

The vampire had vanished before their eyes. How did they know he wouldn't reappear someplace and attack? But… "He isn't what scares me most."

Aidan's hand curled under her chin. Again, he was so careful when he touched her. Like she was glass that could shatter.

Or…

A human in a werewolf's hands.

"You scare me," she confessed.

She saw the pain flare in his beautiful eyes, and Jane hated that she'd caused that hurt. But Jane didn't want to lie to him. "If I change, will you be the one who comes for me?"

"You aren't changing. You'd have to die first, and that shit will *not* happen."

"But what if—"

He kissed her. Aidan's mouth took hers in a kiss that was hot, deep, consuming. Just the way she liked. The way they both liked.

His tongue thrust into her mouth, and she gave a little moan. Her desire for him didn't surprise her. That desire was always there, just beneath the surface. Bubbling, ready to spill out and break free.

His hands dropped to her waist, and he lifted her up so easily, sitting her on the edge of the sink. Her hands lifted to curl around his shoulders but she stopped —

His wound. Watch out for his wound.

His lips lifted from hers, just a bare inch. "Nothing you do can hurt me." His eyes seemed to glow as he stared down at her. His beast was closer than she'd realized. "Know that. And know that you are *not* dying. That isn't an option."

Good to know. "Kiss me again." Because when he kissed her, when the passion and pleasure swept between them, she could pretend that her life wasn't about to fall apart. She could pretend that maybe she had a future with her werewolf.

That her life wasn't going to crash and burn into flames.

He kissed her. Her mouth was open, ready for him, because she loved his taste. Rich and masculine. Sometimes, Jane thought she might get a little drunk off him. Her nipples were tight, eager, and they pressed to his chest. Her legs curled around his hips as she arched against him.

He was aroused. She could feel the thick length of his cock shoving against the front of his jeans. She'd rather prefer it if he was shoving into her. Thrusting them both into oblivion. That would be awesome.

Her hands slid between them. She caught the button of his jeans. Yanked it open and carefully pulled down the zipper.

He wasn't wearing underwear. When you could shift into the form of a wolf, you had a tendency to wear fewer clothes, not more. The better to shift fast and not destroy needless shit that was in your way.

When the zipper slid down, his cock thrust toward her. Her fingers curled around him, stroking. He was hot and thick and hers.

For that moment, *hers.*

"Jane, don't play," Aidan rasped.

"Who said I was playing? But my clothes are in the way, don't you think?"

And just like that, he'd yanked her shirt away. He tossed her bra, threw it behind them, and then he was kissing her breast. Taking her nipple into his mouth. Sucking her and making Jane gasp. He laved her nipple. Drove her wild. And she knew her panties were getting wet. "Aidan!"

He shifted her position, pushing her until her back touched the cold mirror. She kicked away her shoes and he yanked down her jeans and her panties. She was completely nude before him, and Jane didn't even feel a moment's hesitation.

With Aidan, when they were like this, there was never any room for fear or doubt.

His hand went between her spread thighs. That dark tanned hand, so strong and powerful, touched her lightly. Sensually. She bit her lower lip. He had reinforced walls in his office — when werewolves and their enhanced hearing were close on a normal basis, it paid to invest in some serious sound-proofing — so she knew she could scream and no one else would hear.

Soon enough, Jane figured she *would* be screaming.

His fingers slid into her. Thrust and teased. His thumb pressed to her clit, stroking her just the way he knew she enjoyed being touched. Sometimes, she thought Aidan understood her body better than she did. Harder, a little rougher now, he stroked.

"Aidan!" She didn't want to play. She needed him inside of her. "Now!"

But he shook his head. "Not yet."

He dropped to his knees before her.

Strong Aidan, so powerful. So —

"I will not lose you." His words sounded like a vow. Then his mouth was on her. Warm and wet, his tongue touched her clit and she just imploded.

The pleasure hit her with stunning force. Her head tipped back against the mirror and she gasped. Zero to implosion. She whispered his name, she rode that blast of pleasure and still...she wanted.

Him.

In her.

"Aidan!"

He rose up. His expression was harder. The angles of his face were sharper. His eyes, if possible, were even brighter. He positioned his cock at the entrance to her body. No condom. Werewolves didn't carry diseases — they couldn't — and she was on protection so pregnancy wasn't an issue. They were flesh to flesh, just the way she wanted to be with him.

His hands clamped around the edge of the sink. He drove into her, hard and deep and the pleasure she'd felt just kept going. Her sex trembled with the contractions of her release, the pleasure was so fierce that her whole body shuddered.

He thrust in and out, driving deep, his rhythm fast and furious, his hands still gripping the sink so hard. She grabbed him. Her hands locked around his sides as she urged him to move even faster. To drive deeper. Each glide of his body into hers had Jane moaning. Had her —

Screaming.

The pleasure was too powerful to be contained. So she didn't even try.

Then he was exploding within her. The hot surge of his release filled her. He drove deep once more, then stilled. His bright gaze locked on her, and Jane saw the pleasure in his stare.

Mine.

Sweat had slickened their bodies. Her breath still came in desperate heaves. She didn't want to move but—

The sink gave a loud groan. Something shifted beneath her. She started to tumble, but Aidan jerked her up and into his arms. Jane looked back. He'd been gripping the sink so tightly…

He'd broken the granite. The sink was sliding from the wall and collapsing.

And she laughed. With a vampire, with murder…with the secrets she still had to keep, Jane found that she could laugh, with him.

Only him.

Aidan carried her out of the bathroom. They curled together on his couch. Exhaustion pulled at her, and Jane intended to close her eyes for just a moment. Just a little while. Then she'd clean up and get her ass over to the ME's office. She'd see if Dr. Bob had examined the body. She'd see…

In a moment.

A moment…

CHAPTER THREE

Jane was asleep in his arms. Aidan stared down at her, lost for a moment. Her thick lashes cast shadows over her cheeks. Beautiful Jane. Strong. Smart. Sexy as hell.

And dangerous. So many feared that she was dangerous.

Carefully, his fingers slid down her body, moving gently over her stomach, over the luscious curve of her hip and then…lightly tracing the mark on her right side.

A brand. The shape curved on her skin. It almost looked like a horseshoe on her body, one that had been carefully burned into her skin with a soldering pen. She'd been a child when a vampire had captured her, had killed her parents before her eyes, and had permanently marked her with that brand.

*Not a horseshoe. The brand curved at the top, and then it seemed to have two legs that jutted to the left and the right…*Omega. The Greek Symbol for the end.

Many of his kind feared what Jane would be. Many had wanted her dead as soon as they'd learned of her existence. He'd fought for the right to keep her at his side. His job was to protect her, always. His fingers skimmed over the brand.

If I change, will you be the one who comes for me? Her words whispered through his mind and his eyes squeezed closed. Kill Jane? If she ever became a vampire, was that really what he was supposed to do? Could he?

Would he have any other choice?

Slowly, he slipped from the couch. She kept sleeping, her breathing deep and steady. He grabbed fresh clothes from the closet. He kept clothes at the bar because he never knew when he might have to transform.

And running around naked after a shift was one surefire way to catch attention in the city. As he pulled his shirt into place, he opened his office door. Jane continued sleeping behind him. Good. She needed her rest, especially with a new vamp in town.

He paced away from his office. Stared down below at his bar. It was a Friday night, and Hell's Gate was packed. Hardly surprising. The werewolves and the humans blended together below him. The humans were completely unaware that they danced with paranormals. That was the way the werewolves liked for things to be. Their existence was supposed to be secret.

But vamps were different. They had a tendency to leave blood and death in their wake. They wanted attention. Wanted the truth to come out.

Wanted chaos.

He glanced around the bar and caught the eye of Paris Cole, his oldest friend and his right-hand wolf. Aidan inclined his head and Paris immediately headed for the stairs. The crowd parted instantly for Paris, though the tall, African American wolf made a point of pausing to smile at the pretty ladies he saw. Typical Paris. A charmer, and often, a pain in Aidan's ass. But...

Someone I can count on.

Aidan had been betrayed before and, no doubt, he would be betrayed again. When power was on the line, a guy always had to watch his back. *But I can depend on Paris.*

As Paris neared him, worry flashed in the guy's light, golden eyes. Paris's gaze dipped from Aidan to the closed office door. "Everything okay with our cop?"

Our cop? Aidan's brows rose.

Paris delicately cleared his throat. "What I meant was...how's Jane tonight?"

The same way she was every night. *Mine.* "A new vamp is in town."

Paris swore. "When will they learn? This city isn't theirs anymore."

No, it wasn't. It belonged to the wolves, but it was like there was some damn vamp beacon in place because the undead always circled back to New Orleans. Aidan rolled back his shoulders. "The vamp said he wasn't here to start a war."

"And you didn't buy his bullshit."

"Vincent Connor." Just saying the name pissed him off. "Find out everything you can about him and spread the word to the pack that we need to be on alert." If Vincent decided to make an undead army in the city, they needed to be ready.

Paris nodded and turned to leave.

Aidan caught his arm. "Something else…" He heaved out a hard breath. "The guy vanished. Right in front of my eyes, he disappeared."

Paris laughed.

Aidan didn't.

"You're…serious?"

Aidan stared at him.

"How can he do that?" Paris's forehead wrinkled. "*Can* vampires do that? I mean, I know they get more power with age but…"

"For all I know, the guy has been gorging on werewolf blood." A quick way to increase a vamp's power. "Or maybe he's the oldest SOB that I've ever come across." *That's why I need to learn everything about the guy that I can.*

"He's after Jane."

Aidan forced his back teeth to unclench. "He may have already killed a human. I'll be stopping him before he hurts anyone else." It was a promise. Aidan's hand fell away from his friend's arm. "And put extra protection on Jane's detail."

Paris whistled. "You know she doesn't like it when you throw guards at her."

Too bad. He'd rather she be pissed than dead.

Or undead.

"We're going to need Annette. Get word to her that I want a meeting."

Paris took a step back. "You're calling in the voodoo queen?" His expression hardened. "Aidan, how do you even know she's on our side?"

He didn't. "She still owes me." And with a vamp *vanishing* before his eyes, he needed to understand exactly what was happening.

"You don't think…" Now Paris was hesitant. "That she's helping him, do you?"

"I don't know." Annette Benoit, voodoo queen extraordinaire, had been forced to help a vampire before. Was that happening again? "That's why I need the meeting."

Paris nodded. "Then I'll make it happen." Though he sure didn't sound happy about the situation. When it came to voodoo magic, Paris liked to keep his distance. Not that Aidan blamed him. They all knew how strong Annette was.

Aidan turned toward his office, and that was when he heard…

Jane, crying.

***

The nightmare would never leave her alone. No matter how much time passed, no matter how strong she *thought* she was…it would return.

Maybe because it wasn't a nightmare.

It was a memory. And it was so real…so strong…

She could actually feel the rope as it cut into her wrists and ankles. She could feel her own blood as her skin ground against the rough hemp.

Jane wasn't an adult in that memory/nightmare. She was just a child, barely eleven years old. So scared. In so much pain. The pain wouldn't stop. The vampire just laughed when she cried.

She was tied down, secured on the top of an old table. In the basement of *her* house. When she turned her head, Jane could see her mom. Her mother was tossed on the floor, her limbs all twisted and a big pool of red underneath her body. Her dad…he was there, too. Another quick turn of her head showed Jane her dad's form.

His eyes were still open, but she didn't think he saw her, not anymore.

"There, there...no need for tears, little one. It's all for you." That voice was back. The voice she hated. Mean and cold and cruel and she wouldn't look at him. She just *wouldn't.*

"We waited a long time for you. You'd better not disappoint."

She looked back at her dad. This was her house. Her mom's house. Her dad's house. They were supposed to be safe there. *Why aren't we safe?*

"You can scream if you want," that cold voice told her.

It was all the warning she got. Pain came then. So hot. Burning, branding. She screamed and screamed but it didn't stop. And she could smell something — something funny. Something —

It's me. I'm burning.

Her voice broke and her cries stopped.

"Good girl."

She didn't want to be good. Not if he liked that.

"I'll be back soon." He stroked back her hair, and his green eyes gleamed down at her. "We'll take a little break. Let you get a bit of strength back so that we can finish things up." His blond hair was swept away from his face. A face that seemed so normal.

It isn't. He's not normal. He's evil. Monster. Monster. Monster!

Vampire.

There were no tears on her cheeks. She'd stopped crying after...*Daddy*.

The green-eyed man — *monster* – shut the door on the way out. Her home. He had taken over as if he owned the place. *They had*. In the middle of the night, monsters had come for her. Her mom had told her that monsters weren't real. That she should never be afraid of them.

Her mom had been wrong.

She heard faint squeaks. The softest of rustles. Her eyes had closed. When had they closed? She should look around and see what was happening.

But she was afraid and she didn't think she wanted to see anything else.

Her right side kept hurting. Throbbing. She could still smell that terrible scent in the air. *I think that's me.*

"Mary Jane..." A soft voice called. "Mary Jane...are you okay?"

Don't be here. Don't. Run away.

"Y-you didn't tell them I was here."

Now she did cry. One long tear slid down her cheek.

"I'm gonna...I'm gonna get you out."

She shook her head and kept her eyes closed. But she felt him pulling on the ropes that held her ankles down. There was a faint sawing motion. It sounded so loud to her ears. She was afraid *he* would hear. "Stop." The barest of whispers.

But the rope gave way. Her legs were free and her feet *hurt* because it felt like needles were shoved into them. She bit her lower lip as hard as she could, trying to hold back her cries. Now wasn't the time to scream. She knew that.

Her eyes opened.

Her dad's sightless eyes stared back at her.

No, look away. Look away!

Then the rope was gone from her wrists. Sawed away. He'd cut her wrists with the knife he had, but she didn't care about that small pain. Then he was pulling her, pushing her toward the window. Such a small window. They were in the basement. And that window was up high.

"I'll go through first," he said. He shimmied up and vanished.

I don't want to leave mom and dad. But...they were already gone. They'd left her. They weren't suffering anymore. No one could ever make them suffer again.

"Mary Jane!" He reached down for her. His hand was small, barely bigger than hers. Dirty. Bloody. "Come with me, Mary Jane!"

Had he been hiding, during everything? Hiding and waiting? He'd seen everything, too, just as she had. She looked up into his eyes — eyes that were the exact shade of her own. He'd been crying. He never cried.

Her gaze darted back to his hand just as she heard the basement door opening—the faintest of clicks from the top of the stairs. The monster was coming for her again.

She grabbed for the dirty little hand, and he pulled her up, yanking with all of his strength. Her body slid through the narrow opening of the window. Her shoulders. Her chest. Her stomach. Her—

The monster grabbed her feet.

"*No!*" she screamed. And then she held that dirty little hand even tighter. "Drew, help me!"

***

"*Jane.*"

Her eyes flew open. The basement—her old home—vanished. She was in Aidan's office, naked, on Aidan's fancy leather couch. Her heart drummed hard enough to shake her chest as Aidan crouched over her.

She sat up, fast, but he didn't move back.

"You were having your nightmare again."

She swiped a hand over her face. Since they spent plenty of nights together, he knew all about her sleep issues. But then, he knew how she'd come to have that not-so-lovely scar on her right side, too. She'd told him most of the story.

Most of it.

Some details had been left out. Not because she didn't trust him, but because she knew him too well.

"Back in the basement?" Aidan asked carefully. His hand was on her shoulder, lightly stroking the skin.

Chill bumps rose onto her arms. "Y-yes." She hated that stutter. Hated any fear. Fear was for the weak. She'd always wanted to be strong. Strong enough to save her family.

But they were gone.

"The vampire who burned you…he can't hurt you anymore, sweetheart."

She knew that. She and Aidan had killed the bastard. She'd hoped that with Thane Durant's death, she'd get some peace. That maybe the nightmares would stop.

No such luck.

"I should get dressed. Get to the morgue." Dr. Bob had taken the body in for examination. It wouldn't take him long to learn what she needed…

Was it a vamp attack? Is the dead guy going to wake up with new fangs and an appetite for blood? If so, then she and Aidan had to be on hand to stop the fellow. *Victim to monster all in the blink of an eye.* She'd seen that happen before.

Unfortunately.

Aidan eased back as she rose to her feet. Jane locked her knees so they wouldn't tremble. She

didn't like showing weakness in front of Aidan—
or in front of anyone. She hurried toward the
bathroom—

"Are you going to tell me…" Aidan's deep,
rumbling voice followed her, "who Drew is?"

She froze. "Drew?" Her voice broke on the
name, dammit. Schooling her expression, she
glanced back at Aidan. "What are you talking
about?"

"Not what. Who. And you were the one
talking about him." He cocked his head as he
studied her. "You were just calling out for him,
begging him to help you."

Her face felt numb. "I don't remember." She
spun away from him but—

He was there. Freaking super speed. Aidan
blocked the bathroom door. He stared down at
her and said, "Liar."

Jane flinched.

"Why keep secrets from me, Jane? I thought
you trusted me."

"Get out of my way." She was not having this
conversation, not while she was completely
naked. *I don't want to have this conversation at all.*
But she'd been playing Russian roulette with him
for weeks now. Jane had known how dangerous
it was to let down her guard with him, but she'd
been helpless to stay away from her wolf.

Now she was about to pay the price for her
mistake.

Aidan's eyes narrowed but...he moved.

Her breath expelled in a relieved rush as she hurried into the bathroom. She grabbed her clothes and dressed as quickly as she could. Jane risked a quick glance in the mirror. Yes, she looked nervous, dammit. Whatever. Squaring her shoulders, she opened the bathroom door and marched back into his office. "Aidan, look—"

But she stopped because Aidan *was* looking at something. He was staring down at a small, black picture frame.

A familiar frame.

Jane frowned. She crept toward him.

"Is this Drew?" Aidan turned the frame toward her. The photo she saw had her heart clenching. She was smiling and her arm was wrapped around the shoulders of a handsome, dark-haired man.

"I thought that picture burned," Jane whispered. She'd lost pretty much everything else when a deranged vampire had sent his freaking minions to burn her out of her apartment. That precious photo—she'd thought it was destroyed. "Did you save it from the fire?" Dumb question. He must have—

"Actually, I took it long before the fire." He turned the photo back around to face him. "I took it the first night we met. It was on your nightstand, you were passed out cold and I...I didn't think you'd remember me when you woke up."

Because he'd used his alpha power to try and make her forget that whole fateful night. Only she hadn't forgotten.

Turned out I wasn't exactly human so his power didn't work on me. Jane swallowed and said, "You know, doing stalkerish things like that will get you in trouble."

"You look happy in the photo. I wanted to be able to see you that way every day." His gaze rose to her face. "I often see you scared. I see you determined. I see you furious." His lips curled. "I even see you when you're turned on and you sure as hell know I love to look at you that way…" Aidan exhaled. "But happy? It's hard to get you to smile, Mary Jane."

"Jane," she said automatically, though she didn't really mind when he called her Mary Jane. Only Aidan called her that.

Well, Aidan…and Drew. But she hadn't seen Drew in a very long time. *Since we took that picture.* She'd been telling him good-bye that day.

"I like to see you happy."

She closed the last bit of distance between them and took the picture from his hand. "Then don't steal my stuff."

"It's an old habit."

Her thumb smoothed over the wooden edge of the picture frame. "Oh, yeah? From when?"

"From the days when I had nothing. The street was my home and I had to fight for everything I wanted."

Her thumb stopped moving. Aidan didn't speak much of his past. She knew there were plenty of dark spaces there. Lots of blood and pain, but he didn't talk about them.

"You...weren't with your pack?"

"There was damn little of my pack left after my parents — after they died."

He'd stumbled a bit at the end of that sentence. Aidan wasn't the type to stumble with his words.

"Those who were left, they didn't exactly have a lot of time for a kid. They didn't know I'd turn out to be an alpha. To them, I was just a reminder of my father's...mistake." His jaw hardened. "I was told, again and again, not to repeat that same mistake. To never be like him."

Just what horrible crime had his father committed? And did she really want to know? *Some things are best forgotten.* Jane thought of her own family and of the secrets she'd kept. "We don't have to be like our parents. We *aren't* them."

"No." He nodded. "We aren't."

She glanced down at the frame.

"When I was on my own, I took things to survive," Aidan confessed.

Did he expect her to judge him for that?

"Food, clothes. The things I needed."

She waited, silent, hoping he'd tell her more.

"Later, I took things that I wanted."

Her gaze flew to his face.

"A poor kid, looking in from the outside. He wants what others have. He wants the things that make them…happy."

"Just what kind of things are we talking about?" She was a cop, after all.

He laughed. "Like I said, old habits."

"Aidan…"

His arms crossed over his chest. "That's Drew, isn't it?"

So he was done with his sharing session and it was back to her?

"He has your eyes."

"I'd rather hoped you hadn't noticed."

"His eyes are the reason I'm not a jealous bastard right now. He's related to you. I can see that."

Yes. "My brother." The words sounded foreign to her own ears. Mostly because they were. She hadn't spoken about Drew to anyone in so long.

Too long.

"Where is he, Jane?"

She put the frame down on his desk and took a few quick steps back from him. "Why, Aidan? So you can hunt him down and see if he's like me?"

She expected him to lie to her. Instead…

"Yes. If he's a vampire-in-waiting, I have to know."

That was what she'd feared. "Then what will you do? Give him protection? Some werewolf guards to follow him the way they do me?" And she hated that crap. "Or will you ensure that he dies a non-violent death?" Her stomach twisted. "Because that's the key for the transformation, the violent end. Maybe you'll find Drew and slip him a little poison. Let him fall asleep and never wake up. Then he wouldn't be any problem to you at all."

Aidan hadn't moved.

And the room suddenly seemed very, very small.

Or perhaps Aidan just looked bigger. *That happens when he gets pissed. The guy's energy seems to fill the space around him.*

"Is that what you think of me?" Aidan finally asked. "That I'd kill your brother?"

She would be honest with him. They both deserved that. "I think you're an alpha werewolf and, as you've told me yourself, you have an instinct to attack vampires."

His hands had fisted. "You just fucked me."

Um, yes. She didn't need a reminder of that. Her body still ached in interesting places.

"You just fucked me, and now you're accusing me of plotting to murder your brother?"

Oh, shit. Definitely pissed. "I didn't accuse you!" *Just to be clear.* "I asked, okay? *I asked* because I've been scared as hell that you will go after him. And I'm scared — scared because no one else knows about him. He has a normal life. One that doesn't include me and my craziness. I want things to stay that way for him."

Aidan glared at her.

She glared back.

"You don't trust me." Hurt flickered on his face, just for an instant.

"No, I do trust you." This was the part that hurt her. "I trust you to do what's best for your pack. That's what an alpha does, right? The pack comes first, I know that. So if you were to think that my brother was a threat…" She couldn't finish.

But then, she didn't need to do it.

Aidan understood. "You're more important than my pack. You should know that."

She wanted to believe him. But…Their relationship was so screwed up. *So why does it feel right when I'm with him? Why do I keep wanting him so much? Needing him?*

"Drew is hundreds of miles away. He isn't a threat. Just forget about him."

Aidan didn't speak.

"I have to go." She grabbed her jacket. "The ME will be waiting on me. I just — sorry for shooting you," Jane mumbled and rushed for the

door. Her fingers closed around the door knob.
She expected Aidan to stop her.

He didn't.

He must be really pissed.

She opened the door, but looked back at him.
He wasn't even glancing her way. He was staring
down at the photo. That old picture of her
smiling with her brother. She'd been younger
then, maybe twenty-one. Twenty-two? That was
the last time she'd seen her brother.

For damn good reason.

"Promise me." The words slipped from her.
"Promise me that you won't kill my brother. No
matter what happens."

His fingers tightened around the frame. But
then, as if catching himself and remembering just
how much strength he truly possessed, Aidan
very carefully put the frame down on his desk.

"Promise me," she continued. "And I will
give you anything you want."

His eyes narrowed on her. "What don't I
already have?"

"I don't know." More chill bumps were on
her arms. "But think of something I can give you.
Something you don't have to take." She stared at
him a moment longer. "Good night, Aidan."
Then Jane slipped away.

***

Aidan glanced back down at the photo on his desk. A smiling, happy Jane stared back up at him.

Drew.

I will be finding you.

He hadn't promised Jane. Mostly because he hated to make a promise that he wouldn't be able to keep. If her brother proved to be a threat, to either Jane or to the pack...

I will deal with him.

And as far as the thing he wanted...the thing he couldn't take...

He couldn't look away from the bright smile on Jane's face.

One day. If he was patient enough, if he fought hard enough, he would have exactly what he wanted.

***

The werewolf alpha was sending his dogs after the woman.

Vincent Connor eased back into the shadows as his prey marched out of Hell's Gate. He'd been watching that noisy bar for a while. Humans had gone in, werewolves had acted as if they owned the place — probably because they did — and no one had noticed the vampire lurking outside.

Because he hadn't wanted to be noticed.

Normally, werewolves would smell his kind, but he'd taken a little precaution to ensure no one would scent him before he headed to Hell's Gate.

It hadn't taken a big leap of knowledge to realize that Aidan Locke would keep Mary Jane Hart close. When you had a prize like her, you didn't let her stray easily.

Mary Jane left the bar, not looking back. She walked fast with hard, angry strides that almost made Vincent smile. Not that he'd had a whole lot to smile about in the last century or so. Too much blood. Death.

Boredom.

Mary Jane wasn't boring to him. Quite the opposite.

When she left, two werewolves followed her. Sure, they looked like humans, but he knew better than to be fooled. He could tell that they were beasts just by the way they walked — that predatory stalk was obvious. The way the men would stop every few moments, their heads stiffening, their necks shooting up as they sniffed the air around them — *dead giveaways*.

The two werewolves kept Mary Jane in their sight as she hurried through the city. And he — well, he followed them.

After all, he'd journeyed to New Orleans for one reason. Mary Jane Hart. He could play nicely with the werewolves for a time, if that niceness got him what he wanted. And if raising a flag of truce didn't work...

Then he would just take what he needed. He was very, very good at taking.

CHAPTER FOUR

"He's not going to become a vampire." Dr. Bob Heider took off his tortoiseshell glasses and rubbed the lenses. "The guy's blood showed no signs of any mutation. You don't have to worry about this one." He put his glasses back in place then gestured toward the body on the slab. "He's not rising."

Some of the tension left Jane's shoulders. She and Dr. Bob hadn't always gotten along so well, but now things were going much better between them. He wasn't bullshitting her on the paranormal cases—after all, word had come down that she was the lucky detective who got to handle the monsters—and she was slowly finding her footing in the land of the supernatural.

"Have you been able to tell what killed him?" Jane leaned closer to the body. "Any puncture wounds to show that a vamp attacked?" Because a vampire could have attacked the guy, but not transformed him. In order for a normal human to become a vampire, the human had to get the vampire's blood so the transformation would occur. No blood, no new vamp.

Unless you happened to be born waiting to be a vamp...like me.

Dr. Bob nervously cleared his throat. She looked up at him. The overhead lighting reflected off the guy's very high forehead. His hair was receding fast, despite the sweep-over attempt that he'd tried this week.

But he didn't meet her stare. Instead, he kept looking down at the clipboard in his hands, as if every secret in the world were written there.

Maybe the secrets were.

"Dr. Bob?" Jane prompted.

Sweat beaded on his forehead.

Crap.

"Y-you saw the claw marks on him," he said.

"Hard to miss them. But I wondered if maybe the killer was just trying to throw us off — make us *think* a werewolf had attacked."

Dr. Bob shook his head. "I measured the wounds. They're all are the same." He put his clipboard down. She realized that his fingers were shaking. He eased closer to her. His gaze nervously swept toward the closed door, then back to her. "*The measurements are all the same.*" He lifted his shaking fingers, spreading them just a bit as he curled his fingers. Then he made a clawing motion at her.

Her brows shot up. "What in the hell are you doing?"

"Werewolf attack," he whispered, then threw another nervous glance toward the door. "Oh, shit, do you think your guards can hear me? I don't want to get my throat ripped out."

She grabbed his hand before he could do one of those annoying-ass claw motions again. "No one is ripping out your throat. You *work* for the werewolf alpha, remember?" He'd been on Aidan's payroll long before she came into the game. Aidan paid the ME well to make sure that paranormal murders didn't leak to the press.

Most humans didn't know about the paranormals. Aidan wanted to keep things that way.

"Aidan doesn't like it when his own kind kill." Dr. Bob licked his lips and beetled his bushy eyebrows at her. "You know what happened the last time a werewolf turned on him."

Yes, she did. Death. But Aidan hadn't been the one to kill the wolf who'd betrayed him.

"I think this human...his name is Alan Thatcher—I think he was killed by a werewolf."

"Alan?"

"His prints turned up in the system. Guy had a charge of marijuana possession when he was eighteen. The charges were later dropped, but his prints were still on file."

She nodded.

"I don't think our vic was killed at the scene." Dr. Bob tapped his chin. "There wasn't enough blood at the scene, not based on the type of injuries he received. A werewolf killed him, then took his body to the cemetery."

"The scene was staged," she murmured, dropping his hand. And that wasn't good. A werewolf killer on the loose, one who wanted people to know about his crimes? *Aidan definitely won't like this.*

And I don't like it damn much, either.

Jane's gaze slid back to the victim. Alan Thatcher. "Why you?" She would find out. That was her job. To give justice to the victims. That was why she'd wanted to become a homicide detective in the first place. Sadness filled her as she stared at all of his wounds. "This sure looks like a whole lot of rage to me."

Dr. Bob gave a grunting sound of agreement. "Seems to me as if the perp didn't just want to kill the vic...the attacker wanted to destroy him completely."

"Disfigure him," she whispered. Alan had been so handsome. Before. "A whole lot of rage," she said again. "And maybe hate." Jane rubbed the back of her neck. "Run every blood analysis and test that you can think of on the guy, okay? If he was special to the killer, maybe there was a reason why. Something that we don't see, not yet." And while he did that, Jane would learn every detail she could about Alan Thatcher's personal life.

She turned and headed for the door.

"Are you…all right, Jane?"

Dr. Bob's question made her pause. A wry smile curled her lips as she looked back at him. "You sound worried about me."

He puffed up his chest. "No. Not at all."

She waited.

His chest deflated. "You're human."

Not according to Aidan.

"You have to be careful in their world. I'm in it only as little as I can be."

He was warning her. That was almost cute. "And here I didn't think you cared."

No humor glinted in his eyes. "They use humans. We do their dirty work." His stare trekked to the body on the slab. "We clean up their messes."

"This isn't a mess. It's a man's life. And I *will* find his killer."

"Even if that killer is in Aidan's pack? Because he controls all the werewolves in the city. Once word gets out that a wolf did this…" He exhaled. "Those two outside probably already heard us. You know wolves have that freakish hearing."

Jane just shook her head.

"They're probably calling him right now—"

Okay, he might be right on that point. She shoved open the door and strode into the hallway. Sure enough, her guards were there. Garrison was easy to spot with his messy mop of bright red hair. The guy was generally her lead guard. Mostly because he'd sworn some blood oath to protect her after she'd saved his ass. Only he was currently on his phone, hunched over and —

Jane grabbed the phone from him. "Aidan? Yeah, it's me. And what Garrison was trying to tell you is true." She glared at Garrison. *Seriously, I wasn't even done with Dr. Bob.* "We've got a werewolf killing in the city. And *we* need to stop him."

***

Jane strode down the New Orleans street, her steps fast and angry. She could hear her guards behind her. Keeping their careful distance. Was this really supposed to be her life? Constant guards? Aidan needed to back off with this shit. She was —

A sharp cry sounded behind her. Jane whirled around. Her blond guard was on the ground, unconscious. A street lamp's light fell on him, clearly showing his slumped form.

"Jane, *run!*" That was Garrison's yell. Her head whipped toward him. Garrison's claws were out and he was facing off against a shadowy figure. "Get out of here!"

The figure lunged for Garrison. The shadow picked up Garrison and held him at least a foot in the air, like the werewolf was some kind of rag doll.

"Stop!" Jane yelled. She yanked out her gun. "Let him go!"

The figure threw Garrison. The redheaded werewolf hit the lamp post with a hard thud. He didn't get back up.

And the shadow turned to face Jane.

She kept her gun up and aimed right at his heart.

He stepped toward her and illumination from a nearby street lamp hit his face. Not the face of some hideous monster, but a man. Strong features. Sensual lips. A small cleft in his chin. Thick hair. Intense eyes.

"Hello, Mary Jane. I've been looking for you, for a very long time." He took another step toward her.

"Move again, and I will shoot." Both of her guards were unconscious. And this joker — he thought he was just going to stride right up to her?

"I'm not here to hurt you."

"Right. You're just here to hurt the two guys who were with me."

He shrugged. "They were following you. I was afraid they meant you harm."

His voice held no accent, and he had a deep, rumbly tone. Rather like Aidan's.

The guy was about Aidan's height, his shoulders were almost as broad, but he didn't carry the raw, animalistic edge that Aidan did. This man — he was more suave. Controlled power. But the danger was still there. Plain to see.

"I was trying to protect you," he said. "I'm sorry if I did something wrong."

Was he telling the truth? Doubtful. "I don't know who you are, buddy, but around here, if you attack first, that's a one-way ticket to jail. You just assaulted two men."

"They aren't men."

Her hold on the gun tightened. It was way after midnight and the street that housed the ME's office wasn't exactly booming with traffic right then. In fact, they were the only ones around. She'd intended to rush over to the police station and do a background search on her victim.

That's not happening now.

"You're under arrest," Jane said.

His gaze swept over her. "You aren't alone."

Uh, no, she wasn't. But her guards were currently unconscious. "You have the right to remain silent."

"I know that you think you are alone. You think that you don't have options. You're scared, and you have to be tired of the fear."

"Listen, buddy—"

"Vincent. My name is Vincent Connor." He smiled.

There was no flash of fang, but his smile still unsettled her. Mostly because it looked far too intimate. As if the two of them shared some special secret.

"You don't belong with the wolves," Vincent said.

Crap. *He knows way too much about me and about this town.* "Put your hands up, now!" Jane barked at him.

His hands slowly rose. "I'm not here to hurt you."

"Obviously—you're just a crazy man. You're out here, spouting about wolves and attacking innocent men. Maybe you don't belong in jail. Maybe I need to find you a nice psych ward for the rest of the night." It was a good thing she'd brought along her cuffs. Jane inched toward him. He wasn't moving. His hands were still up. For the moment, he seemed to be following her orders. She grabbed one of his wrists and locked the cuff around him.

His head turned as he stared down at her. "Don't pretend with me. You don't have to do that. I know exactly what is happening in this town."

She went behind him, caught his other wrist, and cuffed him. With his hands behind his back, she felt a bit more secure.

Okay, not really.

"Garrison!" She called to the fallen man. "Garrison, get up!"

He didn't move. So much for werewolf back-up. If her guards were just going to get their asses handed to them at the first sign of a fight, what good were they?

"If you stay with him," Vincent told her quietly, "he will kill you."

A cold chill slid over Jane's body.

The man — Vincent — glanced over his shoulder at her. "A vampire isn't meant to stay with a werewolf."

"You're crazy."

"Stop." No anger was in his voice. He said the word almost as if it were a caress. "Don't pretend with me. You never have to do that. I'm not here to judge you. Or to hurt you. I want to help."

Garrison groaned.

"Y-you were the one outside of the cemetery, weren't you?" She hadn't been able to see the vampire's face, not clearly. He'd been running toward her, a big, menacing shadow. *Because he's a big guy.* Then he'd just...vanished.

"I was there for you."

"You need to stay the hell away from me."
She pressed her gun into his back. "Because my
last meeting with a vampire didn't go so well."

"We're not all the same. Humans are good
and evil. Werewolves, too. Why would you think
that vampires would be any different?"

Because—

He snapped the cuffs. Just ripped them
straight apart. She'd only seen one other guy ever
do a move like that—Aidan.

The vampire whirled toward her. Her finger
squeezed the trigger because she was not about
to let him attack her. If he thought she would be
his meal for the night, he needed to think again.

The bullet slammed into him, hitting his
chest as he turned, at nearly point-blank range.
He grunted at the impact, but didn't so much as
stumble back.

*Because I hit him with silver. A silver bullet
won't take out a vampire.* But blood loss would hurt
him. So she'd just keep shooting—

He grabbed the gun, his fingers curling over
hers. "It hurts like a bitch to get shot."

She stared at him. He was right, it did. She'd
been shot before so she knew that truth.

He smiled. This time, she could see his fangs.

"I'm not here to hurt you."

So he kept saying.

"Your lover…he's the one you have to fear."

What?

"And he's coming…"

Vamps had enhanced senses. So if the guy said Aidan was coming…*then he is.* "You need to get your ass out of here."

"You'll need me, Jane. When he turns on you, I'll be the one to help you."

"Aidan won't turn on me."

"Yes, he will." Vincent sounded so absolutely certain of that fact. "It's his nature. The beast lives to destroy us."

"There is no 'us' here. I'm not like you." She was still talking to him for one reason—to buy time. Because if Aidan was coming, she wanted to keep the vampire there with her. Together, she and Aidan could stop him. "I'm not a vampire."

"Not yet."

"Not *ever.*"

He laughed. "You sure about that? If you want to know what your future holds, then perhaps you should pay a visit to the voodoo queen in town."

He's talking about Annette Benoit. Because when it came to voodoo in New Orleans, Annette was the real power. Everyone else was just a sideshow for the tourists.

"Ask her to scry and see what the future holds." His voice turned into a whisper. "Though I don't think you'll like what you find."

"*Jane!*" Her name was a roar that seemed to shake the street.

"And here's the lover, rushing to the rescue…" Vincent didn't seem at all worried.

He should have been.

She looked to the right and saw Aidan rushing toward them. He was little more than a blur, so fast, so—

He hit the vampire. Just slammed his body into Vincent's. They both went hurtling to the ground. Aidan lifted his claws, aiming them for the vampire's throat. *He's going to take Vincent's head.*

But…the vampire wasn't fighting back. *And he hadn't hurt me.* He hadn't killed Garrison or her other guard, even though he'd had the chance. Garrison was rising slowly to his feet right then. The other guard was groaning.

And the vamp isn't fighting. Something was very wrong with that scene.

"Aidan, stop!' Jane yelled.

His claws sliced toward the vampire's throat. Blood spilled. The vampire still didn't fight back.

Jane grabbed Aidan's arm, yanking as hard as she could. "Don't kill him!"

Aidan's head turned. His gaze met hers, and Jane had to swallow down her fear. He was still in the form of a man. He was *her* Aidan, but his gaze—that bright blue stare was pure beast. So much rage and hate blazed in his eyes.

"He's not fighting back," she said.

Aidan's expression didn't alter.

"He doesn't care," Vincent snarled, still on the ground. "I came to this town to help you. *He doesn't care.* Take a long hard look at him, Mary Jane. This is what he is. He's the killer. He's the beast. And soon enough, you'll just be his prey."

A snarl broke from Aidan. She felt the rush of power in his body. His muscles jerked beneath her touch. His bones snapped.

He's transforming. Right here. Right now.

"Get...away...Jane..." Aidan ordered, each word a dark rumble. "Get..."

Fur burst from his skin. His body seemed to double in size.

She stumbled back.

"See...him..." The vampire blasted at her as he rose. Blood dripped from his throat. "See what he really is."

Aidan was on all fours now. Transforming fully.

Garrison grabbed her arm. "You need to get away from them."

Aidan was going to kill the vampire. "Why aren't you defending yourself?" Jane asked Vincent, truly confused. He was strong, they all knew it.

Vincent gave her a sad smile. He acted as if his blood wasn't currently soaking his shirt.

"Because you need to see that we aren't all evil. We aren't what he says. *You* aren't."

She shook her head.

Garrison wrapped his arms around her stomach and lifted her up. "Come *on*, Jane!"

Aidan wasn't a man any longer. His shift was complete. A giant wolf had taken the place of the man. He tossed back his head and howled.

"No." This was wrong. Something just didn't fit. The vampire wasn't trying to save himself. He was just standing there. Defenseless.

She broke from Garrison's arms. "Aidan, stop!"

He froze, just inches from the vampire. Froze for the briefest of seconds, and then he leapt forward, slicing out with his powerful claws.

But the vampire vanished before those claws could rip into him.

The wolf howled. Frustration and fury fueled the long, echoing cry.

Like even the people in New Orleans can ignore that cry. She glanced around the street, but it was still empty. Thankfully.

Garrison grabbed Jane once more. He sure was grabby that night. He pushed her behind his back, putting his body between her and Aidan.

The wolf pawed at the ground before Garrison.

"Aidan." Garrison's voice broke a bit. He cleared his throat and tried again. "Tell me that you have control in there. Tell me—"

The wolf's head butted against Garrison's leg.

"Shit, *shit*," Garrison rasped. "Jane, you're gonna need to walk away. *Slowly*. Do not run. That will just make him want to chase you. That's what happens when the wolf is in charge. It's all animal. You run, he chases you down. You—"

"His animal isn't in control. He's Aidan. Wolf or man, he's Aidan." Jane sounded a whole lot more confident than she felt. The wolf had circled around them and now he was right by her side. Jane slowly lifted her hand toward the beast. "He's Aidan."

Aidan with some very, very big teeth.

He sniffed her hand. His eyes—those same brilliant blue eyes—gleamed up at her.

"Aidan," Jane said his name again, only stronger this time. More determined. "Get your ass back into human form before you start to freak out some tourists."

The wolf stared up at her.

Her heart drummed in her chest. She knew he could smell her fear. Aidan had told her once that he didn't like it when she was afraid. That the scent was wrong, coming from her.

She stared at him.

He licked her hand then he slid back onto his haunches. He stared up at her as the change swept over him again. Hard. Brutal. The snapping of bones was a sound she'd never be able to forget. The fur seemed to melt away. Smooth muscle was revealed. Powerful shoulders. Naked skin.

And soon Aidan crouched before her. He rose, slowly, never taking his gaze from her.

"Aidan…"

He wrapped his arms around her, pulled her tightly against him, and held her there, right against his heart. "I was afraid…" His voice still sounded more like a beast's growl than a man's rumble. "Afraid I wouldn't get to you in time."

A bit hesitant, her arms curled around him. "It's all right. I'm fine."

A shudder slid along his body. "This time."

A vehicle's headlights suddenly lit up the street. Jane stiffened. Humans, coming now? Oh, jeez —

"It's just Paris. Get in the SUV, Jane." His voice was still rough but, more *Aidan*. "I don't know where that vampire went, and I need to get you out of here."

She wasn't about to argue. The night had been more than weird enough, thank you very much. She was ready for it to end. When the SUV rolled to a stop, she jumped in the back, and a naked Aidan followed right behind her. "Scout the area," Aidan ordered Garrison through the open back door. "See if you can catch the bastard's scent."

"I didn't catch it before," Garrison admitted glumly as he rubbed his forehead. "The guy just—attacked. No warning. He came from fucking nowhere."

And that was where he'd gone, too. Just vanished. Disappeared.

Garrison slammed the SUV's back door shut, sealing them inside.

"Take us to the apartment, Paris," Aidan said. "As fast as you can." Then his fingers caught hers. He squeezed her. "You're safe now."

But...was she?

Jane looked at his fingers. The claws were gone, but they'd be back. With Aidan, they always were. His beast stayed close.

***

Vincent smiled as he watched the SUV's tail lights vanish when the vehicle turned the corner.

A successful night.

He'd been able to get a little one-on-one time with Jane. Sure, she'd shot him, but the wound had been worth it.

And as for Aidan Locke...

Now maybe she'll start to see just what you really are. The guy pretended to be a hero, but he wasn't. There was nothing heroic about the werewolf. Vincent knew the man's secrets. Soon enough, he'd make sure that Jane knew them, too.

Vincent swiped his hand over his bleeding throat. He didn't feel weak, not yet, but the blood loss — both from the bullet wound and Aidan's attack — wasn't acceptable. He had to always be at full power, at least while he was in New Orleans.

He slipped down the street, making sure to stay in the shadows. Some of the wolves were searching for him, but they'd gone one way and he'd gone another. Vincent wasn't about to be captured. If they got too close, well, he could always eliminate them.

Another few turns and he saw a small tour group huddled together. One person stood before the group, wearing a long black cloak.

"This is the LaLaurie Mansion," the figure in the cloak announced with a dramatic wave of his hands. "Terrible, horrible crimes were committed here by Dr. Louis LaLaurie and his wife Delphine. They tortured their slaves. Performed fiendish experiments…"

A few gasps came from the group as they eyed the house.

They were all busy staring up at the imposing structure. No one noticed him when he slipped toward the group.

There are always stragglers in a group like this…

"Madame LaLaurie was rumored to be the ringleader, the one who ordered one of her servants to have her mouth sewn shut! Madame and her doctor husband created human spiders, they chained their victims to operating room tables..." The tour guide turned away, telling more of his grisly tales as he headed down the street.

The small group followed him.

All except...one woman. She stopped. She tilted up her camera and snapped pictures of the house.

Vincent smiled. "You like...scary stories."

She gave a little jerk, then turned toward him in surprise. He was still in the shadows. The better for him to hide the blood soaking him. The woman's hair was pulled back in a ponytail, giving him a delectably tempting view of her neck. She laughed, the sound high and nervous, before she said, "Isn't that why we're all on the paranormal tour? Because we like to be scared?"

He wasn't on any tour.

She turned away. "Better hurry up. The others are getting ahead of us."

He moved quickly, catching her arm. "I want them to get ahead."

"G-get your hand off me."

"I'm sorry." He was. He didn't normally feed this way. "But I have a need..."

She twisted against him. The woman opened her mouth to scream—

His left hand clamped over her lips. He bit her, his fangs sinking deep, and her blood spilled onto his tongue.

CHAPTER FIVE

Aidan was still asleep. Jane tip-toed around the apartment. *Their* apartment, she supposed. After her place had been torched, she'd planned to find a new place to live. She was still in that whole new-home hunt. But, meanwhile, Aidan had told her that he kept an apartment in the city, one that they could use for as long as she liked.

He'd had a heavy emphasis on the *they* part.

The apartment wasn't Aidan's home, not his real one, anyway. He had a massive, antebellum mansion—a serious freaking mansion—out in the swamp. But the place was pretty much werewolf central, and Jane didn't like staying there. The one time she'd visited the place, all hell had truly broken loose.

So she and Aidan had been compromising with the little apartment in the French Quarter. A place that had top of the line security and a real killer view.

She felt safe in that apartment.

Even with a vampire loose in the city.

Normally, Jane worked nights. Since she was the cop on the paranormal beat, it paid to stay up when the monsters were out. But to learn information about Alan Thatcher, well, she intended to do her research on him during the day.

When I'm not as likely to run into a vamp again.

Jane tip-toed toward the door. She and Aidan hadn't talked when they got to the apartment. They'd collapsed. Or rather, he'd collapsed. She'd huddled in the bed, the vamp's words playing in her head again and again.

What had bothered her most...

I'm afraid he's right. If I do change...what will Aidan do? What did she want him to do?

Jane opened the door and slipped outside.

There weren't any werewolf guards waiting to tail her. She didn't normally have a day shift of guards. Vamps weren't out during the day — they were weaker during the sunlight hours. So her guards just kicked in when the sun set.

She hurried down the stairs, moving down to the first floor, and a few moments later, Jane was outside of the building. The streets gleamed, and she could see the heavy suds washing down the gutters. The street cleaners got out early in the city. Bourbon Street was their number one spot each day — she didn't even want to think about the things they cleaned up there.

It wasn't a long walk to the Voodoo Shop, even with a quick pit-stop.

Voodoo Shop. Simple name, straight to the point. A CLOSED sign hung in the window, but Jane didn't let that stop her. She walked up the narrow porch — the shop had once been an old home, and actually, she still thought Annette Benoit had a place upstairs — and she knocked on the door. For good measure, Jane called out, "It's the police! Let me in!"

And then she waited, her right shoe tapping against the wood beneath her. A few moments later, she heard the soft pad of footsteps rushing toward the door.

Her shoulders straightened.

The door opened with a squeak. Annette Benoit's narrowed eyes swept over her. It was just a few hours past dawn, and it really didn't seem fair that Annette looked so insanely gorgeous that early.

Annette's soft chocolate cream skin glowed as if she'd just gotten a freaking facial. Her hair — long and perfectly straight — slid over her shoulders. Her deep set eyes showed no signs of sleepiness. Instead, her light brown gaze was curious as it slid over Jane.

"You're still human," Annette announced, as if surprised.

That couldn't be good.

"Yeah," Jane muttered as her hand lifted and she pushed the door open a bit more. Annette had only opened it a few inches. *Not very welcoming.* "We seriously need to talk…"

Annette's lush lips pressed together. She looked over Jane's shoulder—

"I came alone."

Annette seemed to relax.

"I don't really want an audience for this little meeting."

Annette's head tilted to the side as she studied Jane. "What is it that you do want?"

Jane lifted the bag of beignets that she held. Based on their previous meeting, she knew Annette had a weakness for them. "I want a reading, and I'm prepared to pay."

Annette's eyes gleamed. "A reading will cost more than a bag of beignets."

"I figured as much. Like I said, I'm ready to pay. Name the price."

"You really believe in my voodoo?"

After everything Jane had seen? "Name the price." She pulled out some cash—

But Annette waved that away. "A few twenties won't cover this." She started nibbling on the beignets. "But a favor will. Agree that you owe me, Mary Jane Hart. Promise that you'll pay the debt to me when I come calling."

Annette could be so weird. "Fine. Whatever." Jane looked over her shoulder. "Can we get off this porch already? You know there are too many eyes and ears in this town."

The voodoo queen waved her inside.

And Jane quickly entered, then shut the door behind her.

***

Humans. He hated them. Hated their smug smiles and the stupid, useless waste that was their lives. They thought they were so superior — at the top of the fucking food chain.

But they had no clue.

He was the apex predator. The one that everyone should fear. Hell, they should freaking worship him. It was time the world understood that truth.

He flipped on the TV, ready to see the morning news. He knew the cops had found the little surprise he'd left in the cemetery. After all, he'd called and tipped them off. Told them that there was trouble on Ann Street and that a beat cop needed to get over there.

He'd even circled back and seen that wonderful swirl of blue lights a bit later on.

His kill had been found. Soon, everyone would know what was happening. They would know about his power, and there would be no denying the truth…

Werewolves were real.

He watched the news. Watched the stupid weatherman make small talk with the pretty, blond anchor. Watched while they talked about a mugging near the Riverwalk. Watched while school kids were shown singing in some stupid recital.

Where's my body?

The minutes ticked by. More stupid stories about the humans.

Nothing about him. Nothing about *his* kill.

Fury burned in his blood.

And claws broke from his fingertips.

***

Jane glanced at her watch. "Could we get on with this? I have a case waiting."

Annette's brows rose. "Jane, you and I both deal with the dead. You're a homicide detective — any case you have can just keep waiting. Not like the guy will get any deader."

"But the trail can get colder." Jane leaned forward and pointed toward the black scrying mirror that sat on Annette's table. "So do what you need to do and let's get the show on the road."

The temperature in the room seemed to instantly drop a good five degrees.

Wrong word choice.

"I'm sorry," Jane said, and she meant it. "You're not a show. I'm just...I'm being a bitch."

Annette smiled at her. "Nothing wrong with being a bitch. Men like to use that word because they think it makes us seem weaker. I don't think so—I'm a strong bitch and proud of it."

It was so easy to like the woman. Even though Jane was pretty sure Annette had a serious dark side...Jane strongly suspected Annette had been behind the mysterious death of the voodoo queen's ex-lover...*But in Annette's defense, the guy was a homicidal maniac.* And Annette hadn't killed him outright. She'd used her magic to do the job. *That's why I can only suspect that she took him out.* Suspicions didn't hold up in court, so Jane hadn't pursued the case. And...

And Annette had saved my ass. Because Annette's ex-lover had been hell-bent on killing Jane, too.

Jane huffed out a breath. "There's a new vampire in town."

"I know."

Jane's brows rose. "Has he been to see you?"

"No, I saw him. *Here.* In my glass." Annette's fingers slid over the dark scrying mirror. "I knew he was coming."

"Um...yeah, and you didn't think to *warn* anyone that a killer was coming to town?"

Her fingers kept sliding over the mirror. "You think he's the bad guy," Annette murmured.

"He *is* the one who drinks blood. Vamps don't exactly have a good track record."

"Yet...you're a vampire."

Her heart drummed too fast. "I'm not."

Annette just gave a little smile. "I'll need a few drops of blood, if you want a strong reading."

She'd feared as much. Jane offered her hand to the other woman. "Don't cut me deep. I'm not really a fan of blood and bleeding and pain."

Annette pulled out a long, wickedly sharp knife.

"What the hell?" Jane blurted. "You just keep that thing under your table all the time?"

Annette curled her fingers around Jane's wrist.

"Tell me that it's super sanitized," Jane spoke quickly. "That it has *never* been used on anyone else before—"

Rolling her eyes, Annette pricked Jane's finger. Then she squeezed three small blood drops onto the mirror.

And just...stared at it.

Jane leaned forward a bit more, now sitting on the edge of her chair. She saw absolutely nothing in that mirror. Though the heavy piece was not even a mirror, not really. More like a big chunk of black glass.

But Annette had gone statue still and the woman barely seemed to breathe. "Your father…"

Jane didn't need to relive that particular torment again.

"He can't wait…" Annette said, her voice husky, "for you to be just like him."

"*What?*"

"She hid you…but he told them where you were. He knew you'd do…great things. Terrible things. Beautiful things…"

Jane shivered.

"He…regretted it, though…tried to help." Sadness flickered over Annette's face. "Too little…too late."

Jane glanced back down. The mirror still looked like black glass to her. "I'm going to have to say that I'm a little confused here." *A lot confused.* "Could we maybe focus on the new vamp in town?"

"*No.*" Annette's voice had gone gravel rough. She seemed to stare straight at Jane only…*her eyes look just like the black glass.* The light brown color was gone. Only darkness remained in Annette's eyes.

"You still want to be the hero." Annette's words were curiously flat. "Even though that's not what you're meant to be."

"What am I meant to be?"

"The end."

Jane shot to her feet. "You're wrong."

"He will kill you."

"Who? Who's going to kill me? The vampire — Vincent?"

"Kill, then you rise."

"I have to die violently for that to happen, right? So tell me when and where and I can change this fate. I can change everything." She was sweating and shaking and desperate.

"There is no changing what will be." Annette's cold voice and her soulless eyes were sinister. "You *are* the end."

"I won't be," Jane vowed. The mark on her right side seemed to burn and she realized that her fingers were pressed hard to it. "Tell me when and where."

"Don't be the hero," Annette whispered to her. "Just…don't be."

Then she blinked, once, twice, and the blackness faded back into the light brown of her normal eye color. Annette collapsed into her chair.

Jane stood before her, her hand still on her side, her body tense, and her mind rebelling. "That's not," she finally managed to say, "the news I was hoping for."

Faint lines appeared near Annette's mouth. Lines that hadn't been there before the reading.

"If you don't like what I see, then you shouldn't ask to know what's coming."

Jane swallowed. "What was that bit about my father? Not cool, Annette. Seriously not cool considering I saw him die before my eyes when I was eleven years old."

"The dead talk to me all the time." Annette rubbed her temples. "And I didn't say your step-dad came to visit me."

Jane took a step back and bumped into her chair.

"You're a born vampire, Jane. Sure, there are some truly random events that cause the birth of a human who is a vamp-in-waiting, but that random event didn't happen with you." Annette's hand fell from her temple. "And I have to wonder...how long have *you* known that your birth father was a vampire?"

"He wasn't."

"Jane..."

"He wasn't a vampire when he first married my mother!" Those words tore from her because...she'd seen the pictures. She knew what her father had been like...before. When her brother had been younger, there had been so many happy pictures of him and their parents. She'd seen those pictures.

Smiling. Laughing. Living.

"He was attacked. He...changed. He hurt my mother." This was Jane's shame. So much shame.

"I figure it must have been right after the attack...he came home to my mother. I-I was conceived." *Don't think about what happened that night. Don't think about the pain and terror that had been in mom's eyes when she talked about her pregnancy. Don't.*

"My brother said our father was a monster." She hated this part of the story. Jane hadn't known...but Drew had. "He would whisper that, over the years. Whenever I asked about my real father, Drew said it was good that he was gone. That dad was a monster. Only my mom kept telling me...monsters aren't real. Almost every night she would say it. *Monsters aren't real.*" Jane licked dry lips. "It wasn't until much later that I realized she wasn't trying to convince me. She was trying to convince herself."

"I'm sorry," Annette said, sounding as if she truly meant the words.

"So am I." She was her father's daughter. Conceived when he'd stopped being human. But her brother...*He isn't like me.* That was why she wanted Drew to stay safe. To stay very far away. "It would really help things out if you would tell me exactly when and where I'm supposed to die."

Annette held her stare. "It doesn't work that way. Things aren't...so clear."

"It seemed clear enough when you were telling me that I was the end."

Annette's long lashes shielded her eyes. "I think it's…soon, Jane. It felt soon."

Hell. "What am I supposed to do?"

"I don't know."

"Did you see who killed me? Was it the vampire? Is Vincent the one I have to watch out for?"

Now Annette's brow furrowed. "He was there. So was Aidan. They were both there but…I don't know who kills you."

She spoke so matter-of-factly. As if Jane's death were just a done deal. To her, maybe it was. "I won't let it happen." Jane spun away from the other woman. "Thanks for this little glimpse into my future hell, but I will change it. I'm not going to become a monster."

She was nearly at the door when she heard Annette's sad whisper.

"You already are…"

***

Jane didn't slam the door when she left the Voodoo Shop. Just as she hadn't pounded furiously when she arrived.

Blowing out a hard breath, Annette slumped deeper in her chair. She wished Jane's fate had been different, but wishing didn't exactly change anything. It—

A faint creak sounded behind her.

In a flash, Annette was on her feet, the knife in her hand as she lunged toward the man who'd somehow slipped past her security system and into her shop.

"Easy!" Paris Cole said, his voice low as he dodged her knife strike. "I'm not here to hurt you!"

Her teeth clenched. *Werewolves. Freaking werewolves.* "Sorry if I don't believe you," Annette gritted out. "I don't have the best track record with werewolves."

His golden gaze darted between the knife and her face. "Your ex was a bastard to us both. I'm sorry I ever called him friend."

Her grip tightened on the knife. "These days, I just call him dead." Because he was. "How long have you been here?" Her stomach clenched as she waited for his response. Werewolves could move so silently. Paris wasn't an alpha, but he was still plenty powerful, and the guy was Aidan's right-hand. If he'd overheard her talk with Jane...

"Long enough," Paris replied grimly.

"You shouldn't eavesdrop on private conversations!"

"When it comes to the pack, I do just about anything." His body was battle ready. "Now are you going to stab me with that knife or can we talk like normal people?"

She slowly lowered the knife, putting it back on her table. It wouldn't be much good against him, anyway. It wasn't made out of silver. "We aren't normal people."

"True. But then, I've always thought normal was highly overrated."

Her gaze slid over him. Paris. Handsome Paris. The ladies' man. The charmer. The guy who usually wore a grin but... "I know what you are."

"A werewolf." He shrugged. "Guilty as charged."

"More. A werewolf in sheep's clothing."

He gave a little pout—one she was sure plenty of ladies had found incredibly sexy. "I think you just insulted me," Paris drawled.

"You are far more than you seem. The easy going façade doesn't fool me. Not for an instant. You're a predator to your core."

"Kind of goes along with being a werewolf..."

"You're Aidan's assassin."

He stiffened. That sexy pout was long gone. Good.

"I know," she said softly. "There is very little that I don't see."

"In that black mirror of yours?" He headed toward the table and picked up her mirror.

Now she was the one to stiffen. It wasn't as if a mirror like that one was particularly easy to come by. She'd built the power in it slowly.

Don't let him know. Never let anyone know what matters to you. That way, people couldn't hurt her as easily.

Gazing into the darkness of her mirror, Paris mused, "You saw Jane turning in this mirror."

She didn't speak.

"You know that can't happen. She'll have too much power if she rises as a vampire."

She wondered if he was afraid. "Do you think she'll be stronger than Aidan? That he won't be able to stop her?"

He shook his head. Sadness flashed across his handsome face as he set the mirror back down. "No, I'm afraid he won't have the heart to do it."

Did Aidan truly love Jane that much? She'd wondered...

Love or the pack? Which would he choose? That she hadn't been able to see.

"I came to talk to you about the vampire in town," Paris announced, his voice turning brisk.

She put her hands behind her back. "Seems like plenty of people are curious about him."

"Did you work a spell for him?"

Now she laughed. "Do I *look* like I want to be helping vampires?"

"For the right price, I think you might help anyone."

She schooled her expression. "Now I'm the one insulted." She pointed to the front door. "How about you haul your handsome ass out of here? I think we're done."

He marched—toward her. Not to the door. "He vanished, right before Aidan's eyes. Just disappeared."

Oh, no…someone knows how to use some very powerful magic. Part of her was impressed. Another part was very scared.

"I don't know about you," Paris continued in that deep voice of his, "but that seemed a bit abnormal to me. I've come across plenty of vampires and I've never seen one do that."

Her hands twisted behind her back.

"Did you give him a spell?" He leaned in toward her. She could feel the threat then, stirring in the air around them.

Aidan's assassin. "No."

He studied her, as if trying to decide whether or not she was lying. This time, she wasn't.

"Then how did he do it?" Paris's scent—rich, masculine, oddly sexy—circled her.

"Maybe…maybe he knows a few spells, too."

"So he has a witch working for him? Someone like you?"

She wasn't a witch. "It would explain…how he found Jane."

"No, plenty of people know about her. It's hard to keep someone like Jane a secret for long."

He stepped back. "What do you know about Vincent Connor?"

"Nothing."

He smiled at her. Flashed dimples. *A wolf in sheep's clothing.* "Come now, that's not true. Just moments ago, I heard you tell Jane quite a few things about him...for instance, you said he was there when she died."

"Y-you need to leave."

His eyes narrowed. "I'm not here to hurt you." His voice had softened. Paris almost seemed sincere.

It was good that she knew better than to believe a werewolf's words.

"If you learn more about Vincent..." Paris pulled a card from his pocket. "Call me. You'll be well paid for the information that you offer."

She forced herself to take the card. Their fingers brushed and — dammit — she felt a little electric surge at the contact. The last thing she wanted was to get involved with another werewolf.

Especially one who might try to kill her.

Or Jane.

If Aidan can't do the job, will his assassin take care of eliminating Jane when she turns?

He turned away from her. Took two steps. Then stopped, snapping his fingers. "Oh, one more thing..." Paris glanced over his shoulder at her. "Good to know you think I'm handsome."

"I said you were a handsome *ass*."

"No, you said I *had* a handsome ass."

She hadn't. She—

He left.

Her shoulders fell. Annette grabbed the mirror. "Does he kill her? Does Paris kill Jane?"

But in the glass, all she could see was the blood. Jane's blood. And not just three little drops.

A river of blood.

CHAPTER SIX

Talking to grieving family members was the worst part of her job. Death was a bitch, no one liked it, and no, staring into the heart-broken eyes of Alan Thatcher's sixty-two-year-old mother hadn't been an easy task. It had been gut-wrenching.

Jane paced in Alan's dorm room. The guy had been a senior at Tulane, majoring in chemical engineering. Just a semester away from graduation. His whole life ahead of him. And now…

A grave is waiting for Alan.

There was nothing in his room that she could use. The guy had been normal. A human with human friends. He'd had a pretty ex-girlfriend, one who'd posted lots of pictures on social media sites of the two of them. He'd had a caring family. He'd had everything.

Now it was all gone.

"Why did he pick you?" Jane whispered. The guy had a New Orleans Saints shirt on his bed. Game tickets were in the garbage can.

She raked a hand through her hair. A knock sounded at the dorm room door and she stiffened—

"Hey, Thatch! You in there?" A loud male voice called.

Before Jane could answer, the door swung open. A tall, dark-haired guy stood there, looked to be around twenty-one, maybe twenty-two. He blinked in surprise when he saw her.

"Oh, didn't realize Thatch had...company." He flashed her a broad smile, one that showed a dimple in his left cheek. "I'll come back. I can talk to him later."

"No, you can't." Dammit, she *hated* this part. Jane pulled out her ID. "I'm Detective Jane Hart."

The guy hesitated in the doorway. "Is Thatch in some kind of trouble?" His pale green eyes were worried. "He's a good dude, I swear. Smart, you know. Wicked smart. He helps me with my math when I need it and, sure he likes to party a little hard, but who doesn't—"

"I'm sorry," Jane cut in. "But Thatch is...he's dead."

The fellow's expression didn't alter.

Shock? Another reaction that she'd seen all too often.

Jane stepped toward him.

He stepped back, shaking his head. "What? *What is that?* No. Not Thatch. *No!*" He covered his face. "*Thatch!*"

"I'm sorry," she said again. The grief was kicking in for him, and it was a terrible thing to do, but she wanted to question him before he gave in to the pain he felt. "Alan Thatcher was killed last night."

The guy's hands slid away from his face. "He was...he was heading out to party last night." His voice was so rough now. Gravelly.

"Where did he go to party?" That would be a lead she could use. She'd retrace Alan Thatcher's footsteps and figure out just how his night had gone so terribly wrong.

The fellow's smile was bitter. "Where does everyone go these days?"

She had no clue. Jane wasn't exactly big on trending party scenes.

"The hottest club in town. Hell."

She sucked in a quick breath.

"Hell's Gate," the guy continued as he blinked quickly. His eyes had filled with tears. "I was supposed to go, too, but I got slammed working on my research paper. Never made it there. Shit. *Shit.*"

"What's your name?" Jane asked him carefully. She wished she was better at handling the victims. They just made her feel bad because she hurt for them. It was too easy for her to understand their pain and their rage. Easy, but she had no words to comfort them. *I give them comfort when I lock up the bastards who hurt their loved ones.*

"Quint. Quint Laurel." He shook his head. "Does his family know? Thatch was always so close to his family. Especially his mom."

"They know. She knows."

His eyes closed. Then, hoarsely, Quint said, "What...what was done to him?"

"I don't think you really want to know that." Her gaze slid over to the cork board on the wall. A picture of Alan Thatcher was up there, with his arm around his pretty ex-girlfriend. A big smile was on his face. "Better for you to just remember him this way."

"Jesus...that means it was bad, right? So bad you don't want to tell me."

She didn't respond.

"*Jesus.*" He said again. "Thatch."

She had to ask her next question. "Did Thatch have trouble with anyone on campus? Any enemies?"

"Nah...nah. I mean, he and Gena had broken up, because she'd been caught hooking up with that jerk Beau, but it wasn't a thing." His brow furrowed. "I don't...I don't think it was a thing. Thatch was pissed at Beau, and I think Beau felt the same way, especially when Gena started calling Thatch again but..." He rolled back his shoulders. "That's just stupid drama. Not the kind of thing a guy would get killed for."

You'd be surprised why people get killed. But a college romance gone wrong? That hardly connected with the slashed remains she'd found. Still… "Does Beau have a last name?"

"Yeah. Beau Phillips. Doesn't live on campus. Think he has some place in the Quarter."

She'd find him. Jane offered Quint her card. "If you think of anything else about Alan Thatcher that you feel I should know, call me."

He stared down at her card, his expression fierce. "You a good detective?"

Her brows climbed. "I like to think so."

He grunted. "You'll…catch the guy?"

"That's the plan."

His stare rose, lingering on her face. "You look young."

"Not as young as you." *And appearances can be deceiving.* "I know how to do my job. Don't worry."

"Sorry, I just…he was a good guy, you know?" Quint shoved the card into his pocket as he turned away. "Good guys should have good lives." He shuffled out of the room, his shoulders hunching forward, his feet dragging.

***

Hell's Gate was different during the day. No big throngs of people waiting to get inside. No mass of bodies jumping on the dance floor.

It was quiet. Peaceful. Almost tomb-like.

Aidan smiled a bit as he lounged at the bar. The door to Hell's Gate had just been thrown open with a bit too much force — Jane's usual entrance style at his place. Did Jane realize she always strolled in as if she owned the place?

I can make that happen. He'd be happy to share everything he owned with her. Always.

His fingers tapped on the bar as he watched her. Beautiful Jane. Her long, dark hair slid over her shoulders and her eyes — dark like her hair but framed with gold flecks — locked on him with obvious purpose.

"You left before I woke up," he said. Though that wasn't really true. He'd been awake, but he'd also been aware that she was trying to slip away without talking to him. Had the vampire's words gotten to her?

He'd already talked to Paris and learned all about Jane's little side trip to see Annette.

Another problem he'd need to face, soon enough.

"I need to see your security footage from last night."

"Well, hello, to you, too, sweetheart," Aidan murmured. "You look lovely, and yes, my day has been just grand." He reached for his whiskey glass and took a quick swallow. "Thanks for asking."

"Aidan...it's not even noon."

He waited.

"And you're drinking now?"

I've got plenty of reason to drink. Trust me. Her impending death? Fuck, yes, that was putting him on edge. Because despite what Annette had said, he would find a way to change Jane's fate. He didn't want to lose her. He couldn't.

"Is everything...okay?" She asked as she crept closer. Concern softened her face. "Did something happen?"

I found out that you're supposed to die soon. That you'll become a vampire. Then I'll have to make a choice.

Would he make the same mistake his father had made?

"What could possibly be wrong?" He forced a mocking smile. "Don't mind the booze, sweetheart. You know it doesn't influence me the way it does mortals."

"What's happened?"

"Oh, you know...the usual. Got a city to run and a paranormal killer to stop." He shrugged. He'd drained the whiskey. "And I got a fun little phone call a bit ago."

Her shoulders stiffened. A very small move, but Aidan watched her carefully and he waited. Would she tell him about her meeting with Annette? So they could face the shit that was coming together?

"Who called?" She slid a step closer. Her face had gone blank, deliberately so, he knew.

A crack appeared in the glass he was holding. *She's not telling me. Jane is still holding back.* "Dr. Bob," he tossed out the name because that was true enough. One of his phone calls had come from the ME. "He's on my payroll, after all. So he wanted to make sure I got all the results of his autopsy on last night's victim." Aidan gave a low laugh. "I'm pretty sure the guy wants to put a new roof on his beach house in Gulf Shores, so I figure he's looking for some bonus pay."

"And he's still working with the idea that a werewolf committed the crime?"

"It would certainly appear that way. All of the evidence supports a supernatural killer, only not of the vamp variety." *Werewolf.* He pushed away from the bar because she'd stopped moving toward him. The scent of apples and lavender filled the air. So did the sweet scent of woman.

Jane.

"But we both know," Aidan murmured as his hand rose and the back of his knuckles trailed over her silken cheek. "That appearances can be deceiving."

It was so easy to get lost in Jane's eyes.

Will it be as easy when she becomes a vampire?

"Aidan...your fangs are showing," Jane said this simply, no fear in her words or on her face.

He smiled. "The better to bite, my dear."

He expected her to back away, but she didn't. Jane moved closer. Her hands locked around his shoulders and she shot onto her toes. "We didn't talk about last night."

"Maybe because neither of us knew what to say."

"Or because we didn't want to lie to each other."

His jaw hardened. "Do you lie to me a lot, Mary Jane?"

She swallowed, the movement of her throat delicate. "I try not to, Aidan Locke. I want you to know everything about me. You matter to me more than anyone else has in a very, very long time." Her voice had softened with emotion.

Aw, Jane. My Jane. In a flash, he'd picked her up and sat her on the bar top. He put his hands on either side of her body, caging her there as he leaned in toward her. Her breath came faster now as she stared into his eyes.

"But I have lied to you," she said, and she sounded miserable. "And I'm afraid I'll do it again."

"Jane…" *I've been lying, too. I know it's fucked up, but I'm trying to protect you.*

"If what we have is built on lies…then what does that mean, for us?"

He kissed her. Not hard or desperately or wildly. Just a soft press of his lips because sometimes, he knew that she needed softness.

Fuck, sometimes, he did, too. The world was brutal and dangerous and he wanted to hold on to every tender moment that he had with her. There hadn't been much tenderness in his life. Not much love, either. Not until Jane.

Was it any wonder he was ready to fight his own pack, to fight heaven and hell and anything in between, in order to keep her with him? "It means," he murmured against her lips, "that we have to stop lying. It means we have to share every damn thing that is happening. Total trust is what we need. We're stronger that way."

Her hand slid against his jaw. He loved it when she touched him. Inside, his wolf ached. The beast needed her just as much as the man did.

"Then time for confession." She exhaled on a quick, little ragged breath. "The vampire last night scared me."

"I won't let him—"

"*I* won't let him hurt me. I'm carrying wooden bullets in my gun now. Wooden bullets in the gun and a silver knife strapped to my ankle." Her lips curved into a wan little smile. "The better to kill all monsters."

Werewolves and vampires weren't the only monsters out there.

"But I have to wonder…" Her lashes lowered. "If I do change, if something happens, if I die—"

"It won't—"

"People die every day, Aidan. Death is a fact of life." Now she was staring into his eyes again. "You can't protect me from every single danger out in the world. You can't lock me away from every threat, can't keep me wrapped up in cotton."

Did she think he hadn't considered locking her away? He was just enough of a bastard that he had. She was the one person in the world who made him completely happy. She fucking completed him—filled that dark hole inside that was where his soul should have been. Taking her, locking her in his home in the swamp, keeping her away from any and every danger…hell, yes, he'd thought about it. Time and again. But in the end…

Jane wouldn't want to live that way. She'd hate me. And her hate is something I can't handle. He needed her to look at him with love in her eyes. Because when she did, Aidan felt like less of a monster.

"I agreed to the guards you have trailing me at night, but…when the vamp came at me last night, they were no good."

He'd chewed their asses out over that fact.

"You can't stop every threat."

"Doesn't mean I won't try." She needed to understand that. With Paris's words ringing in his ears…*Annette saw her changing, man. I'm so*

fucking sorry. Your Jane is running out of time.
Aidan intended to do everything possible to save her.

"I've lied to you."

And I to you, sweetheart.

"I told you that my parents were killed by vampires. By the bastard who branded my skin." Jane shook her head. "But that wasn't completely true. The man who died that night — Jason Hart — he wasn't my biological father. My mother...she married him when she was pregnant with me. But he wasn't my father." She laughed, but the sound held pain. "I wish he had been."

"Jane..."

"I heard her talking once, on the phone to someone. About how she wished things had been different. That Drew and I *had* been his children. She said...she said everything would have been better. That *we* would have been better."

"I'm sorry."

Her lashes fluttered.

"I know her words must have hurt you, but she was wrong. You *are* better, Mary Jane. There is no one better than you."

Jane licked her lips. "When you say sweet shit, it makes me want to jump your bones."

A quick laugh came from him, totally unexpected. *That's my Jane — still surprising me.*

"But I'm kind of trying to bare my soul to you right now," she continued, "so the bone jumping has to wait." She squared her shoulders. "My real father was a vampire."

He didn't speak.

"You're supposed to have some kind of reaction."

If your real father is still alive…

"From what I've been able to piece together, he…he changed. Drew swore he was a good man, once, but he remembered…Drew remembered him coming home one night and being soaked in blood." Her voice went small and sad as she said, "I think that was the night I was conceived. Drew heard yelling and fighting. Attacking." Her cheeks had paled. "I think he must have been newly transformed. I like to…to believe he wanted to stay with his family. That the reason he came home was because a part of him still wanted to be with his wife and son. Only…something went wrong."

I've seen newly turned vamps drain their entire families. Kill without any hesitation.

According to the stories, that was exactly what his own mother had done. But Jane didn't know about her. Another secret. Another lie.

"My mother became pregnant with me, and we…we never saw him again. None of us. I've never met my father. And Drew's memories— well, they are the memories of a child. My mother didn't exactly talk about our real father to us. But she did…she did move us around a lot. Maybe all that time, she was really running from him, and I didn't even realize it."

"Jane…"

"He hurt her that night." Jane's fingers slid to Aidan's throat. "I know that for certain because I saw the scars she carried on her neck. Long and deep, always there. She'd rub them sometimes while she looked at me, and there was so much pain in her eyes."

Hell. Jane—

"I don't like to think about how I may have been conceived." Her lips were trembling and tears gleamed in her eyes. "Whatever—whatever happened that night, my mother still loved me. *She still loved me*," Jane said desperately, almost as if she were trying to convince herself.

Aidan wrapped his arms around her and held tight. "I know she did. How could she not? You're fucking loveable, sweetheart."

She gave a choked laugh. "Aidan…"

"I love you." Saying the words out loud was still new for him. And his heart burned as he said them, but they were true. He did love Jane.

"Then make me a promise."

"Anything." That was simple. He eased back, just enough to stare down into her eyes. "I will—"

"If I do change, if the vamp was right, if—" She pressed her lips together. "If I turn into a vamp and I'm hurting others, you have to stop me. Don't let me become a murderer."

She'd just asked him to kill her.

Fuck.

The door to his bar opened, the creak overly loud as he stared down at Jane. His nostrils flared, and he instantly recognized Garrison's scent. The wolf was hesitating in the doorway, probably realizing he'd just interrupted at the wrong time. But Aidan *had* called and ordered the guy to come by.

Mostly so he could rip him a new one for failing in his guard duty with Jane. He'd already berated the guy once, but once wasn't nearly good enough.

"You didn't promise," Jane said.

He kissed her once more. Harder this time. Rougher because the emotions in him were rough, then he shoved away from the bar. "About time you got here," Aidan said to Garrison.

The guy winced as he took a few steps inside. "I am so freaking sorry about last night—"

Not sorry enough. But you will be. That was pack business, though, and he'd chew the guy's ass out again in a moment. First...

Jane jumped down from the bar. She cleared her throat. "I, um, I'm not leaving before I get what I came for."

If she was looking for his promise—

"Security footage," Jane said. "From last night. My vic came here, and I need to see exactly who he was partying with before he died. I've been running down leads all day and my last one—the victim's ex-girlfriend and a bozo guy named Beau Phillips—turned out to be a dead end. Both were alibied completely. They were at a *church retreat* with about ten other couples. Those couples *and* the priest backed up their story. A priest." Her smile was mocking. "You don't get a better alibi than that. So I need that footage, Aidan. I need to keep working this case."

"Of course." This was something he could give her. "I'd give you anything you needed, Jane. I hope you know that."

Her head tilted as she studied him.

Anything that didn't involve tearing out my own soul.

Paris strode into the bar, pausing behind Garrison. Paris's gaze swept around them all and he whistled. "Did I just interrupt a party?"

"Paris, will you take Jane up to my office? And give her the password so that she can access last night's security feed. I'll be up soon. Just need to…handle a little business with Garrison here."

If possible, Garrison's skin paled even more.

"Right. Happy to escort our detective upstairs." Paris gave a little salute to Aidan. He and Jane headed for the stairs but, halfway up, Jane glanced back, frowning at Aidan.

"You didn't promise."

No, he hadn't. He just stared at her, waiting for her to understand. *That's one promise I can never give.*

Her delicate jaw hardened and Jane turned away. She finished climbing the stairs in silence. He waited until she was at the top, until he heard the door click closed behind her and Paris and then...

He braced his legs apart. Crossed his arms over his chest. Glared at Garrison. The young wolf was third generation, came from a damn good family, but he was still learning. Still too reckless in some ways. "The vamp got the drop on you last night."

"I didn't scent him! Me and Jagger—neither of us caught his scent. We're supposed to smell vamps, but we didn't, at least, not him. Not until he was right on us." His words came out in rapid-fire succession. "And he was so fucking strong. I felt like I'd been hit by a truck."

Definitely not your average vamp. "And you didn't find his trail last night?"

"I..." Garrison glanced at the floor. "No." His head slumped forward. "I'm sorry. I'm so fucking sorry."

Frustrated fury beat within Aidan's body. He knew Garrison had tried. The guy was young, a bit of an asshole sometimes, but when it came to vamps, Garrison gave his all. Vampires had killed his family. Aidan had been the one to go in and find a young, desperate Garrison alive in the carnage. So maybe—shit, not that he'd ever admit it out loud—maybe he had a *small* soft spot for the little bastard.

"I...I didn't find him." Garrison's thin shoulders straightened a bit. "But I did find the woman he attacked last night."

Aidan's brows climbed.

"She's alive. And...I've got her outside."

Well, well. Now they were talking. "Bring her to me."

CHAPTER SEVEN

"Stop," Jane said as she leaned over Aidan's desk, her gaze on his computer screen. "Stop right there."

Because she'd just seen her victim.

On the screen, Alan Thatcher was strolling into the club, laughing, with a tall, blond guy walking right next to him.

"He didn't come alone."

Paris was quiet as he sat in the chair to her left.

"Play it forward," Jane said, even as she memorized the grainy features of the blond. Handsome-ish guy. Young. Looked like a college guy and that *was* a Tulane shirt he was wearing so, yeah, *definitely* college.

The feed kept going. Alan headed into the crowd. Started talking to a pretty redhead. *So much for him wanting to get back with his ex.* Alan's blond buddy hit the bar.

"Looks like a typical night," Paris murmured. "Two guys going out to pick up pretty women."

"Only the night didn't end so typically." She leaned a bit closer to the screen. "Alan just left the blond. Aren't guys supposed to act as each other's wingmen or some crap? He's—"

She stopped.

Because Alan wasn't flirting with the pretty redhead any longer. Instead, he was sneaking toward the upper level of the bar. He kept glancing over his shoulder. No one tried to stop him. With the crush of bodies in the club, no one even seemed to notice him. He went up—

But a big, barn-sized bouncer—who also happened to be a werewolf, Jane had seen him a few times at Hell's Gate—caught Alan on the second floor. He grabbed Alan by his shirt-front.

And a few moments later, Alan was being tossed out the back of Hell's Gate.

Paris's fingers—incredibly well manicured for a werewolf—tapped lightly on Aidan's desk. "So to be clear…because I know this shit looks bad…Aidan wasn't at Hell's Gate last night. Not when this Alan Thatcher was here." He gestured toward the time stamp on the screen.

Jane's head turned so she was staring into Paris's eyes. "And where was he?"

"Uh…well, you know…"

"You have no clue, do you?"

"I'm not the one dating him," Paris muttered. "Maybe *you* should know."

"*Paris.*" She put some bite into his name.

"Secrets are the fucking devil, aren't they?"

She straightened, rubbing the back of her neck. "I am trying to find a killer."

"And I'm trying to stop one."

She frowned at him.

But Paris just stared up at her. "I like you."

"Okay…" Where was this going?

"So I'd hate for things to end with an implosion, okay?" Then he stood. "That's why I am saying this with the utmost affection for you. *Get the fuck out of this town, Jane.*"

"What?"

"Get out, for the next week or two. Go on a cruise. Go to Disney World. Just go somewhere."

She paced away from him.

"A new vamp is here. One who came looking *just* for you. Come on," Paris continued, his normally charming voice roughening. "You know that's bad news. It can't end well."

"If I run, won't he just follow me?" She headed out onto Aidan's balcony. Paris was steps behind her. "I mean, you think I haven't already considered running?" As soon as Annette started her scrying, Jane had been flipping through her options. "But if the vamp found me here, won't he just keep hunting? Is there really any safe place for me?"

"Jane…" Frustration bubbled in her name.

It was a frustration she understood. "I'm going to tell you a secret." She looked back over her shoulder at him. "Aidan. Aidan is my safe place."

Surprise flashed on his face.

"I've thought about running, but the danger won't go away if I do. I'll just be on my own out there — easier prey."

He swore.

"But with Aidan, I'm stronger. We're stronger together." She absolutely believed that. "I don't know how much time I have, but you know what? No one does. We all go through life, doing the best that we can. We wake up each day and we never know — will this be it? Is this the day it ends? We don't think like that, though, we don't think constantly about the end because we can't." Now her voice was the one to roughen. "Because that's not living. That's just fear. And I won't be afraid. I won't let this thing…" Now her hands rose and pressed to her heart. "This thing that's waiting inside of me…I won't let it win. I will be happy." *While I can.* "That's all any of us can do, you know? Live and be happy." She turned away from him. Jane marched to the end of the balcony and curved her fingers around the wrought iron railing. "Running and being alone at the end won't change anything for the better."

Silence.

Her gaze drifted over the street below her. A black SUV was parked in front of Hell's Gate. As she stared, Garrison rushed out of the building and headed for that SUV.

"Ask Aidan…" Paris's voice was so low. So gruff. "Ask him about his family. Make him tell you."

She opened her mouth to reply but —

What is Garrison doing? He'd opened the back door on the left side of the SUV, and he appeared to be hauling something out.

"Oh, sweet hell," Jane said as her fingers tightened around the railing.

He wasn't hauling *something* out. He was pulling a woman out. She was crying and hitting him but he'd — cuffed her?

"No, no, no." Jane spun around.

Paris blinked.

"Garrison," she snapped out. "Garrison is fucking up my life again." The first time she'd met the guy, he'd shot her. And now — now he was abducting a woman? That wolf was about to drive her mad.

She raced back down the stairs, with Paris following close behind her.

***

Well, well, well…there was certainly a lot of action happening at Hell's Gate.

From his safe perch a few bars down, he watched as a cuffed woman was dragged into the bar. Interesting. Very interesting.

The detective was inside. Not surprising really. Aidan Locke was there, too.

But the woman who was crying as she was carried into the place — *that's new*. Hell's Gate had been a perfect place for him to get his prey when he hunted. Packed with so many people, *the* place to be, he'd slipped so easily into the crowd.

And he planned to hunt there again. *Tonight*. The place had felt oddly right for him. Especially with all the rumors that swirled around town about it being a secret hiding spot for monsters.

Now, with this new twist…Hell's Gate appealed to him even more.

He was definitely going to have to meet with Aidan Locke. Looked like they might have more in common than he'd realized…

***

Garrison brought the crying, fighting woman into the bar and stood there, smiling, as if he'd just done the best good deed of his life.

"Aidan!"

He winced at Jane's cry.

"What in the hell is happening here?"

Garrison's smile dipped a bit. "I thought Paris was keeping her busy," he mumbled.

Jane rushed down the stairs and flew toward them. "Is that a gag in her mouth? And why is she *cuffed?*"

"She was bitten by a vampire!" Garrison explained, his cheeks flushing. "I'm thinking it was the same asshole who tried to grab you!"

"No one grabbed me," Jane threw back at him as she pulled the gag from the woman's mouth.

"H-help me..." the woman whispered, her voice hoarse.

Aidan pinched the bridge of his nose. Cleaning up Garrison's messes...that shit was turning into a full-time job.

"Get the cuffs off her!" Jane demanded. Then her voice softened as she stared at the woman. "It's okay. I'm a cop. I'll make sure that no one hurts you."

Aidan just watched the scene. He knew exactly how this would play out, so he wasn't overly concerned about the drama. A few well-placed words from him, and the crying woman would forget the whole scene.

Should I feel more? Am I turning into a fucking psychopath? Maybe he'd already been one, and he just hadn't realized it.

"Look at her neck, Jane!" Garrison pointed to the marks that the woman bore. "He *bit* her! I had to take precautions. For all I knew, he had her under some kind of compulsion! I found her, caught the scent of blood in the air…and she was just lying passed out in an alley. He'd fed on her and just left her there!"

"I-I want to go home," the woman whispered.

"It's okay," Jane said again, her voice reassuring. "Although I can certainly understand why you're afraid." She glared at Garrison.

Paris whistled. He'd taken his time heading down the stairs and now he was standing near the bar, watching the scene unfold with gleaming eyes. "This is certainly not how I expected the morning to go."

"I need another drink," Aidan muttered.

Paris nodded. "Maybe three?"

"I-I don't have the handcuff keys with me," Garrison stammered. "I think they're out in the SUV."

Aidan shoved away from the bar. He stalked toward the woman—the marks on her neck definitely looked fresh. When she saw him approach, her eyes widened. Fear had her blanching.

"He's not going to hurt you," Jane said.

No. She'd been hurt enough. The bite marks on her neck and the way her body trembled…just how much blood had the vamp taken from her?

"I shot him," Jane spoke quietly. "I should have known…with the blood loss, he'd want to feed."

"F-feed?" the woman repeated as her trembles got worse.

Aidan walked behind her. He caught the cuffs in his hand and snapped the silver. He was looking at Jane when he broke them, and at the sound of the metal crunching, she flinched.

"Something you have in common," Jane said. *What?*

But the woman who'd been in the cuffs was lunging for the door, so Aidan didn't get to question Jane. He moved fast to intercept the human, not touching because he didn't want to terrify her any more than was necessary, but positioning himself directly in her path.

Because he'd moved at his enhanced speed, he caught her by surprise. She staggered to a stop, nearly barreling into him, then she screamed, *"What is happening?"*

Jane didn't like it when he used his powers to *influence* humans, but in order for the werewolves to remain hidden in this town, sometimes, he had to do things that she didn't like.

Or that I don't like.

"We think you were attacked," he told the woman gently. "And we're trying to help you."

She held up her hands. The broken cuffs still circled her wrists. "I-I think you kidnapped me."

Garrison growled. "No, dammit. I *found* you. You were unconscious in the alley. I was helping. I was saving you!"

The woman — with her dark hair tumbling out of a ponytail — whirled to glare at him. "You gagged me! You handcuffed me! You threw me in the back of your car!"

Jane winced. "This looks really bad, I get that."

"If you're a cop, help me!" the human yelled as she whirled to face Jane.

Paris stayed at the bar and poured himself a drink. "I think you all have this."

Jane held up her hands, palms forward. The good old I'm-No-Threat stance as she faced the woman. "Did you know that you're bleeding?"

"What?"

"Your neck. You have wounds there. And blood is soaking your shirt."

The woman's hand flew up to touch her neck. "I...he..." She shook her head and pointed to Garrison. "What did you do to me?"'

His cheeks had reddened, a dark red to match his hair. "I get that the cuffs were the wrong move, but when I found you and you woke up, you started freaking the hell out. I needed you to come here so the alpha could talk to you—"

"So who could? What's an alpha?" Her voice rose to an ear-splitting shriek. "What is happening?"

Jane took another step toward the woman. "Everything is okay. We are not going to hurt you."

But the human was shaking hard and still screaming. "I don't believe you! You — you're going to kill me!" Then she whirled for the door, shoving against Aidan. "Get out of my way! Get out of my way! *Help! Someone help me!*" Her cries were high and desperate. Utterly terrified.

He had to stop her terror.

Aidan's hands closed over her shoulders. He exhaled on a low breath, and, staring into her wide, frightened blue eyes, he called up his beast.

"*Help!*"

"You are safe," he told her softly.

She'd opened her mouth to scream, but at his words, she stilled.

"You are protected. You are with friends."

Jane rushed toward him. "Aidan..."

"You think there's a fucking choice here, Jane?" Garrison had taken the choice away by — yes, *kidnapping* the woman. And Aidan's job was to clean up the pack's mess.

"You don't have to control her. It's not right. She's been through so much."

It was precisely because of what she'd been through that he had to control the human. His back teeth clenched. He hated the way Jane was looking at him right then. Like he'd disappointed her. Failed her.

Turned into a monster before her eyes.

Oh, sweetheart. The truth is that I'm always a monster. Sometimes, you just get fooled by the man.

The human wasn't fighting. She stood docilely before him. "What's your name?" Aidan asked her.

"Mary Vester."

Mary. She had the same first name as his Mary Jane. He swallowed and knew he would go easy with her. "Mary, what happened to your neck?" He pulled up a little more power, even though Mary was proving very easy to influence. Not like Jane. He'd tried to control her, when they first met, tried to make her forget a particular case she'd been working on, but Jane hadn't forgotten.

His power — the power of an alpha wolf to control and influence those around him — hadn't worked on her.

The first sign that Jane had been something...more.

Mary's hand rose once more, and her fingertips fluttered over her throat.

"*Remember* what happened," Aidan pushed.

She blinked. "He bit me."

"Who bit you?"

"The man in the shadows." Her brow furrowed. "He was...he was on my paranormal tour. I stopped to take pictures of the LaLaurie Mansion, and he was — just there." Her hand fell away from her neck and she stared at her fingers. "What happened to my camera? I need my camera."

Garrison cleared his throat. "I have it. In my ride. It's okay, I promise."

"We should take a look at the pictures on the camera," Jane said. "See if Mary got a shot of her attacker."

"I didn't," Mary's voice flowed now, soft and easy. No terror. No horror. "There was no time. He moved so fast—he was on me. He said...he said he was sorry."

I just bet he was.

"But he—he had a need." Mary kept her gaze on Aidan. When he used his power, he knew she couldn't look away. "He needed my blood."

"Because I shot him." Jane sounded disgusted. "I'm so sorry, Mary."

Not your fault, Jane. I'm the one who sliced his throat open.

"He drank and he...he carried me to the alley. Put me down carefully. S-said thank you before he left."

Paris sat his glass down on the bar with a thunk. "What a polite bloodsucking bastard we have on our hands."

"I tried to get up," Mary continued. "But...I got dizzy. So I just closed my eyes for a moment...and when I opened them—"

"Let me guess," Jane filled in. "This redhead…" Her thumb jerked toward Garrison. "He was looming over you?"

"Yes."

Well, they knew the rest of the story. "Did you get a good look at the vampire?" He thought it was Vincent, but he wanted to be sure. If there was another vamp in town…

"T-tall. Your height. I just…it was dark and I-I couldn't see that much." But her hand moved to Aidan's shoulder. "I grabbed him…here. It was wet. Blood?"

"That's where I shot him," Jane said.

"He was a vampire." Mary's eyes widened in horror. "That's what he was, right? Bloodsucking…that's what— *he was a vampire! A vampire bit me!*" Her terror was back.

"You're safe," Aidan said again.

"Aidan…" Jane warned. "Don't."

His gaze shot over to her. "You think it's better for her to relive the attack? To look for monsters everywhere she goes for the rest of her life?"

"I think someone else shouldn't play with her mind. It's her choice."

Her choice. Right. He focused on Mary once more. "Do you want to remember the attack?"

Mary's breath sawed in and out.

"Do you want to remember that vampires are real? Do you want to remember that a vampire drove his teeth into your throat and drank from you?"

Her eyes filled with tears. "No."

There. Her choice. "Then it didn't happen."

Jane gave a frantic shake of her head.

"It didn't happen. You were on your paranormal tour, you got separated from the group, and you fell asleep outside of my bar." He smiled at her. "Garrison found you. He brought you inside to make sure you were all right. And he's going to be taking you home now. Home…where you'll be safe."

Mary was silent for a moment, then a quick smile spread over her face. "I'd like to go home."

Right. He motioned to Garrison. The guy bounded forward. "I knew you'd do it," Garrison said quickly. "You always make them forget so I knew—"

He grabbed the guy's shirtfront and jerked him forward. "The next time you get the urge to kidnap a human…*don't*," he whispered into the younger wolf's ears. "Because maybe I won't clean up your mess again."

"I'm sorry! I wanted to help, I—"

That was Garrison's problem. He wanted to help, but he kept making things worse.

"Get her camera, bring it to me." He kept his voice low. "And get her home." He released Garrison and stared at Mary once more. "You didn't meet me. You didn't meet anyone but

Garrison. And you think he's one kind Good Samaritan."

Mary turned her bright smile on Garrison.

Garrison looked miserable as he stared back at her. "I'm sorry," he said again. Then he took her hand.

The broken handcuff gleamed. "What's that?" Mary asked curiously.

Jane spun away and paced toward the bar. Her angry mutters drifted back to Aidan.

Aidan took Mary's wrist, and he yanked away the silver that still lingered on her — on both wrists. "It was nothing."

Mary nodded. Garrison curled a hand carefully around her waist and gave her a little push toward the door.

"Mary…" Aidan called, stopping her. "If you ever see that vampire again, you're to immediately come to Hell's Gate. I will protect you, understand?"

"Yes."

Then she was gone. Garrison led her outside and the door closed behind them.

He exhaled slowly.

Paris looked over at him, raising an eyebrow. Just one. The one elevated brow was Paris speak for…*What the hell do you want me to do now?*

Aidan jerked his head toward the stairs.

Paris got the message. He cleared out fast. Jane just stood there, her hands flat on the bar, her tense back to Aidan.

He waited until Paris's footsteps had faded away, then he stalked closer to her. "I let the human make the choice."

"Bullshit." Her head was bowed. She never glanced his way. "The woman was traumatized. She was in no shape to make *any* choice."

"She didn't want the memory of her attack. You think she's the first? Humans don't want to remember monsters. They have enough stress just in their *normal* lives. Dealing with the fact that werewolves and vamps are real — that these monsters are walking the streets — humans can't deal with that shit." He was adamant on that fact. "It's easier for them to forget. Easier for them to get on with their lives and be happy again. If she'd remembered, she just would have been afraid. Every damn day and night." He waited a bit. Then Aidan said, "Like you are."

Jane spun to confront him. "I'm not afraid."

"Yes, sweetheart, you are. You think I can't see it? You think I can't *smell* it?" And he hated the scent of her fear. "It's been there, all along."

"Stop it."

"When you wake up at night, screaming because the memories won't stop for you…because you see the vampire killing your family again and again…do you know what I wish?" He wasn't going to hold back. Not on this. Not now. Not with her.

"What? What do you wish?" Her words were angry, tight.

"I wish that I could make you forget."

She sucked in a sharp breath.

"I wish I could make you forget every second of pain you've ever had. I wish you'd just be happy." It was the stark truth. Take the terrible memory away from her? Control her mind enough to do that? Yes, he was bastard enough to want just that.

The silence in the room was thick. Heavy. Jane would see that he was right. She'd understand the choice he'd made and —

"I am afraid."

There, yes, she understood —

"But that's okay." Her chin notched higher. "I can live with the fear. I can live with the anger. I can live with all the emotions that sometimes feel like they are ripping me apart — and you know why?"

"Jane —"

"Because they are *mine*. My emotions. And my memories. Yes, I see that fucking bastard killing my family. I feel the rage beat at me. The helplessness. I *hate* those memories."

She understood. She did. She —

"But before she died, my mother said she loved me."

Aidan blinked at her.

"My father…stepfather…no, dammit, he will *always* just be my dad to me…He looked at me. Even when that bastard was torturing him, even when the vamp was *killing* him, my dad looked at me. He smiled and told me that I would be all right." A tear leaked down her cheek.

"I can't stand it when you cry." It tore him apart. *That's why I want to take all of Jane's pain away. Her pain guts me.* "It's better to be without the pain, better to —"

"It's better to have the memories. The fear and the pain — everything. It is better to have them. Better for me to remember that even at the end, even with all the terrible shit that was happening to them, my parents still loved me. They died loving me. I have that, Aidan. *That* memory, and it gets me through the days when I question everything around me. I wouldn't trade that love, not for anything. I wouldn't wish the memory away, I would never want to forget." Her eyes gleamed as she stared up at him. "Just because you have a power, it doesn't mean you should use it."

His chest burned. "Jane, that woman didn't want to remember the attack."

"You didn't want to expose your pack. Pack is first." Jane nodded. "That *is* something I seem to have trouble remembering." She pushed away from the bar. "Get Paris to send a copy of your video footage to me at the station. I have a case to work."

He caught her arm. "Jane, don't leave."

She looked down at his hand.

"The world can't know about supernaturals. There would be chaos. War. You see how humans fight each other now — because of different beliefs, different races, different religions. What do you think would happen if they knew there were real monsters roaming the streets? It would be fucking Armageddon."

"I think all humans aren't evil. I think some people truly do have good inside of them." Her smile was sad. "Just as I think some monsters do, too." She pulled away and walked slowly for the door. But her steps stopped and she said, "He didn't kill her."

Aidan was staring down at his clenched hands. But at her words, he glanced up.

She wasn't looking at him. "The vampire could have killed Mary, but he didn't."

"He *attacked* her, Jane."

"But he left her alive."

"It doesn't mean anything."

"I think it does." She pushed open the door. "Maybe it means he isn't as completely evil as you think." She left him.

Jane…no, he fucking is.

But Jane was gone, and he knew she didn't want him going after her. Not then.

Hell.

CHAPTER EIGHT

Travis Maller loved a good party. He'd finished his big chemical engineering test, scored a B on that fucker, and he was more than ready to let off steam.

He pushed through the crowd at the bar. There were always crowds in New Orleans. That was why he loved the place so much. He'd grown up in freaking Wharo, Mississippi, a speck on the map with all of eight hundred people in the city limits. He'd hated the small town. Hated everyone always knowing everyone else's business.

In New Orleans, no one cared what you did. You could get lost in the crowd. You could party your ass off all night on Bourbon Street.

No one cared.

Thatch had loved this city just as much as I did.

When he thought of Thatch, pain knifed through Travis. He and Thatch had been at this same club just the night before. And now his wingman was dead. Shit, *shit, shit.*

Travis motioned to the bartender. "Give me the hardest shit you've got."

The bartender, a big guy with piercings in his ears, lifted his brows. "Celebrating?" He started to mix the drink.

"Celebrating and mourning. Both are going to take me to oblivion." And that was just where he needed to be. He grabbed the drink when the bartender shoved the glass toward him. Travis tipped it up, angling the glass toward the packed dance floor. "Here's to you, Thatch. One night you're in Hell, and the next...buddy, I sure as shit hope you're in heaven."

He downed the drink in one gulp then slammed the glass on the bar. "Another."

The bartender started pouring.

"Keep them coming." *Gonna miss you, Thatch.* Coming back to this place had seemed fitting. Paying a final respect. Missing the hell out of his wingman. Thatch had been the one to choose Hell's Gate as their party spot the night before. He'd been the one to push to get inside.

*And now he's gone...*Travis tilted back his head as he drained the second glass. And as he gulped down that alcohol, his gaze shifted to the second floor of the club. An area that was off-limits. A big, dangerous looking SOB stood at the top of the stairs. He had dark hair and his arms were crossed over his chest as he stared down at the crowd.

No, not at the crowd. At me. The guy was looking straight at Travis.

And then...the guy lifted his hand and pointed.

"He wants you to come upstairs," the bartender said.

"Who the hell is he?"

The bartender gave a long, slow sigh. "You're gonna wish you didn't even have to find out..."

***

Aidan stared at the human who sat across from him. Travis Maller. The guy held a drink in one hand and his slightly unfocused gaze told Aidan that the human was already well on his way to being smashed.

"Thanks, Saul," Aidan said to the werewolf who'd brought the guy up to him.

Saul gave a little nod then turned to head back to his bartending duties.

Aidan tapped his fingers onto the desk as he stared at Travis.

"So...what?" Travis asked nervously. "You're the BFD here or something?"

Big Fucking Deal. "Or something," Aidan allowed. His gaze swept over the man. Yes, this was the fellow he'd seen on his security footage. Paris had made sure to show him this guy's face. "You were here last night."

Travis's expression darkened. "With my boy. But he's fucking dead." He lifted his glass, as if saluting the dead man. "Heard today. Thatch was mugged or some shit on the way home."

Or some shit. Yes, that had happened. "Why was he trying to get into my office?"

"What?" Travis blinked. "No, no, he was here to party. Why the fuck would he want to get in this place?" He glanced around, seemingly confused.

Why, indeed. "Why did you come to this bar?"

"To party. To get laid." Travis shrugged.

Jane wouldn't like what came next...but Jane wasn't there. Aidan leaned forward and locked his gaze on the human. He needed answers and he didn't have time for bullshit. *"Why did you come to this bar?"*

"Because Thatch said he wanted to get inside. Thatch picked the place, I just followed his lead." Travis Maller's answer was instantaneous.

"And did Thatch tell you why he wanted to get into my office?"

"No." Travis blinked. "Um, what are we talking about?"

"Get your ass back down to the bar. We're done." The human didn't know anything that could help him.

Travis hurried out of the room.

Aidan watched him go.

Alan Thatcher. He was the one with the answers. Unfortunately, it wasn't easy to get answers from the dead.

***

Jane headed toward Hell's Gate. It had been a long day. A day of chasing leads, of talking to the family, and of dealing with political bullshit at the PD.

The death of Alan Thatcher was being handled with extreme care. Jane's boss, police captain Vivian Harris, had been in charge of the afternoon press briefing. When a good-looking, wealthy college student was killed, yeah, a press briefing was needed. *A Cover-Our-Asses* briefing. Vivian had fed the reporters a BS story about the guy being killed in a mugging gone wrong.

Jane had stood silently behind her captain, her stomach in knots.

Vivian was a werewolf, part of Aidan's pack. She didn't want to leak any intel about the paranormals, but she *did* want Jane to find Alan's killer.

That's my job now. To protect the human victims.

There was a long line of folks waiting to get inside of Hell's Gate. The street was overflowing with bars — why didn't some of those people head into a different venue? Muttering to herself, Jane skipped that line and headed straight for the door.

And she plowed into a big, blond guy.

"Sorry!" His breath—heavy with the smell of booze—blew across her face. "I've got...got to go..."

She stared up at him. Thick blond hair, young twenties, strong face, Tulane t-shirt...

He brushed around her.

"Stop!" Jane called out.

That's the guy who was at Hell's Gate with Thatch on the security video. She'd been showing his picture to folks at the Tulane campus all day. While she hadn't found him, Jane had learned a name to go with his face. Travis Maller. Right before she'd come to Bourbon Street, she'd even gone to his off-campus apartment, the guy hadn't been there.

Because he was back in Hell's Gate.

At her cry, Travis Maller didn't stop. He just quickened his steps.

Dammit. Jane yanked out her badge. "I'm a cop!" She rushed after him. "And I need to talk to you!"

Travis cast a frantic glance over his shoulder—then he turned and ran straight into the throng on Bourbon Street.

"Oh, come on," Jane muttered. Then, shaking her head, she gave chase.

***

Aidan had just stepped onto his balcony when he saw Jane rush after Travis Maller. His gaze swept the crowd on the street below him. New guards were supposed to be watching her back but...

This is my Jane.

He jumped off the balcony. When he hit the street, his knees didn't even buckle.

"Did you see that shit?" One man's voice called out, the words breaking a bit. "That SOB just jumped —"

"You're drunk," Aidan snarled back as he pushed his way through the crowd. "You didn't see anything." That was the beauty of humans. Most would explain away the paranormal activity that they saw with their own eyes.

Just drunk. I imagined it. Guy was probably on the ground the whole time. Yeah, they did half of his job for him.

He rushed forward.

He didn't see Jane.

His nostrils flared. *I don't need to see her. I can track my Jane anywhere.*

And she'd turned left. So did he.

***

"*Stop* running, dammit!" Jane grabbed Travis by the shoulder and slammed him against the

wooden wall of an abandoned building. He'd
fled down a side street—a deserted street that
was nearly pitch black because the street lamps
barely flickered. "I'm not going to hurt you!"

"Don't arrest me!" He shoved against her.

Jerk. Jane shoved back, hard, then she
whipped out her gun. "And don't attack a cop,
dumbass."

He stilled.

"That's better." Her breath sawed out of her
lungs. "Are you Travis Maller?"

He nodded, miserably. "I'm sorry."

Jane tensed. "For what? What have you
done?"

His knees seemed to give way and the guy
slid down until he hit the ground. Jane kept her
weapon aimed at him.

"Drinking didn't make it better..." His words
were slurred. "Not a damn bit..."

"What are you trying to make better?"

He tilted his head back, looking up at her.
"My best friend is dead."

"I know. *That's* why I need to talk with you."

"Then you know." He sighed and his
shoulders shook. "I killed him."

***

When he heard the confession, Aidan stilled.
He'd caught up to Jane's guards and he'd put his

hands on their shoulders, stopping them from closing in.

Jane seemed to have the situation well under control. *She gets pissed when I keep rushing into her life.*

She was already pissed enough. He didn't want to get even deeper into her bad graces.

Jane's body was poised to attack. Her gun was held securely in her hand. And her eyes were on the crying man at her feet.

"Looks like she's got this," Aidan said to the werewolf guards he'd assigned to Jane. "Go back to the bar. I'll...linger." Just to make sure.

Just...because it was Jane.

And because I need to hear what happens next.

The werewolves hurried away. Aidan eased a bit closer to Jane and the human...the sobbing human.

***

"I left him fucking alone," Travis said, rubbing his hands over his face. "I was his wingman. I was *supposed* to stay with him. Instead, I hit on some girl I met at the bar, and I never looked back."

Guilt. Yes, Jane knew it when she heard it.

"He left the bar alone." Travis pressed the heels of his hands to his eyes. "I did that. If I'd been with him, he wouldn't have died. No one would have messed with us. Not the two of us. But Thatch was by himself. Easier pickings. And some sonofabitch killed my best friend."

Jane didn't lower her weapon, not yet. Her heart ached for the guy, yes, but she wasn't going to take a chance on being played.

"It's my fault," he whispered.

Time to wrap this up. "My name is Jane Hart, and I'm the homicide detective in charge of Alan Thatcher's case."

His hands lowered. He blinked up at her.

"I could have told you that sooner, but as soon as you saw my badge, you cut and ran."

"I-I...I thought you were coming about the weed." He winced. "I...had some in my apartment. I swear, I was just holding it for a friend, and I—"

"My job is to find the person who killed Alan Thatcher."

He licked his lips. "You...you have leads?"

Yeah, I'm after a werewolf. Only Aidan has fifty werewolves in the city at last count. "I have leads."

He pushed himself to his feet. "You—you were going to Hell's Gate."

Jane lifted her brows. *So?*

"That guy who runs the place—shit, I don't know his name. But the one who has that big, fancy office upstairs...he called me up there, was asking me all kinds of questions about Thatch." He raked a hand through his hair. "I...know he asked the questions, but I can't remember exactly what he said."

Her eyes narrowed. She just bet he couldn't "remember" — courtesy of Aidan. "You had a lot to drink tonight," she murmured. "That's obvious by the smell."

"Thought it would make...him being gone easier."

"Nothing makes it easier to deal with the dead." No, that wasn't true. Giving them justice — that made things a little easier. "Let me call you a cab. Get you home safe."

"No." He shook his head. Weaved. "I'm walking. Clear my...clear my fucking head that way."

Fine. She handed him her card. "When you're sober, we'll talk more. I need to know if you saw anyone suspicious around Thatch last night. I need to know *why* he was heading up to Aidan's office at Hell's Gate."

"Can tell you now..." His hand fisted around her card. "Didn't see anyone. Fucking terrible wingman. And don't know any Aidan..."

Yeah, he did. "He's got the fancy office."

Travis just frowned harder at her. "What?"

He is no help to me now. She needed a sober chat with Travis, not this drunken insanity. "Are you sure you don't want that cab?"

But he'd already started to stumble away. Jane watched him, her body tense, until he vanished around the side of a nearby building. Then she put her gun back in the holster, she straightened her jacket, and she turned to face the dark shadows. "Are you going to keep skulking all night or are you coming out, Aidan?"

Silence. She tapped her foot. Seriously? What was he waiting for? Christmas wasn't coming soon.

He stalked out—looking all menacing and strong and dangerous. Typical Aidan.

"How did you know I was there?"

She rolled her eyes. "Because I saw you on the balcony at Hell's Gate. And I *know* you. When I gave chase after Travis, it didn't take a huge leap of logic to realize you'd be right behind me."

"Because I have your back." He took a few more slow steps toward her.

"Because you're a semi-stalker."

He stopped. "I'm...not. I wanted you safe."

"And I've got a gun with wooden bullets in it to stop vamps and a silver knife strapped to not one, but two ankles tonight. I am safe." She put her hands on her hips. "You used your power on that guy, didn't you?"

"I wanted answers, same as you."

"Did you get those answers?"

"He didn't know anything, not about the killer or about why Alan Thatcher tried to get into my office."

A dead end, or so it would seem anyway.

Aidan was a few feet away from her. His hands were loose at his sides.

"You know the killer is in your pack." Since they were facing off, why not be as clear as possible? "Are you planning to call everyone in? You could question them—force them to admit who is guilty—"

"My power doesn't work like that on other werewolves."

She'd suspected as much since she'd never seen him try to influence any of the wolves, but still, she'd needed to ask. "Then still call them in so I can question everyone."

"They want to keep who they are secret, Jane. Most of them are leading completely ordinary lives. Just being human."

"Look, you have fifty werewolves in this town—"

"Fifty?" He blinked, looking confused.

"You...told me that, once." She was sure of it. The number had been jarring at the time.

Aidan had fallen silent. Not a good sign.

He rolled his shoulders in an uncomfortable-looking shrug. "The number is really closer to four hundred."

What. The. Actual. Fuck? "Then why did you say fifty?"

"Cause I didn't want you to freak out. This was all so new to you!"

She was freaking out. *Four hundred*?

"Look, Jane, some are kids, they don't even know what they are yet. Some are elderly — they just want to be left the hell alone. Good people, not all killers. If I pull them in, if I line them up for you to question, then I'll be destroying their trust in me. I'm the alpha. I'm supposed to be their protection. I need their trust."

And I need you. Jane swallowed. "I have to interview potential suspects…"

"That's why I have Paris working to see who has an alibi for the time of Alan Thatcher's murder and who doesn't. I'm narrowing down my wolves. Once I get a list going, we'll go from there."

Her muscles ached because she was so tense and stiff. "Are you holding back on me, Aidan? I thought we were partners." *He'd lied to me about the number of wolves in this town.* "Partners don't keep secrets."

His eyes glowed in the darkness. "No, they don't, *Jane.*"

Shit, he was talking about her biological father being a vampire. Her hands fisted at her sides. "I have work to do. So if you don't mind…"

But he was there, right in front of her, the distance between them completely eliminated. "I mind, quite a bit."

"Aidan…"

His hand lifted and curled under her chin. At his touch, heat seemed to shoot through her body. She always responded that way to him, no matter how furious or scared she might be...his touch always got to her.

Just as he did.

"I'm sorry."

She found herself leaning forward a bit. "Come again? Because I thought you said—"

"I'm sorry that I'm not the man you want me to be."

What kind of apology was that?

"I'm sorry that I let you down." His voice was gruff. "I don't...I don't always understand humans the way I should." Then he released a hard breath. "That's not true, dammit, I'm not good with anyone generally—humans or werewolves. Emotions weren't supposed to matter to me. I was raised—after what happened, I was taught..." But his words trailed away.

"Aidan?"

"Emotions were bad. Desires that were too strong—they were bad. I was supposed to stay in control. *Always.* And the last thing I was ever supposed to do..." Now his voice was low. She had to strain to hear him say, "It was fall for someone like you."

***

Travis stumbled down the street. He shouldn't have drank so damn much. He knew that. He was weaving. His head was spinning. And he was about seventy percent sure that he'd be vomiting all over the street at any minute.

It was a good thing the city cleaned the streets each morning. There were plenty of drunk assholes like him out at night, only most of them were still on Bourbon Street, living it up.

He couldn't be in the crowd anymore. Because every time he turned around, he could swear that he saw Thatch. His buddy — his buddy was looking for him. His buddy needed him...

But I wasn't there.

Going back to Hell's Gate had been his shittiest idea to date. Being there hadn't made the pain easier. It had just made everything worse.

He stopped at a crosswalk, his breath coming in shallow pants. Maybe he should have just let the detective get him a cab. Travis looked down at his hand. Her card was still curled up in his fist. She'd had a good voice. Determined. Husky. She'd sounded as if she really had wanted to help Thatch.

But I couldn't remember shit to help her.

He started to step forward into the street.

A car horn blared at him.

Someone grabbed his shoulders and yanked him back. "Easy, buddy!" The voice was loud, grating, and…familiar. "You almost got yourself killed!"

Travis glanced back at his rescuer. "I…know you."

The guy's hold on his shoulder tightened. "Well, of course, you do. I'm your friend."

He…was. Sort of. Hadn't Thatch introduced them at a party a few weeks ago?

"I'll take you home. Come on, my ride is waiting."

A walk to clear his head didn't seem like such a good idea any longer. Not when his stomach was churning, and he'd nearly strolled himself straight into oncoming traffic. "Th-thanks, man."

"My ride is right here." The guy pointed to a nearby SUV. "Come on, I'll help you."

He could actually really fucking use some help. Travis leaned on the fellow as they approached the vehicle.

"You sure got hammered tonight," the guy said as he opened the passenger side door. "Celebrating?"

"Thatch is dead." He just announced it. A really shitty move because his Good Samaritan might not have heard the news, but the words just kind of tumbled out of him. He eased into the passenger seat and closed his eyes. "Fucking dead."

"Yeah, I know." The words didn't sound sorry or stunned or anything like that.

They were...happy?

I had way too much to drink.

But Travis forced his eyes open. The vehicle's interior light was on, and the guy — he *was* smiling at Travis.

"Thatch is dead," his rescuer told him, "and soon, you will be, too."

"I — "

Something sharp drove into his stomach. Felt like a fistful of knives. He tried to scream but the dude had slammed his left hand over Travis's mouth.

One hand was over his mouth and the guy's other hand —

He's stabbing me! Stabbing...

"Don't worry." The man slid his hand back. "You won't die right away." He wasn't holding a knife. Freaking *claws* – bloody claws — had sprouted from his fingertips. "I've discovered I like to play a bit with my prey."

***

"Someone like me?" Jane's voice was very, very soft. "What is that supposed to mean?"

He had shit for timing, Aidan knew it. Shit for timing and he had no charm to speak of. When you were used to just telling people something and seeing them immediately react — having that absolute control — you didn't exactly learn a whole lot of tact.

And Aidan had been an alpha since he was twenty-one. That was the age the alpha instinct kicked in. You would either be a normal werewolf — having some increased strength, superior senses, and some wicked sharp claws that burst out when you hunted or when you were pissed — or, if you had the right bloodline and the right genes...you could be an alpha.

An alpha was an altogether different beast.

A typical werewolf couldn't transform into the body of a wolf...an alpha could.

A typical werewolf could persuade humans, but not control them. An alpha could control completely.

A typical werewolf couldn't survive injury after injury after injury...An alpha had blood with special healing properties. An alpha's blood healed not just the alpha, but it could also be used on other wolves who'd been injured in order to speed up the recovery process.

And an alpha...an alpha was born with the desire to destroy vampires. Innate. Blood and bone deep. When a vamp was near, most werewolves felt the urge to attack. It was just part of their DNA. But when an alpha confronted a vampire...

"Aidan, what exactly did you mean...someone like me?"

Tell her. "You know alpha werewolves...they're drawn to the vamps-in-waiting."

"Right. Yeah, you told me this before. And I *don't* like that our attraction might be due to some genetic mumbo jumbo."

It wasn't mumbo jumbo. It was evolution. As long as Jane stayed the way she was, then the beast in him wanted to protect her. Wanted to be as close to her as possible. Vamps-in-waiting—female vamps-in-waiting—could join with a werewolf to produce very special offspring.

A potential new alpha. Jane didn't know that part. She didn't realize that alphas were so rare these days because there weren't enough women like her left in the world.

"I want you," he told her clearly, "because you're *you*. It's not some genetic thing."

She watched him.

"Do you ever wonder about my parents?"

Jane took a step back. "Your parents?"

"I...I need to tell you about them." He had to make her understand what could happen. And why he was going to take steps to stop the hell that waited. *I already put in a call to Annette. She is going to see what magic she can use, if there was any magic that could change the future.*

"Paris mentioned them." She pressed her hand to her right side. She did that a lot—especially when she was nervous or afraid. As if touching the old scar would remind her that she'd survived worse. She could get through whatever was coming next.

Did she even know she made that little move? That it was one of her tells?

"What did Paris say?" He'd have to warn his friend to watch his mouth. Aidan's secrets were his own to reveal.

"That I needed to—"

She broke off when her phone rang.

Shit.

"I have to get it. This late...it's probably my job. I'm sorry."

Her job. Another murder?

She put the phone to her ear. He stepped a bit closer. His enhanced hearing would let him hear every word that she and the caller said.

"Detective Hart." Her voice was clipped.

"I have your card, Detective Hart." The caller's words were low, whispered. Aidan still heard them perfectly.

"My card?" Her breath rushed out. "Are you calling about a crime?"

Had to be, if the guy had—

"I stole it from the man beside me. I'm afraid it has a lot of blood on it now." Once more, the caller's voice was a whisper.

Jane had gone statue-still. "Who is this?"

"I think you've been looking for me."

Jane stared straight at Aidan.

"If you want me so badly, why don't you come and find me?"

"Tell me where the hell you are," Jane gritted out, "and I'm there."

"No, no...not that easy. *You* figure it out. Hurry, before the unlucky bastard with me joins the dead."

The call ended with a click.

"Tell me you recognized that voice," Jane said.

Aidan shook his head. The fellow had obviously been trying to disguise his voice but...*I don't think I know him.*

"Shit, shit." Then she spun on her heel and started running toward the street.

"Jane, stop!" He raced right with her. "You don't know where to go. You don't even know if he was serious—the guy could just be jerking you around. Some punk asshole—"

She whirled toward him. Her chest shook with her heaving breaths. "He's back in the cemetery. That's what he meant by the whole 'joins the dead' line. He has a victim and he's about to kill the guy, and I am *not* going to stand around wringing my hands while that happens. I'm stopping him." Then she was running again, and Aidan was right beside her.

CHAPTER NINE

In New Orleans, the cemeteries were called Cities of the Dead. They'd earned that moniker for a good reason — with the tall, rising crypts and mausoleums that filled the cemeteries, the places actually *did* look like cities. Cities populated by ghosts and phantoms.

The dead weren't under the ground. They couldn't be, not with the flooding that the city had to endure — and *had* endured — for centuries. The dead slept in their crypts. The tourists flocked to their cemeteries looking for a paranormal thrill, and a killer...

Well, it seemed that a killer had marked one of the cemeteries as his own private hunting grounds.

Jane's gun was in her hands as she crept between the crypts. Before she'd gone in the cemetery, she'd taken the liberty of putting silver bullets in her gun and ditching the wooden ones. For the time being. Since all signs were pointing to the killer being a werewolf — Dr. Bob sure was convinced of that fact — she'd wanted to have the best possible weapon for this fight. Aidan was at her side. They'd just entered the cemetery —

"I smell blood," he said.

Dammit. "Lead the way." Because she didn't want to waste time searching. If he could track their victim, that would just make things easier. "Get to him. If he's still alive, he needs our help."

Aidan rushed forward, but he moved too fast. She scrambled to keep up with him. She hurried to —

"Jane..."

A low whisper, one that froze her in her tracks.

She spun around with her gun up. She *knew* she'd heard that voice, just as she'd heard it the last time she'd been in this damn cemetery. Was it the same voice that had called to her then? Jane wasn't sure and she didn't see anyone. She could hear the thud of Aidan's footsteps. He was rushing to the victim.

But I think the killer is watching me. "Show yourself!" Jane snarled.

He didn't. He...

"What are you, Jane?"

Was it Vincent? He'd been outside of the cemetery before. Was the vamp the killer she sought?

Jane saw a shadow move to the right of a tall, crucifix statue. She lunged forward. "Freeze!"

It was so dark. She caught the outline of a man's back. Strong. Muscled. *Bare?*

He took a step forward, moving away from her.

"I said, *freeze!*" Jane yelled at him.

***

The scent of blood was overwhelming. Fresh. *Fresh blood.* Aidan ran to the victim, following that thick scent and then...

Arms spread, as if reaching out to heaven. Body twisted. Blood all the fuck everywhere.

Aidan staggered to a stop. The guy hadn't just been killed. Deep claw marks covered his face and body. So much blood. This wasn't just a kill. This was...

Sadistic. Out of control.

A beast playing with his prey.

He'd heard talk of this before, but during his time as alpha, Aidan had *never* come across anything quite like this.

Travis Maller, you poor bastard. The guy's blood was still dripping onto the crypt beneath him. The kill was so fresh, it—

Travis's body jerked.

Fuck, he's still alive. Aidan leapt toward him. He shoved his hand on the worst of the guy's wounds, trying to staunch that terrible flow of blood.

Travis's eyes rolled as he glanced around, crazed. His body jerked, spasmed. He tried to talk, but spittle and blood just burst from his lips.

"We'll get you help," Aidan promised him. "Stay calm, okay? Just stay *calm.*" The human wasn't going to live long. Not on his own. But Aidan knew how to help him.

My blood. It can give him strength. It might even help him to survive this hell.

Aidan lifted his hands away from the gaping wound. *Not like I was doing much good there, anyway.*

He let his claws out. Then he took one long, lethal claw and sliced it across his forearm.

"M-monster!" Travis screamed.

Now he managed to talk?

"Yeah, well, I'm the monster trying to save you. So just calm the hell down, got it? Take my blood and—"

But Travis was fighting him now. Frantic, desperate and—

He stilled.

"No," Aidan snarled. He grabbed the guy's head. Tried to force his blood into Travis's mouth. "You don't die yet, you hear me? Take a few fucking sips. Drink, come on, you asshole, try to live!"

But Travis's head just sagged back. The last bit of strength he'd had was gone. That last scream—

Monster.

That scream had been his death cry.

Aidan's teeth ground together. His head sagged forward. And then he realized...as some of the desperation faded...

Where is Jane?

Fear came then, coiling around him like a snake, and he surged away from the body. "*Jane!*"

***

When Jane heard Aidan bellowing her name, she tensed. The unknown assailant was still just a few steps in front of her, his face shielded by shadows. Had Aidan found the victim? Was Travis all right?

"*Jane!*" Another roar of her name, only this time, it was much closer. She knew Aidan was tracking her by scent. But she still called out, "I'm here, and I'm not alone! I've got the bastard who—"

The dark shadow flew at her. Fast. Too fast...Aidan fast. And something hit her hard in the stomach even as she fired her weapon. Once, twice, three times.

The bullets slammed into her attacker's chest. He let out a terrible *howl* and then he seemed to leap right over her as she fell to the ground. It took a stunned moment for Jane to feel the pain.

It didn't register at first. The adrenaline was too strong. She was still trying to shoot the bastard who'd knocked her out and—

Blood. Her blood pumped from the wounds in her stomach.

"Jane!"

She tried to rise, but couldn't. Then Aidan was there. Crouching over her, his blue eyes wild and desperate, glowing with his beast.

"Get him," Jane whispered as she shoved her hand over the wound. Damn, but it hurt. And it was deep. *The bastard clawed me.* "I shot him with silver, so he's going to be weak. You get him—"

"I'm not leaving you."

"Aidan."

He lifted her hand. Stared at her wound. The glow of his eyes shined even brighter.

"You...can't hurt."

Yeah, well, she could. She was. "He's getting away! I need you...to stop him..." Talking was getting harder and her head seemed to be spinning. She would get up and give chase on her own, in just a few moments. When a bit of the weakness passed.

When...

Aidan lifted her into his arms. "I won't lose you, Jane."

He wasn't...was he? The pain had faded. That had to be a good sign.

Or maybe…maybe she just couldn't feel anything right then. His arms were around her, but her body seemed numb and—

"You need my blood. You're *taking* my blood."

The hell she was. She wasn't some vampire. That was her nightmare. She would not—

"It will help heal you." He was lifting his arm to her mouth. She tried to turn away because there was *no* way she was going all vamp and drinking his blood.

"Jane…you will die."

What? No, it was just a flesh wound.

"He carved you up, sweetheart. Deep. And I will kill him for it."

Her lashes were trying to sag closed.

"Just take a little of my blood. A little…" His forearm was near her mouth. He had to be holding her with one arm. Typical werewolf strength. She would have made some smart ass comment about that but…

Too hard to talk.

"Travis Maller is dead."

She jerked at those words.

"You're not dying, Jane. *Drink. Take my fucking blood.* Save us both…"

Save them both? What—

Her lips parted.

Something warm, wet…oddly sweet touched her lips. She shuddered because she knew it was his blood. This was so wrong. She should be revolted. She should fight him but...

I like it.

Then her eyes closed and a cold darkness pulled at her.

I like it too much.

***

Jane sagged in his arms. Aidan forced his blood past her lips. She didn't realize how bad the wound was, but he did. She would take his blood, she would heal. She would *live*.

And the sonofabitch who'd hurt her would pay.

He stood with Jane in his arms, holding her tightly. The SOB had fled, but Aidan could still hear the echo of his pounding feet. It would have been so easy to give chase. To stop the killer. To rip out his throat.

But then I might lose Jane. And that wasn't a risk he could take. If she died this way, such a violent death, then she'd come back as a vampire.

I'd be the one sent to kill her. It would be on me. It would be –

Sirens screamed in the distance. His head jerked up as he listened — those cop cars were racing their way. The killer had called Jane, had baited her into coming after him. Had he also called other cops?

Was he staging some kind of scene? It sure looked that way.

Aidan growled as he held her tighter. The cop cars were coming in fast, and they were nearing the entrance to the cemetery. If they saw Jane, they'd take her to their human doctors. Those doctors would try to fix her.

She wasn't ready to be fixed yet, not by their science.

So he didn't go to the entrance. He just ran straight for the big, stone wall that surrounded the cemetery. He ran faster and faster and when he got to that wall...

He held Jane against his heart and he jumped right the fuck over the wall.

***

She'd shot him. And the shots freaking *burned*.

He ducked behind an old building, one with boarded up windows and the scent of rats clinging to its exterior. He huddled low and gritted his teeth as the pain seemed to roll through his body.

The bitch, the *bitch*. He'd been distracted by her because her scent...it kept messing with his head. So he'd lingered at the cemetery. He'd gone closer to her.

And she'd shot him.

His claws were out. His fingers were trembling. And he seemed to be growing weaker with every single moment that passed.

What in the fuck?

He was supposed to be invincible. A god among the stupid humans but that cop, she'd brought him down. His eyes squeezed shut as he battled the pain. He hoped that bitch was dying in that cemetery. Another body to join the dead. He'd sliced her as hard and deep as he could.

Sirens echoed through the night. The other cops, rushing in. He'd intended for them to find Travis's body *and* the pretty detective's corpse. A double kill like that—no way would it not make the news.

Only he hadn't been able to stay around and make sure the detective died. Her scent—shit, it had messed with his head.

She shot me.

The burning wasn't stopping. He just seemed to be getting weaker and weaker and...

He lifted his trembling hand. One of the bullets had hit him near his heart. He started clawing at his chest, wanting that terrible pain to stop. That burning...he was burning from the inside, out. He clawed and clawed and —

His claws scraped over the bullet. He pulled it out, clenching his teeth to hold back his scream of pain.

This shouldn't happen! No one hurts me! No one!

If the cop wasn't dead, he'd get her...he'd make her suffer. Torture, so much torture. She'd beg him to end her suffering. She. Would. Beg.

His fingers burned when the bullet touched the skin there. Small tendrils of smoke rose from his hand, but he didn't drop the oddly heavy bullet. He lifted it up, squinting his eyes.

Silver.

She'd shot him with silver.

He threw the bullet away and began clawing at the wound on his left shoulder. A few moments later, with smoke trailing from his fingers, the second bullet was out.

Time to get the third...

Silver. Detective Hart had known the score about the paranormal world. She'd used silver on him.

He couldn't wait to use his claws on *her* again.

***

Annette Benoit didn't like the werewolf mansion in the swamp. When a woman almost died at a particular spot, well, it wasn't as if it left the best impression on her.

But the werewolf alpha had summoned her out to his place and when a werewolf like Aidan issued an invitation...

No one has the option of refusing.

She slammed the car door shut and glanced over at her driver, the always too handsome Paris. He'd been very stoic during the drive. He'd appeared at her shop and only said that Aidan needed her.

She wondered just what the emergency was that waited inside the mansion, but before she could even take a step toward the house, another car was rushing up behind her. She turned her head, blinded a moment by the vehicle's bright lights. She didn't have any kind of enhanced vision, so the lights made it hard for her to see *anything* beyond the big bulk of the SUV.

Someone jumped out of the driver's side of that SUV. "Hurry the hell up!'

Ah, she knew that voice. Garrison. One of Aidan's younger minions.

At his order, someone did hurry the hell up—the passenger side opened and a man with slightly stooped shoulders hopped out. He rushed for the mansion's front door, a small bag gripped tightly in his hands.

Paris put his fingers at the small of Annette's back and gave her a light push toward the house. She hadn't even heard the guy move toward her.

"Aidan needs science and magic tonight," Paris said.

Her stomach was twisting with fear. "What kind of magic?"

They crept up the steps that led to the entrance.

"The kind that will save the woman he loves."

Annette sucked in a sharp breath. *Jane.* She'd feared this, especially after her last scry. "There isn't anything I can do."

"Yeah, well…" Paris's voice was grim. "I wouldn't tell Aidan that shit. I'd *think* of something. You're the strongest voodoo queen that's ever lived, right?"

She wouldn't say that. She might *think* it, but she wouldn't—

"So use whatever mojo you can, and make sure that Jane lives through the night."

Through the night. Her breath eased out. "I'll see what I can do." But she wasn't about to make any promises. Annette headed into the house. Werewolves were everywhere, and the tension in that place was thick enough to suffocate her.

"Upstairs," Paris said. "She's in his bedroom and—"

"I remember where his bedroom is." Because during her last memorable visit to the mansion, she'd snuck Jane *out* of that bedroom. Annette had thought that she was saving Jane.

I wasn't.

The guy with the bag had already started climbing the stairs. He was an older guy, balding, and wearing a white lab coat. He wasn't hesitating at all as he rushed to the higher floor. In fact, his movements were jerky, tense. *Worried?*

She climbed quickly, too, her mind whirling. The guy up there had to be a doctor and from the way he was acting, he certainly knew the werewolf score. He seemed to either personally care what happened to Aidan or...

The doctor threw open the door that led to Aidan's bedroom. "Jane!" His voice was hoarse. Scared.

The doctor disappeared inside. Annette squared her shoulders. She didn't know what she'd find in that room, but she knew that if Jane slipped away that night, Aidan Locke quite possibly would go mad.

***

Jane was too pale. Too still.

"What in the hell happened to her?" Dr. Bob Heider demanded as he rushed toward the bed — and Jane. But as he neared the bed and got a better view of Jane...he swore. "Claw marks. *Wolves!*" He whirled toward Aidan. "Did you do this shit to her? I told her it was a mistake to get involved with someone like you! You aren't meant to be with humans! You're too wild, too rough, too—"

"Sew her up," Aidan said, his voice flat and cold. Emotions were ripping him apart on the inside and it took all of his self-control not to let his beast out. Only this wasn't a time for the beast's fury and rage. This was a time for the man. Jane needed him.

He would be strong for her.

Bob had flushed a dark red. His eyes were watering. "She needs a hospital!"

"Sew. Her. Up."

Bob whirled away from him and stomped to the bed. "Jane…" He touched her cheek with a trembling hand. Jane didn't stir.

She'd taken Aidan's blood, both at the cemetery, then here at his house. He'd *made* her drink. The wound was already healing, not nearly as deep. But still…*bad*. "Clean the wound. Make sure there is no chance of infection, then sew her up."

"I heard you the first time!" Bob snapped back at him.

Aidan's fists clenched. *Don't attack the doctor. You need him, for the moment.*

"I deal with the dead! I'm not supposed to work on *living* humans!" But Bob had opened his bag. "I need to sterilize first…*dammit, dammit…*" Then he rushed in the bathroom.

The bedroom door opened once more. Aidan's gaze flew to land on the new visitor. Annette. The voodoo queen looked nervous, too hesitant. Paris stood just behind her.

Annette's gaze darted to Jane, then back to him. "What happened to her?"

"Ambush." *Don't let the rage escape. The beast can't come forward now. Jane needs the man.* "Bastard werewolf in the cemetery. He killed again. Another human victim. Then he attacked Jane. She shot him, but he clawed her." *Nearly ripped out her insides.*

"Did you kill him?" Annette asked.

I wish. "My priority was Jane. I had to get her to safety."

There was a little gasp from the general area of the bathroom. "You...you didn't do this." Dr. Bob. Getting on his fucking nerves. "I-I thought..."

"If you don't get to work on Jane in the next five seconds," Aidan told him, rage cracking through his words. "I will start peeling off your skin."

The room went dead silent.

Dr. Bob ran for the bed.

Aidan stood there, his whole body aching because Jane was hurt. She'd come too close to death. He needed her to open her eyes. To look at him and smile. Or to just look at him and give him hell. He liked it when she did that, too.

Annette crept toward the bed.

Paris took up a position near Aidan's side. "You think threatening the doctor is the best idea? I mean, you weren't really going to..." His words trailed off when Aidan looked at him. Just looked. Then Paris gave a low whistle. "That close to the edge, are you?"

He was already over the edge.

Annette stood at the foot of the bed. Her hands were twisted in front of her. "This isn't what I saw."

Aidan wasn't sure what the fuck that meant. He marched toward her. "Use a spell. Get one of those damn dolls that I've seen you manipulate. Make her survive."

"Survive the night?" Her stare darted from him to Paris. "That what you want?"

"I want her *always.*"

"Be careful what you wish for..." she murmured.

Jane was the only thing he'd ever wished for. "I do not have time for the bullshit that keeps coming my way." He wanted to be clear. "Jane. She matters. Make it so that she lives."

"So that she survives the night?" Annette asked carefully.

"Why the hell do you keep saying that?" Aidan shouted.

Everyone jumped.

Bob jumped, then stilled, his gloved fingers poised over Jane's stomach.

Annette swallowed. "I just want to be sure I understand what you're asking for. Spells are very particular. One wrong word can bring a world of hurt."

He leaned in toward her. "I am already in a world of hurt. So is Jane. That's why I need you. I need her pain to stop. I need her to pull through. Survive the night? Hell, yes, I want that. If she makes it through tonight, then she'll just keep getting stronger. I gave her my blood to make sure of that."

Her lips parted. "You...you gave her your blood? But she's human..."

No, not technically true. *Vamp-in-waiting.*

"I've done it before, and if she needs it, I'll do it again. Alpha blood heals, and I wasn't just going to let Jane die in my arms." He gave a hard, negative shake of his head. "That isn't an option."

"It may be."

Breathing was hard. The wolf clawed at his skin, demanding his freedom from the inside.

"She'll survive the night," Annette told him. "Beyond that, I can promise nothing."

He wanted her to promise him everything. That Jane would recover fully. That Jane would have a long, happy life. That Jane would live to be ninety-eight and surrounded by a giant family that loved her and needed her and —

"Drew..."

Jane's soft whisper cut right through him. He spun to face the bed. Jane's eyes were still closed, but she'd definitely spoken that one word.

"Drew…" Again, her brother's name came from her. So soft. So desperate. "H-help…me…"

Aidan locked his gaze on Paris. "Find the brother. Bring him to me." Because anything Jane wanted, he would get for her.

Annette started chanting. Bob was working with his surgical instruments. Jane was bleeding and Aidan…he did something he hadn't done before in his entire life.

He prayed.

Survive the night.

***

Police Captain Vivian Harris stared at the body. Another human, slashed and tortured and left to die in a New Orleans cemetery.

This was bad. So freaking bad.

"Cover the body," she ordered a nearby cop, a young guy in uniform. What was his name? Something Mitchell. Michael? Mason? Jane had worked with the guy before, had spoken pretty highly of him…

So maybe they could count on him right now. "I want the scene secured. No reporters get in here, got me? Not a single one is to photograph the body. I'll get the ME out here immediately, and I don't want this crime scene contaminated. We have a killer to stop, and we *will* stop him."

The young cop's gaze was on the dead man. "What...what kind of knife do you think the killer used?"

She didn't think the killer had used a knife.

Vivian recognized claw marks when she saw them. After all, she had her own set of claws that sprang out when the time was right.

A wolf, hiding in plain sight among the humans. It was the way most of her kind lived.

"Not normal stab wounds," the young cop continued. "They're more slashes, spaced out just the same and—"

"No reporters," Vivian interrupted him, her voice clipped. "If I see a shot of this scene on tomorrow's news, I will hold you personally responsible."

He snapped to attention. "Yes, ma'am."

"Good. Now I'm going to call Detective Hart." *Again.* "She'll be lead on this case, and I want her ass down here." She'd been trying to call Jane all during the ride to the cemetery. Where the hell was the woman? Vivian paced away from the scene, yanking out her phone. She waited impatiently for the call to connect and then...

Music. Hard rock. The music reached her ears, a sound that others at the scene didn't seem to notice.

Because they aren't werewolves. Sure, she wasn't an alpha. Vivian couldn't do a full-on shift like Aidan, but her senses were enhanced, and there was no fight she hadn't ever won. Superior strength was always a plus.

But that music...

Vivian slowly followed the sound. It was her favorite band. She loved rock, the harder, the better. And Jane knew that. For her birthday, Jane had given Vivian tickets to *that* band's latest concert. The band had made a pit-stop in New Orleans, and, though she hadn't let on, Vivian had been touched by the gift. Jane actually paid attention to people. To what mattered to them.

Vivian rounded another crypt. Her steps were faster now. She still had her phone to her left ear. It kept ringing.

And the music kept playing.

A quick twist around another crypt and —

The phone was on the ground. Its screen was smashed to hell and back.

Vivian ended her call. The music instantly stopped playing, and, there on the screen, beneath all of the spider-web like cracks, she saw...

Missed Call. Vivian Harris.

The scent of blood was strong around her. Vivian sucked in a deep breath, then she made another phone call. Only this time, she called her alpha.

The phone rang once. Twice...

The call was answered and a gruff voice said, "He can't talk now."

She immediately bristled. "Put Aidan Locke on the phone, *now*. This is Police Captain Vivian Harris, and I have to speak with him about Detective Mary Jane Hart—"

"This is Paris, Viv." The voice had softened. "And he's with Jane now. That's why he can't talk."

Her nostrils flared as she pulled in that heavy scent of blood. "How bad is it?"

"She'll make it." Though he didn't sound so sure. "She has to make it."

CHAPTER TEN

Jane's eyes flew open. She stared up at the ceiling—a really tall, cathedral ceiling—and she tried to figure out just what the hell had happened to her.

Then her hand flew to her stomach. She—

"Don't," Aidan said, his voice a rough rumble. His fingers tangled with hers. "Don't touch the bandage, not yet."

Her gaze snapped toward him. He sat in a chair that had been pulled right next to the bed. Dark shadows lined his eyes and deep lines bracketed his mouth.

"You look like hell," she told him.

But he smiled at her. A smile of such warmth and straight-up joy that Jane had to blink away tears.

"You look like heaven," he said. "My own angel."

She was as far from an angel as it was possible to get.

His fingers smoothed over the back of her hand. "I thought I told you to stop scaring me."

She did vaguely remember him saying something like that. "How bad was it?"

"Bad enough that I had a doctor and a voodoo queen working on you at the same time." He paused. "And I had to give you my blood."

Jane shook her head. "I don't…I don't remember any of that." But chill bumps rose on her arms. *It had tasted good.*

No. Jane gave another hard shake of her head. That was just some—some weird dream. Some craziness brought on by the trauma. She hadn't taken his blood and thought that it was good…had she?

"Probably a good thing. Doubt you'd want to remember your good buddy Dr. Bob stitching you up."

Yeah, she didn't want to remember that. She glanced around the room. "We're at the mansion."

"I wanted you in the safest place possible. This was it."

She pushed up, slowly, until she was sitting in the bed. She was wearing one of his shirts—a giant white button-up that swallowed her.

"Dr. Bob will want to come in soon and see you. He's been checking on you every hour." Aidan rose, as if he were about to head to the door and get the doctor.

But she tightened her grip on his hand. "What happened to Travis?"

A muscle flexed in Aidan's jaw. "He...didn't make it. I'm sorry, Jane."

Dammit.

"*You* did make it. You survived." He swallowed. "And I'll take that miracle."

"How close was it? How close did I come to waking as a vampire?"

"You don't want to know."

Oh, crap. She must have come very, *very* close.

He leaned over the bed, over her. Aidan's gaze held hers. His eyes were so very blue. "I love you, Mary Jane." The words were deep and strong and they made her feel warm inside. "Know this...I will fight anything, *anyone* in order to keep you alive and with me. I don't want to lose you."

She had to blink away tears and then she thought—*why stop them.* Jane realized just how close she'd come to losing *everything.* She jerked him closer, locking her arms around him, and Jane held Aidan as tightly as she could—so tightly that she never wanted to let him go. "I love you," she whispered.

Her words were so true. This hard, stark, primitive connection between them—it was just the beginning. Physically, she was completely attuned to him. But emotionally, he got to her. Had, from the very first. He could frustrate her, amuse her, charm her...thrill her. *Love. That's what I feel for him.* For a while, she'd thought that she'd never fall in love with anyone. Her job had consumed her. She'd only let a few friends close. Jane's life had been about protecting herself from the pain of the past. From any future pain that would come.

But...that hadn't really been living.

She eased her hold on Aidan. He pulled back, staring down at her.

Jane kissed him. She poured all of her emotions into that kiss. He'd given her his own blood so that she could live. He'd fought for them both when she was on the verge of passing — of becoming something else.

Aidan. Her Aidan. Always.

A knock sounded at the door. "Aidan?" That slightly pompous voice — ah, she would recognize it anywhere. "I need to check on Jane." The door swung open and Dr. Bob stood there, glowering. "What the hell? *She has been fighting death all night. Don't jump the woman now!*"

"I wanted him to jump me," Jane said. She offered Aidan a weak smile. "That was all me."

He didn't smile back. If possible, his expression became even grimmer. "I would do anything for you. You know that, don't you, Jane?"

She did.

He kissed her again. "I can't lose you."

"*I* need to check my patient," Dr. Bob said, huffing indignantly. "I'd better make sure your *jumping* didn't pop any of her stitches."

Aidan growled, but he backed away from the bed. He shot a fast glare at Dr. Bob. "Watch the tone, asshole. Her friend or not, you don't fuck with the alpha."

Dr. Bob licked his lips. "I-I—"

"I'm grateful to you for saving Jane, so you get a pass this time. But don't pull that shit again." Then Aidan's gaze swung back to Jane and softened. "I'll see you again real soon, sweetheart. I just need to take care of one thing, and I'll be back with you."

She didn't want him to leave. Crazy but…she was feeling vulnerable and scared. Claws to the stomach could do that to a woman. But she kept her weak smile in place and nodded.

A few moments later, the door closed with a soft click as Aidan left the room.

"Jane." Dr. Bob didn't sound so pompous any longer. His shoulders had sagged as he stared at her. "Jane, I thought you were dying in front of me."

Her breath heaved out. "That bad?" Because she felt pretty darn good right then, all things considered.

"That bad." He gave a brisk nod and hurried to the bed. "I saw the claw marks and I…I thought Aidan had attacked you."

"That wouldn't happen." Her words came out instantly.

"I know how strong he is. The *alpha,* just like the cocky SOB just said. He's stronger than every other wolf in this town, and I know the kind of damage he could do to you if he lost his control."

"Aidan doesn't lose his control. And he wouldn't hurt me."

Dr. Bob chewed on his lower lip. "You absolutely sure about that?"

As long as I'm not a vampire, yes. But if I change...all bets are off. Her chin lifted. "I'm sure." If she changed, then she wouldn't be the same person. And Aidan would need to protect the world from her.

Vampires became wild, bloodlust driven monsters. They attacked their families, their friends. The old. The young. Everyone.

Dr. Bob cleared his throat. "You look remarkably well." A pause. "I was scared last night."

Now he was surprising her.

"I...like you, Detective Hart. You don't put up with my bullshit. You don't pull your punches. And you do your job because you actually care about people."

Her eyes widened. This was more emotional than Dr. Bob had ever been with her before.

"I would appreciate it," he continued gruffly, "if you would not get yourself killed. I don't have many friends as it is, and I would like to keep the few that I enjoy."

"I'll do my best," she told him. "On the whole, not getting myself killed part."

He nodded. His expression lightened a little.

"And I'm glad you're my friend," she added. His cheeks flushed a light pink. "Even though you can be a serious asshole most days."

A ghost of a smile lifted his lips.

"I guess I like asshole medical examiners," Jane mused.

"Damn straight." He exhaled heavily. "Now, I'm going to need to take off that shirt and look at your wound. Just—you know, hold your shit together because this is all just medical. Purely professional. Don't go freaking and calling in the big bad wolf on me just because I see you without your clothes."

She rolled her eyes and started unbuttoning the shirt from the bottom. "Bob, I know you're gay. I saw your boyfriend sneaking out after your lunch date one day. Rob the cradle much?"

He made one of his *hmmmph* sounds. His smile stretched a little more. And she knew all was well again.

She stopped unbuttoning the shirt just below her breasts and held the material there. Then she eased back down on the bed until she was lying flat. It was odd. She would have expected the wound to be pulling with her movements, at least aching, but it wasn't.

Though it had started to itch in the last few moments.

Dr. Bob put on his gloves, then he began to carefully pull back her bandages. She kept her gaze on the ceiling as he worked. If she looked up there, if she let her thoughts focus elsewhere, she wouldn't think about the damage that he had to be seeing.

Think about the victims. They weren't lucky enough to survive. Think about them. Alan Thatcher. Travis Maller.

The two victims were connected. So, was their killer connected to them, too? Someone they both knew?

Why was this killer targeting humans? Why Alan and Travis? Had they learned his secret and threatened to reveal it to the world?

But…no. She narrowed her eyes on the ceiling. Aidan had used his power when he questioned Travis. Surely the whole, I-Know-About-Werewolves bit would have come up during that little talk, right?

It took her a moment to realize that the bandage was gone. She could feel air swirling over her skin and…Dr. Bob was just standing there. Her gaze slowly slid from the ceiling to his face. His *horrified* face.

"Guess I'm going to have quite the scar, right?" That was okay. She'd deal with it.

His mouth hung open.

"Dr. Bob?" Fear twisted inside of her. "Is everything okay?"

Then he gave a slow, negative shake of his head.

***

"I want a protection spell for Jane," Aidan said as he paced just outside of the bedroom. His steps were quick and angry. "The most powerful one you've got."

Annette Benoit rolled back her shoulders. "She survived the night. That's what you wanted. That's what happened."

He stopped pacing. "A protection spell. We both know you can do one."

She laughed, but it was a sad sound. "You think you can save her from every danger out there? That you can keep her safe from every single threat? Not even my magic can do that. Jane has a life to live, and every life has dangers. Every second—it's a gamble. There are no guarantees in this world, and you know it."

His hands were fisted. "I know that I need her."

"Poor wolf. You fell hard and now—"

He stared down at his fisted hands. "Now I'm terrified because I don't want a life without her."

She walked toward him. Put her hand on his shoulder. "You think you're the only one? Anyone—everyone—who loves feels this way. When you give so much of yourself to another, you open yourself up to incredible joy."

He lifted his gaze to her face.

"And incredible pain." Pain was reflected in her eyes. "But that's the risk. And it's a risk we all take." Her gaze never left his as she said, "There is no protection spell strong enough. Even you, big, bad alpha, can't protect Jane from everything in this world. If you tried, if you locked her away, would that really be living for her?"

"I'm not talking about locking her away," he said. "I just—" Aidan broke off. *I just feel powerless.* No one else had ever mattered to him this much.

"I know," Annette murmured and she truly did seem to understand. "But magic can't fix everything. You love your Jane? Then just—just enjoy her. Enjoy every moment. Don't look back and don't look forward. No one on this earth—human, vamp, or werewolf—is guaranteed anything. We take our joy where we find it."

His joy...it was all tied up in Jane.

"Thank you for your help tonight, Annette Benoit," he said formally. "I know coming back to this place wasn't easy."

"Just like walking into my favorite nightmare," she said, her lips hitching into a half smile. "So you owe me, wolf."

He already knew that. "Paris will see you back home. He'll also pay you for tonight's work." Aidan turned away.

"The cash is great, but I'll be collecting a favor, too. Just so we're clear."

He'd figured as much. Aidan turned away from her. He wanted to go back to Jane and hear what Dr. Heider had to say about her wounds—

"Is it wise, do you think? Giving her your blood?"

Her voice was so hesitant. Very *un*like Annette.

Glancing over his shoulder, he frowned at her. "I've given my pack blood plenty of times." It had helped to speed up their recovery process when their injuries were particularly severe.

"But Jane isn't a werewolf." Her head tilted to the right as she studied him. "Have you given your blood to a human before?"

"No. It's not like I'm overly tight with humans."

"Right. Not you." She rubbed her neck. "And Jane isn't exactly an ordinary human. Aren't you worried — at all — that there could be repercussions from what you're doing?"

"I'd given her my blood before this attack. She was fine after taking it."

Her eyes widened. "Just how many times have you given Jane your blood?"

"I gave her my blood twice last night." Because she had been so severely injured. "And once before that. And she seems *fine*."

"It's werewolf blood, though. Alpha blood. That you're giving to a vamp-in-waiting." Annette's face showed her worry. "What will that do to her?"

"It will keep her alive."

"Aidan...you know better. Frankenstein isn't the only one who can make monsters."

"Jane *isn't* a monster."

"Not yet. But — "

The bedroom door flew open. Dr. Bob stood there, his eyes wild. "You need to see this — see *her!*"

"What's wrong with Jane?" Aidan shoved him out of the way.

"Nothing...nothing at all!" Dr. Bob's voice broke with excitement. "The stitches were barely hanging on and when I removed them —

Jane wasn't in bed. She stood, studying herself in his mirror, his shirt hiked just beneath her waist. She wore only his shirt and the pair of blue panties he'd put on her the night before.

Jane wouldn't have liked waking naked and so he'd wanted to make sure she was comfortable and—

Jane touched her stomach and twisted her body a bit as she stared harder at her reflection. He saw the slightly raised skin on her right side—that long ago burn that would forever mark her but...

Jane turned toward him. "What happened to me?"

But there were no other marks on her. The deep claws that had ripped into her stomach hours before—there was no sign of the damage from those claws at all.

"Aidan?" Jane's voice was confused, a little scared. "What happened?"

The floor creaked behind him. He knew that Annette had followed him into the bedroom, he'd caught her light, distinctive feminine scent. "This is what I was talking about," she whispered. "You give a vamp-in-waiting your blood...and you don't know what will happen."

"She's healed," Dr. Bob said, his expression still dazed. "I thought she was dying, but you can't even tell Jane was injured! Even as I cut the stitches away, her skin was getting stronger. It's the damnedest thing I've ever seen."

Jane still clutched his shirt in one hand and her other smoothed over her stomach. Then that hand slid to her side and pressed to the old burn mark. "Aidan?"

Jane's scared. "Dr. Heider, Annette — thanks for your help." He moved toward Jane, positioning his body protectively in front of her. "But it's time for you both to go."

Dr. Heider was still gaping.

And Annette — she just looked worried.

"Go," Aidan said again, pushing some power in that word. This time, they left. He waited until the door closed behind them, then he turned toward Jane.

Her eyes were so big. Dark and deep and confused. "I shouldn't look like this. Not after the attack."

Aidan reached out his hand and touched the smooth skin of her stomach.

Jane flinched. Then she was grabbing his hand, holding tightly. "Aidan, what is happening to me? Is something *wrong* with me?"

"Hell, no," Aidan gritted as he touched her soft skin. "You are absolutely perfect."

***

Paris led Annette out of the mansion. Dr. Heider had already fled, as fast as he could possibly go. But Annette found herself lingering. She paused at Paris's car, then glanced back at the mansion.

Paris opened the passenger door for her. How sweet and all gentleman-like. She still didn't get in the vehicle. "You need to watch Aidan's back."

"That's what I've always done."

"No, I mean from the threat he won't see coming." She hated to say this, but fear was blossoming inside of her. "He loves Jane so much. He's bent nature to keep her safe."

"Yes, um, I have no fucking clue what you're talking about."

"He's made a new monster." And his actions were going to change everything. "He gave her his blood—*three times. The lucky three…*" There was a reason the old tale about three blood exchanges had been pushed in popular culture so much. But three blood exchanges didn't make a vampire. Just one would do that.

Three…*three links you.* Three gifts of blood given—given so freely—from a werewolf to a vamp-in-waiting. That could not be good. "She's even stronger now. Jane's healing at an incredible rate." And Annette didn't think enhanced healing would be the only side effect to show itself.

"But that's good, right?" Paris asked as his perfect brow wrinkled. "If she heals fast, then she's less likely to die in that whole violent way that would kick in the vamp genes."

Her gaze lowered. "I don't think it's good." She'd need to scry as soon as she got back to her shop. "I think it could be very dangerous." *Very, very bad.*

In order to save the woman he loved, Aidan may have crossed a line—a line that would bring them all pain.

And hell.

She reached into her purse and handed Paris a small pouch.

His brow wrinkled even more. "What's this?"

"It's a precaution." One that they might not have to use but... "The liquid inside can knock out a werewolf in his prime—an alpha werewolf."

His fingers clenched around the bag. "You were planning to attack Aidan?"

"No, I was planning to save my own ass. When I came here, I didn't know what I'd find." *But I feared it would be Jane's dead body.* "I like to protect myself."

He opened the bag and pulled out the vial. "I can see that."

"Put it in a syringe. Keep it close. If something happens and you need Aidan to...to calm down...use it." Because as powerful as Paris was, he would be no match for an alpha who'd lost his sanity. "It won't kill him, I promise. It will just knock him out long enough for you to secure him."

He was still staring at the vial. "By secure him, you mean lock him down with silver."

That was exactly what she meant.

"How were you going to use this on him tonight? I don't see a syringe here."

"I would have found a way." She didn't mention that she had a syringe hidden in her purse.

He put the vial back into the little bag and pulled the draw string closed once more. "Why give this to me?"

"Because there is a reason you're Aidan's right hand. You can be trusted." He was an honorable man. A rare thing in this world. "And maybe I don't want to see you get ripped apart by your friend."

Paris took a step back. "You think Aidan would turn on me?"

"If you turned on Jane, yes, I do." Without hesitation. "Some bonds are stronger than pack. Time for everyone to start realizing that."

CHAPTER ELEVEN

Aidan lowered to his knees before Jane. His beast was howling inside of him—so desperate for her—but he kept a leash on that wolf. His control *would* hold. Where Jane was concerned, there was no room for error. His touch stayed gentle on her, and he leaned forward, feathering light kisses on her stomach.

Jane's hands settled over his shoulders. "Aidan…"

"I need you, Jane." She was alive. Safe. Strong. Right there with him. And Annette had been right—there were no promises for the future. There was only that moment.

For that moment, he had Jane.

He looked up at her. "If you want me to stop, say the word." He'd always do what Jane wanted. Did she understand the power that she wielded? He was supposed to be the beast in charge of the city, but for her…*I will give her anything.*

Jane shook her head. "Stopping is the last thing I want."

They both needed this—needed each other. Needed the reassurance of being skin to skin. The wild oblivion of pleasure that would sweep them away.

He pressed another kiss to her stomach, then Aidan eased down a bit more, moving lower, lower...

He kissed her through the soft silk of her underwear. A shudder slid along her body and the scent of her arousal teased him. He kissed her again even as his hands curled around her hips. His tongue slid out, licking lightly, but he couldn't get the access he needed, not from that position.

He needed so much more from Jane.

He caught the edge of her panties with his teeth and yanked them down.

Jane gave a little surprised laugh. He fucking loved it when she laughed. Then she said, "My, what skillful teeth you have, wolf..."

"The better to strip you, my dear."

Her laughter came again, but the sweet sound faded when he scooped her into his arms and hurriedly carried her to the bed. He positioned her on the edge of the mattress, letting her silken legs hang over the edge. Then he bent once more, his hands moving to push her thighs farther apart.

And he tasted her. His tongue licked. Again and again. She moaned and jerked against his mouth, but he just kept going. He wanted Jane to come this way, for him. Wanted her to have the first blast of pleasure.

Her hips arched toward him. He kissed her tender flesh and kept stroking her with his tongue, just the way he knew she liked. When the pleasure hit her, he felt it. Her body stiffened. Her sex spasmed.

And he pulled back so that he could watch her come for him.

"Nothing is more beautiful," he whispered, "than seeing you, like this." Aidan rose, stripping off his clothes and tossing them away. He needed to be skin to skin with her. Needed to be deep inside of Jane.

She rolled, moving her body quickly and rising up on her knees. Then she looked back at him, her cheeks a sweet pink and her eyes gleaming. "I want it this way."

Fuck, yes. He'd take her *anyway*. He climbed onto the bed. The mattress dipped beneath his weight. He grabbed her hips, positioned his cock, and drove into her in one long, hard thrust.

Balls deep. Perfect.

She moaned.

He gave a guttural groan.

And then he withdrew, only to thrust deep again. The rhythm was hot and fast, and he should slow down, he knew it, but—

"More!" Jane gasped out. "Don't stop!"

He would do whatever she wanted.

Jane's hands flew down and she shoved her palms into the mattress, balancing herself. He gave her more. Gave her everything. The bed was squeaking, the mattress rocking, and his hips pumped frantically as he drove them both toward the abyss of release.

He kissed her shoulder. Licked the skin. Then he bit her, a light marking that was the way of his kind. When his teeth touched her skin, Jane gave a quick cry. Not of pain, but pleasure, and he felt the contractions of her release all around his cock. His eyes squeezed closed because she felt so incredibly good.

Like she'd been made just for him.

He withdrew, then drove deep once more. The pleasure hit him, surging up hot and wild, and he yanked his mouth from her shoulder because he was afraid he'd bite too hard. That he'd hurt her.

He growled her name, and kept thrusting. The pleasure wasn't ending.

"Aidan!"

His eyes flew open at her cry. She was still coming. He could feel it around his dick. Aidan wanted to give her so much pleasure. So much that she would always remember him — always remember *this* moment.

Always remember the way it felt when they were together.

Her hands had fisted around the sheets. She held them so tight. Her body arched like a bow and he curled around her, both of them absolutely lost.

Give her up?

His heartbeat drummed in his ears.

Hell, the fuck no.

***

"A second deadly mugging has New Orleans residents on alert this morning..." The pretty blond news anchor, Sarah Steele, stared straight ahead, her voice carrying just the right degree of concern. *"Authorities have confirmed that another body was discovered in the St. Louis Cemetery late last night, another victim of a robbery gone wrong."*

"What the fuck?" He shot up from the barstool, glaring at the small TV. It was freaking early and he'd dragged his ass down to this tiny diner because he'd wanted to see people's reactions to last night's kill.

But the reporters were screwing up the story. It was no mugging. Fuck that. And what about the detective? Mary Jane Hart? Was the blond bitch on TV even going to mention her?

Folks at the nearby tables glanced at him, their expressions a bit worried.

They should be worried.

The blond continued, *"Reporter Kennedy Jackson is live at the police station with an exclusive interview with Police Captain Vivian Harris."*

And then a new scene was showing on the screen. The camera focused on an older woman, one with a gleaming badge pinned to her chest. The woman looked all official as a microphone was shoved toward her. "Citizens should be on guard," the woman explained. She had to be the damn police captain that the reporter had mentioned. As if on cue, text appeared beneath her image, text that read *Police Captain Vivian Harris.* "They should be smart. Citizens should always travel with a friend late at night and be aware of their surroundings. And if anyone sees something suspicious, do not hesitate to call the cops. After all…" She gave a tight smile. "We're here to help you."

Fuck, fuck.

"Rest assured," the police captain continued doggedly. "I have my best team working on this case. The killer will be apprehended."

Then — from off camera — he heard a reporter ask, "This makes two murders in a very short amount of time. Are we looking at a serial?"

The police captain's eyes narrowed just a bit.

He realized he was holding his breath.

"No, Ms. Jackson," Vivian Harris said clearly. "We're just looking at a man who enjoys preying on the weak. A coward who hunts in the dark."

His claws wanted to spring free. He wanted to attack. She'd dared to call him a coward?

Vivian Harris stared straight into the camera — *seems like she's looking right at me.* "As I said before, this killer will be apprehended, have no doubt about that."

Really? Then come and get me.

The camera cut away from her and the pretty blond reporter was back on screen.

Or...maybe I'll just come and get you.

***

Aidan's heartbeat thundered in his ears. He was still curled over Jane, the scent of their lovemaking filling the air. And he was already getting hard for her again. Hardly surprising. He pretty much always wanted Jane.

She looked back over her shoulder, smiling at him. "I love you, Aidan Locke."

I would die for you, Mary Jane Hart.

"Want to take a shower with me?" Her voice was light, happy. And why not? She'd cheated death. They were together. They both *should* be happy.

"Absolutely." Slowly, he withdrew from her. She gave a little moan.

And I'll be coming right back inside you when we get in that shower.

He rose from the bed. Maybe his knees were a little weak. Making love to her could do that, not that Aidan would ever admit it. He wasn't supposed to have a weakness. *I do. It's my Jane.*

She rolled over, still smiling up at him. "I don't know how it happened, I don't know what magic you got Annette to pull, but I feel stronger than I've ever felt in my entire life."

He forced a smile for her. "I'm glad."

"Race you to the shower." Then she was zipping past him.

He started to hurry after her but...

Something caught his eye. Something there, in the bed. Frowning now, he leaned over and looked closer at the bed covers. Sure, they'd wrecked that bed. Only...

The sheets were ripped.

He picked up part of the sheet and saw the long tendrils that looked as if claws had sliced into them. Aidan glanced at his own hands. He hadn't let his claws out. He'd been touching Jane the whole time, so he hadn't wanted to risk cutting her skin.

He picked up another piece of the shredded material.

Jane had grabbed the bedding. He remembered that. At the end, when she'd been lost to the pleasure, she'd fisted her hands around the sheets.

These are marks made by claws. I've seen marks like this before.

"Aidan..." Jane's voice called. Light. Teasing. "I won."

***

"I don't like this," Aidan said.

Jane rolled her eyes as she checked her gun. The weapon was good to go with silver bullets. And, for extra paranormal protection, she had a wooden stake strapped to her ankle. "Yes, well, I adore you, but I don't particularly care what you *like* about this part." He'd brought her back to town, but been oddly quiet and reserved during the drive to the cemetery. *Back to the scene of the crime.* "I have a job to do, and I'm getting back to it." Her gaze sharpened as she looked at him. "I'm not a cop because I like playing things safe. I'm a cop because I want to keep everyone else safe."

He stood beside her, his arms crossed over his chest. "Did you forget you nearly died last night?"

"Hard to forget that bit."

He glowered even more. It was probably not the time to tell him that she found his glowers sexy. Her body was practically humming. It was so weird. She couldn't remember ever feeling this good. "I also didn't forget," Jane continued, "that I shot the bastard who attacked me. So if I shot him, he bled. And you — with that absolutely wonderful nose of yours — will help me track him."

"Jane..."

"Come on." She led the way into the cemetery. Dr. Bob had the victim's body on his table, and she'd be heading to the ME's office later for an update on Travis. Just to make sure there weren't any new twists waiting for her. But for the moment, she wanted to try some blood tracking.

The scent of blood hit Jane just after she'd taken a few steps inside the cemetery. Strong. Coppery. A little...woodsy? Her nostrils flared as she inhaled the scent. Then Jane turned to the right. "I was over this way when he attacked."

Aidan caught her elbow. "Jane, do you *smell* the blood?"

"Yes." Her breath hitched. "He must have bled out a whole lot more than I realized." And the crime scene techs must have been damn slouchy at their jobs. They should have cleaned the area far better.

She followed the scent, her steps quickening. Then...

Jane stopped. There were no giant trails of blood on the ground. Well, not except for the stain that was from where she'd been. Someone *had* tried to clean that up. Jane pointed. "I remember falling here. You — you were crouching above me." She threw a quick glance his way.

His face hardened. "Yes."

She lifted her hand, as if aiming a gun. "He was right over there." Where the slightly woodsy scent was coming from. Jane took a few lurching steps forward and then she saw the blood drops. Just drops. As if the killer had been running away and the blood had flown back in his wake.

How do I smell this? The blood drops have already dried and they're so small.

What in the hell was happening? "Aidan?"

But he'd just brushed past her. "It was good of the bastard to leave us a trail."

"Aidan, what's happening to me?"

His shoulders tensed. "I think he jumped over the wall to get out of here, same as I did." He came back to her, scooped her into his arms and said, "Hold on tight."

He was keeping something from her. "*Aidan. Stop.*"

He tensed.

"How did I heal? Why can I smell his blood?" *Why do I feel so good?*

Aidan's Adam's apple bobbed as he swallowed. "I told you...that I gave you my blood."

Jane nodded. "You did that before." When Garrison had been a trigger happy dumbass and shot her. Not that she held a grudge. Well, not anymore. She and Garrison had worked past that unfortunate first encounter.

"There seem to be a few…side effects this time."

Side effects? That sounded so not good. "How long will they last?"

His arms tightened around her. "I have no fucking clue." Then he was running toward the wall. She held onto him as tightly as she could and then—

They were over the wall. He touched down without even having his knees buckle. Carefully, he put her onto her feet then swept his gaze around the area.

A little late to see if anyone saw that move.

But…no one was there.

Aidan threaded his fingers with hers. "Come on." And he was moving fast, but not so fast that she couldn't keep up. They hurried across the street and he crouched next to a boarded-up building.

The scent of blood was strong again. And sunlight glinted off the silver bullet on the ground. A blood-stained bullet.

"He dug them out," Jane said. There were two more bullets nearby. "He's strong, Aidan."

Aidan had turned to stare down the street. His expression thoughtful, he said, "Yes, yes, he fucking is."

Her nostrils twitched. "Where did he go after he left?" Because she couldn't tell. Her *side effects* weren't that good.

"They cleaned the streets," Aidan said, disgust thick in his voice. "This is the only scent I'm getting...right here. If there was more blood, it was washed away when the streets were cleaned this morning."

Dammit.

"Sorry, Jane."

"No, don't be sorry." Carefully she pocketed the bullets. "We learned more. The guy is stronger than I expected. Hell, you're the only one I've seen dig out silver bullets. I didn't realize that was something most werewolves could do."

He was silent.

"I need to go see Dr. Bob," Jane continued, adjusting her plans as she considered things. "But I think first I'll check in at the station with Vivian. She's probably freaking the hell out right now, and if I stop to see her, it will give Bob a little longer to finish his report."

Aidan's head jerked to the right. A low growl built in his throat.

Oh, jeez. What now? "Aidan?"

"He's coming."

She yanked out her weapon. "The killer?"

"Worse." The one word came out as a snarl. "The vampire."

And then he was there. Just strolling down the street toward them. Jane blinked. Had the guy been in the road a moment before? She didn't think so, but now he was just boldly striding toward them.

The vampire took his time approaching them, and when Aidan wanted to lunge forward, Jane wrapped her hand around his arm. "I want to see what he has to say."

"The bastard is in *my* town, without an invitation. He's asking for trouble."

She knew that was true. Vamps and werewolves weren't made to get along. And Aidan never let vamps stay in New Orleans long.

"Jane." Vincent's gaze swept over her. "You're...still human?" He seemed surprised.

Jane had to admit — when she'd woken up in Aidan's bed — she'd been surprised, too. Only now she fully realized that it hadn't been Dr. Bob's medicine or Annette's voodoo magic that had saved her...

It had been Aidan.

"When I got here last night...and saw Aidan rushing away with you held so tightly in his arms..." Vincent lifted one shoulder in a shrug. "I thought you were dying."

"And you jumped in to help save me?" Anger vibrated in her voice. "How nice of you — oh, wait. You didn't help. What *did* you do? Watch from the shadows and count down as you hoped my life ticked away?"

He took a step back.

Aidan's claws had come out, she could see them. She still touched his arm and Aidan's muscles were rock hard beneath her hand. But Aidan wasn't attacking.

He's holding back for me.

"You can't change fate," Vincent said.

"I think we make our own fate. People aren't born with their whole lives mapped out in some little book."

Vincent's expression hardened. "You aren't like most people."

"Were you watching the whole time?" Jane asked him. "When that werewolf brought Travis Maller to the cemetery? Were you here when the poor guy was being murdered?"

"No," Vincent rasped. "I didn't arrive until after."

Aidan gave another low growl. "Would you have *helped* if you had been there sooner? Would you have stepped in to save the human?"

Vincent seemed surprised by the question. "I didn't know him."

Jane's jaw dropped. "He was a person! Didn't matter if you knew him or not — the guy was in pain and he needed help — so you should have wanted to *save* him."

"Vamps aren't like that, Jane," Aidan said gruffly. "They don't care. They'll tear apart their whole families if that gives them the blood they need."

Sadness flashed across Vincent's face. "I have…seen that happen."

"Yes, so the fuck have I," Aidan fired back. "Too many times. I know what your kind can do. I know how all they can live for is the bloodlust— it controls them. It maddens them. It—"

"My kind isn't doing the killing this time." Vincent had straightened his shoulders. "Yours is."

She let Aidan go. The vamp was just asking for trouble.

But Vincent held up his hands. "I'm sorry. I'm not here to provoke you."

"No?" Aidan obviously doubted that statement. "Could've fooled the hell out of me." He lifted his claws. "So this is how things will work. I've played the good guy with you long enough. The beast in me wants nothing more than to cut off your head—"

"Aren't you the blunt one," Vincent muttered.

"But I've held back, fucking barely. Mostly because you haven't killed anyone yet. Jane doesn't like it if I kill without reason." He shrugged. "One of her little rules."

Vincent's eyelids flickered. "Of course, you can only do what Jane likes."

Jane glanced between the two of them. Similar in size, and she had no doubt that Vincent was a powerful vampire. In a battle, who would win?

Sure, the vamp had his parlor trick of disappearing into thin air but...

My money is on Aidan.

"Get your ass out of my town," Aidan told him darkly. "Be gone by the time the sun sets tonight. If you aren't, I will come for you, and I won't hold my beast back."

The vamp lifted his chin. "Jane, I am here to *help* — "

Her laughter was bitter. "Tell that to the woman you attacked and left in a dirty alley."

"I didn't kill her — "

"No, you just took her blood. Nearly killed her."

Vincent shook his head. "I held onto my restraint. She was never in any danger. What was I supposed to do? You'd shot me and your boyfriend there did his best to rip out my throat. You know how blood loss is for our kind."

She made sure her weapon was aimed right at his heart. "There is no 'our' here, buddy."

His gaze darted down to her weapon. "Wooden bullets?"

"You better believe it." Total lie. But the silver bullets in her gun would still cause him plenty of blood loss. "Think you can pull that vanishing act before I shoot? Or before Aidan decides to use his claws to rip off your head?"

Vincent stumbled back a step.

"See, I don't like it when vamps feed on humans. And I really don't like the way you seem to be skulking around every time I blink. Aidan showed you courtesy," the werewolf version, at least, "now it's past time for you to get out of here."

"You're going to regret this," Vincent warned her.

"I highly doubt it." She cast a quick, nervous glance Aidan's way. He hadn't said much, probably because it took all of his self-control and strength not to attack the vampire. *And he's holding back for me.* "The only thing I regret is that we ever met."

"That so?" Vincent turned away from them, presenting his back as far too tempting of a target. "My mistake. I thought you wanted to know about your father. But, hey, guess I was wrong."

Before she could speak, Aidan curled his arm around her shoulder. "He's baiting you, Jane." His voice was rough, ragged. *Definitely using all of his self-control not to attack.*

She knew Aidan's words were true. Jane gave a rough nod in agreement. Then she made sure her voice was nice and strong as she said, "The only father I had was killed by a vampire when I was eleven years old. He was staring straight at me when he drew his last breath."

Vincent stilled. She saw his shoulders stiffen. "I'm sorry...I-I didn't realize..."

"The same vamp spent hours torturing me. I've still got the scars to prove it."

Now he did whirl toward her. "That shouldn't have happened." Vincent seemed genuinely horrified. "You were the beginning of something new—"

"Bullshit. I'm the end." She'd grown accustomed to that burn mark on her body. "Got the permanent reminder to prove it."

Aidan's fingers tightened on her shoulder.

"Keep moving," Jane said to Vincent, her hand steady on her gun. "Because you are done here."

Vincent's eyes gleamed with his fury. "I am sorry. I will find the vampire who attacked you. I will make him pay—"

"Already done," Aidan interrupted. "He's dust in the wind. See, he was the last asshole vamp who didn't listen when I said this town belonged to the wolves."

A furrow had appeared on Vincent's brows. "You avenged her?"

"I killed for her, and I'd do it again in a heartbeat. Never doubt that."

Vincent raked his hand over his face. "Jane, your father—your *real* father—he was troubled, I knew that. But I can't believe he would let something like this happen—"

"Yeah, well, word on my biological dad is that he died a long time ago, too," Jane said. "The vamp who killed my family? Thane Durant? He told me that werewolves had killed my father."

Surprise flashed on Vincent's face. "That's not what happened to Michael, not at all. You were told a lie."

Her lips parted. *What in the hell am I supposed to believe? And why did it just hurt me to hear my father's name? Michael...*

"Thane Durant," Vincent continued darkly, "was a twisted, sadistic, *lying* bastard. You can't believe any shit he told you." His laughter was bitter. "Actually, Thane *was* the one to kill your father."

What? Jane gave a quick, hard shake of her head but... "I guess vamps turn on each other all the time, huh?"

"No, we don't." Vincent inclined his head toward her. "You know then, how you came...to be?"

"I don't need a talk on the birds and bees from you, jerk." She could feel the rage pouring off Aidan and Jane wasn't sure how much longer his control would last. Having a vamp this close to him, well, it had to be like waving a red flag in front of a bull. A very, very big and dangerous bull.

Stampede time is coming.

"Michael was a good man, once. A good father. But he didn't handle the change well. He needed a guide." Vincent sighed. "I let him down, so that's on me."

He actually sounds sincere. Was the vamp bullshitting? Or had he known her father?

"If you want to learn more, I guess you'd better come find me before sunset," Vincent added. "Because I will be gone then." His gaze slid to Aidan. "Alpha, I don't want a war. That's not why I was in town. Believe it or not, I thought I was helping." He rolled back his shoulders. "I won't make that mistake again."

"Damn right, you won't," Aidan snarled.

Vincent turned away once more. He started walking and then…

Freaking parlor trick. He vanished.

Aidan turned Jane to face him. "He's trying to manipulate you." She could see his worry. "Jane, he probably knows dick about your real father. He just wants you to seek him out. He wants to get power over you."

"I don't care." Saying those words made a weight rise from her chest.

Aidan blinked. "Come again?" He threw a quick glance over her shoulder, and a predatory gleam appeared in his eyes as he swept the street.

Probably trying to make sure Vincent hadn't reappeared.

"I don't care what he knows about the vampire who used to be known as Michael." That had been the name her mother had whispered on a few pain-filled nights. *Monsters aren't real. Monsters...Michael wasn't a monster.* Had her mother been trying to convince herself of that fact? "He doesn't matter to me. The past is over, and all I want to do is focus on the future." Her future with Aidan. "The past isn't going to dictate my life. I won't let it. I'm more than some vamp's kid."

His hand rose and slid tenderly over her cheek. "Yes, Jane, you are. You are...everything."

Only Aidan could say those words and make them sound utterly true. She wasn't, of course. She was just a cop, doing her job as best she could. But Aidan made her feel special. Aidan made her feel like she didn't need to be ashamed of her past.

Her Aidan.

Her head turned and she pressed a kiss to his palm.

***

The werewolf was a fucking problem.

Vincent watched as Aidan touched Jane so tenderly. The alpha knew what she was — he knew what she would become. With Aidan

Locke's own twisted past, the guy should be running the hell away from Mary Jane Hart.

Not holding her so gently.

Damn him. He is screwing this up for me.

Jane should have died the night before. Everything would be different this day if she had. But no, she still breathed. She still packed her gun with its wooden bullets.

She was still fighting what would be.

Jane and her werewolf turned away and headed down the street. Probably off hunting for more clues. She was so worried about getting justice for the humans. He didn't get that. She needed to be worried about herself. Surely she could see that?

She'd flinched, just the smallest bit, when he'd said her father's name. *Michael.* The name mattered to her. The man mattered. Poor Jane. She'd probably gone her whole life, wondering about the monster that was her father. Would she like to hear that he hadn't always been so bad? That he'd tried to protect his family? Protect her?

Vincent thought Michael might just be the key to winning over Mary Jane. He'd thrown out the bait, now he just had to wait and see if she took it.

And if she didn't…

And sunset came…

Then I have to work out a new plan. Because he truly hadn't intended to go to war with the alpha.

But sometimes, battles couldn't be avoided.
Sometimes, bloodshed came.
    Death came.
    No matter how hard you fought to avoid it.

CHAPTER TWELVE

"What in the hell happened last night?" Police Captain Vivian Harris demanded as she paced beside her desk.

Jane blew out a long breath. Aidan had gone back to Hell's Gate after dropping her off at the police station. She'd immediately gone in to have a closed-door talk with her captain and now —

"Jane, how close did you come to dying?"

"I think as close as one can get."

Vivian stopped pacing. Her eyes squeezed closed. "Dear God."

Jane jumped to her feet. "I'm okay now. Better than okay."

Vivian shook her head. "Maybe I shouldn't have put you on this beat. Going up against paranormals when you're human...what was I thinking?" Her eyes opened. "I'm sorry."

Jane's spine was ramrod straight. "You have nothing to be sorry for. I *want* this beat." Even as Jane said the words, she realized they were true. She'd thought that the paranormal beat was a pain, that dealing with the monsters and their drama was her job because she was unlucky but…

That's not true. "I know the score. I understand the monsters."

Vivian's sigh was sad. "But that doesn't mean you have to be the one to clean up their messes."

"I want to be the one." And, again, it was true. Jane shook her head, struggling to fully understand the situation herself. "I know it's dangerous and it's crazy but…someone has to be in the middle."

Vivian crossed her arms over her chest. As usual, she wore a finely cut suit. Her hair was twisted behind her head. No-nonsense Vivian Harris. The captain who could make everyone jump.

The secret werewolf.

And Jane's…friend. Though she would never make the mistake of saying those words to Vivian's face.

"I bridge the worlds, human and paranormal. I understand them both." Because of Aidan, because of her own bloody past, Jane did. "I know what the victims feel like. The ones who survive…" She thought of the woman who'd been bitten by the vampire. And she thought of Alan Thatcher and his friend Travis Maller. "And the ones who don't. I know what their families go through." Because she'd gone through the same thing. "I can help them. I want to help them."

And monsters...they weren't all bad. Vivian certainly wasn't. And even Garrison—she could understand him, too. The guy kept making big ass mistakes with his life, but Garrison wasn't evil, not by a long shot. His family had also been killed by vampires, and that attack had scarred him on the inside. He was trying to do his best to make the city safer.

His best was just...kind of off-beat. Slanted. Twisted?

"I want to do this job," Jane added. She almost couldn't believe she was saying those words, but they were true. She wanted to keep working this beat. She wanted to give justice to Alan and Travis. And as for the werewolf who'd attacked her? *I want to stop him, too.* She *would* stop him.

Besides, she was currently riding a high on the whole new and improved version of herself. Maybe Aidan was right and the side effects of his blood donations would be temporary, but until they wore off, she'd enjoy the bonus of extra strength and some sensory enhancements.

"I don't want to lose a good detective," Vivian said. Her brows climbed as she studied Jane. "Because I'd miss you like hell if that happened."

Jane smiled. "Don't worry, captain. I'm not going anywhere." *The rogue werewolf won't get another swipe at me.*

"All right." Vivian straightened. "Then I won't argue with you."

Good.

"I've got the news covered for now," Vivian continued briskly. "They're running with the story of the mugger. Get over to the ME's office — you're the one who can light the best fire under Dr. Bob. The guy is being freaking slow as molasses on this case. I don't know what he was doing all night...."

Jane winced. "He was patching me up. Sorry."

Vivian looked a bit taken back.

"I'll get right over there," Jane added quickly. "I'm sure he's completed the exam by now." She hurried for the door.

"Jane."

She looked back.

"I'm very glad you're all right."

Jane smiled at her. "Me, too." She opened the door. Hurried toward the bullpen and...if she hadn't still had the enhanced hearing, Jane was sure she would have missed Vivian's low whisper as the captain said...

"I would have hated having to kill you if you'd become a vamp."

Jane kept walking, not letting on that she'd heard that last bit, but her heart was suddenly doing a double-time rhythm and her palms were sweating.

Dammit, people needed to not whisper shit when she was around.

***

The police station was busy. Reporters were swarming the steps. Their news vans were all over the place, and he even caught a glimpse of the pretty blond news anchor who'd been broadcasting so damn annoyingly earlier in the day. The blond woman stood in front of the station, a small microphone hooked to her shirt, and her expression grave as she spoke into the camera just four feet in front of her.

Bitch.

The station doors flew open behind the reporter. A woman with dark hair and wearing a battered jacket hurried down the steps. His eyes widened when he realized...

Detective Jane Hart.

What the actual hell? The woman was looking far too hale and hearty. He'd clawed her insides out. Sure, she might, *might* have been able to survive the night, but no way should she just be running around as if nothing had happened to her.

Not unless...

What are you, Detective Hart?

He took a step forward, intending to follow her but then those station doors opened wide one more time.

The reporters pretty much turned at once as they focused on Police Captain Vivian Harris. *The prey I intended to find this morning.* Before he'd gotten distracted by the sight of a too-normal Detective Hart.

Harris waved her hand toward the reporters. "I have another statement to offer regarding our ongoing investigation into the murders of two area men in the St. Louis cemetery..."

She's distracting them so that Detective Hart can slip away. No one else had even seemed to notice the dark-haired detective.

He should give chase. He should —

"The coward who is killing in our streets *will* be stopped. We have new leads that have developed — "

He didn't hear the rest of what she'd just said. *Coward. Coward.* His hands fisted. His claws itched to spring out. He would show her a fucking coward. A growl built in his throat as he focused his fury on his prey.

Vivian Harris.

His next victim. *I've got the perfect cemetery spot already picked out for you.*

***

Aidan knocked once on the door of the Voodoo Shop. He could hear movement from inside, and he knew that Annette was in there. He didn't hear anyone else, though, so he figured she wasn't with a customer. A good thing because he needed to talk to her, right the hell then.

The door opened. Annette lifted her brows at him. "Alpha, it's only been a few hours. Did you miss me?"

He growled.

"Always growling. So not sexy." She sighed and motioned him inside. "Never can just come for a friendly little visit, can you?"

"Are we friends?" Now he was genuinely curious.

"I have no clue." She turned and headed into her private room in the back. He followed and, once inside, his gaze fell on her black scrying mirror.

"It's showing me nothing today," Annette announced glumly. "And I've looked. Over and over, I looked."

His fingers rubbed at the ache in the back of his neck. "You were right."

Surprise flashed on her face. "Want to admit that again? A lot louder? And maybe wait until I can grab my phone and record this important moment?"

He exhaled on a rough sigh. "Jane's...different. Stronger. Her senses are sharper. My blood did something to her." His hand fell back to his side. "I came to you because I need to know how long that *something* will last."

Her fingers tapped over her mirror. "I told you, I'm seeing nothing in here today. I keep trying to call up Jane's future, but nothing is there."

A chill skated down Aidan's spine.

"Maybe I'm just tired," she muttered. "Some alpha and his goon, Paris, did keep me up all night. I'll rest a bit and try again later." Before he could speak, she lifted her hand. *"If* I see anything, you'll be the first to know about it."

"Thank you." But he still hesitated. "The vampire—Vincent—he just appears and disappears at will. And I don't catch his scent, not until it's too late."

"I'm not helping him," she said immediately, as if he'd just accused her.

"No, I didn't think that you were but..." And this was nagging at him. "It's not like you're the only one who can work magic in the world."

Her expression was guarded "You think he has his own voodoo queen?"

"Doesn't have to be Voodoo. Could be a witch. Could be a demon."

Fear flashed in her eyes. "I've thought the same thing."

"A whole lot exists in this world. We're just scratching the surface, you and I both know it." He tilted his head as he studied her. "Have you felt a surge of magic in this city? Since he's been here?" If so, that would sure give credence to the idea that someone might be helping the vamp. Hell, someone *had* to be working spells around him. Vamps didn't just...vanish.

But how old is he? The oldest vamp Aidan had ever encountered had been two hundred.

"I...looked in my mirror yesterday, to see more about him," Annette confessed.

She didn't add more.

"And?" he prompted. *Come on, Annette, don't hold back.*

She licked her lower lip. "I saw him on a Viking ship. His hair was long, braided, and he had a...a big ax in his hand."

"You're telling me this guy was a Viking? How do you even know you saw the right vamp? You haven't met Vincent—or I thought you hadn't and—"

"I know it was him. Big, your size. Dark hair. Square jaw. Broken nose, a little hawkish. High cheeks. Even has a little dimple in his chin."

Okay, fuck, that sounded like Vincent. She'd noticed details about the guy he hadn't even thought of, not until she'd spoken. *Because I was focusing on not killing him, and not staring at his damn face.*

"After he attacked Garrison, Paris brought me some of the vamp's blood. Seems Jane shot him and a few drops were at the scene. I used those to see his past."

A very, very old past. "With vampires, age brings strength."

"On that ship, with that ax...I saw the vampire you call Vincent die." Her finger was making a swirling motion on the scrying mirror. Almost a circle, but...not quite. "He was run through by an enemy. Only he didn't stay dead."

Fuck me. "I already suspected he was a born vampire, too." But his gaze was on her finger. "What are you drawing?"

She blinked, as if surprised. "I-I don't know."

He grabbed a piece of paper from her desk. Snagged a pen. "Draw it again."

Hesitant now, she did. "It's an image that came to me when I saw Vincent rise as a vampire. I didn't even really think about it much." Her brow crinkled as she drew. "So many images fill my head. If I didn't filter most of them out, I'd go crazy." Her voice had thickened as she made that confession. "Here. This thing. This is what I saw, okay?"

Not okay.

"A horseshoe," she said. "It could mean anything."

"It's not a horseshoe. It's the Greek letter Omega."

A tremble slid over her. "The end."

"Not on my watch it's not." But why had Annette seen it when she scried Vincent's past? Before he could push her for more information, there was a sharp rap on her shop's front door. His nostrils twitched but he caught the familiar scent of their visitor.

"Your guard dog is spending way too much time here," Annette murmured, obviously also knowing who the visitor was. "You could try keeping him away. I'm not a threat to you."

His gaze dipped to her face. "Maybe Paris stays near you for an entirely different reason. One that doesn't have anything to do with me."

Surprise widened her eyes, and he heard the quick hitch in her breathing.

Maybe try scrying that, Annette. Aidan had long known that Paris was interested in Annette. But, back then, Annette had been involved with another wolf. One who'd turned homicidal.

He's dead and buried. Annette and Paris are both living. And something tells me Paris won't stand by and watch her go to another again.

Paris let himself inside the shop and he hurried into the back room, obviously having decided that neither Annette nor Aidan were going to invite him inside. "Was just coming up the steps out there," he said, voice a bit breathless. "When I got the call." He still had his phone gripped in his hand. "We found Drew."

Drew. Jane's brother. The name clicked immediately for Aidan.

"He was actually in Birmingham, Alabama, but the guy is *here* now. He's at Hell's Gate. Garrison has watch over the guy."

Fuck. Garrison watching? That scenario had trouble written all over it. But if Drew was in town, then it was time for the siblings to be reunited. Jane had asked for her brother. Aidan would make sure that she got him.

***

The ME's office was cold — as usual — and it smelled of antiseptic and bleach. Again — as usual. Jane strode inside, and her eyes narrowed when she realized that Dr. Bob's desk was empty.

"Dr. Bob!" Jane called but then her nose twitched.

In the back. She hurried to the exam area, pushing open the door and then striding back to the storage locker section.

Dr. Bob was just closing one locker.

"Knew you were back here," she said, a bit impressed with herself. Even over the bleach, she'd smelled the guy's too expensive after shave.

Dr. Bob gave a quick cry and spun around. His hand went to his chest. "Sweet hell, Jane! Are you trying to give me a heart attack?"

She frowned. "I thought you heard me coming."

"No, because you didn't make a *sound*." He straightened his lab coat. "But at least it's just you and not the alpha, too. That guy — how can you seriously be involved with him? He's bad news."

"Don't push me."

But he lifted his hand and pointed his index finger at her. "I got something you're going to want to see. Just got the reports back." He bustled by her, muttering, "*Don't push me. Don't push me? I'm the only one who knows how dangerous this shit is! Not like you can play nicely with a werewolf...*"

"Dr. Bob." A warning edge entered her voice. "Just so we're clear. I love Aidan."

He picked up a folder. The folder trembled a bit in his hand. "I know. That's part of the problem." He offered the file to her. "Read this."

She did. She actually read it twice because she was sure she had to be mistaken. Then she shoved the file back at the ME. "That's wrong. Run the test again — "

"It is *not* wrong. I am not wrong." Now he sounded insulted. "There was *wolf fur* found on the deceased."

"Aidan wasn't in wolf form at the cemetery. He hadn't shifted." She glowered at him. "So you're wrong, okay? He tried to help Travis Maller, not attack him or — "

"I never said he attacked. And I also never said it was his fur."

The ticking of the clock on the right wall was suddenly very, very loud.

"I have a sample of Aidan's DNA on file. I ran it against this specimen." Dr. Bob was watching her with a very guarded expression. "They weren't matches, Jane. I knew this wasn't Aidan's fur. I never told you it was."

"But only alpha werewolves can transform. Aidan told me that."

Dr. Bob nodded. "He told me the same thing when I first learned the truth."

"You're saying that our killer is an alpha?"

"Yes. Aidan isn't the only alpha in town. And, sooner or later, the new beast *will* come for him. Isn't that the way it works?"

She had no clue. But she would be finding out. Jane stumbled back. She grabbed her phone. Dialed Aidan immediately.

Pick up. Pick up.

"What's wrong, Jane?" Aidan asked when he answered after the first ring.

"Bob says the killer is an alpha."

Static crackled over the line. Hell, she *never* got good reception in that place. Jane rushed for the door. "Did you hear me, Aidan? Dr. Bob says the killer—he's just like you."

But Aidan didn't speak.

"Hello?" She hurried through the building.

There was no connection. Just silence. "Hello?"

Dammit. She ran outside, her finger sliding across her screen as she prepared to dial again.

***

Aidan paused in front of Hell's Gate, his hand tight around his phone. Had Jane just said that another alpha was hunting?

Impossible. Not in *this* town. There were no other alphas in his pack.

But maybe that's why all of my wolves are checking out when I question them. Maybe none of them are killing.

Another wolf…someone new in town…

His phone rang again. Jane's beautiful face popped up on his screen. She'd been in bed with him when he took that picture. He put the phone to his ear when he answered the call. "Jane."

"Aidan!" Jane's voice was tight with worry. "Did you hear me? Dr. Bob said—"

"There's another alpha in town."

"Yes." Her breath heaved out the line. "What happens now? What does it mean to have two of you in the area?"

"He is nothing like me." With an effort, Aidan kept his voice flat.

There was a pause. "Aidan, you know I didn't mean that."

Yes, he did. "I'm sorry." But he was worried. Because if there *was* an alpha in town... "He'll have to challenge me. Since he's not of my family..." *I have no family.* "Alphas who aren't related fight for territory. If he's in *my* city, killing under my watch, then there's only one way for this to end," he told her grimly.

I have to kill him.

"I need to know more about alphas," Jane said. "Look, I mean, when do you guys first start shifting into the body of a beast? When does all this happen?"

"Around twenty-one." When a boy finally became a man, the beast slipped out.

"That's...that's college age." Her voice had turned thoughtful. "Travis and Alan were both college students. They knew each other. *They knew him.*"

"Jane?"

"I bet the killer went to school with them." She was talking fast now. "I need to get back to Tulane. I want to search the campus again."

"Jane, that's a bad idea. Wait for me."

"Well, get your ass to Tulane and *meet* me."

"I...have to see someone first." His gaze was locked on the entrance to Hell's Gate. "You need to see him, too. Come to my bar."

"Aidan, I have a lead. I need to follow this lead before someone else winds up dead."

That was Jane. Being the hero again.

While I'm used to being the villain.

"My guards are tailing me. It's broad daylight. And, yeah, by the way, notice I'm not bitching about having guards during the day? I'm *compromising*."

His lips twitched.

"I'm compromising," Jane said again, "and I'm doing my job. Before I head to the campus, I'll switch to silver bullets." Her breath rushed over the line once more. "Just meet me at Tulane as fast as you can, okay? If our killer is an alpha and he's there, you'll spot him."

Yes, he would. "I'll be there as soon as I can."

"Great. And…Aidan?" Her voice hitched a bit. "I love you."

The call ended.

I love you, too.

Aidan shoved the phone into his pocket. He squared his shoulders. Then he headed into Hell.

***

She was being followed.

Vivian Harris paused at the street corner, her gaze trekking slowly around the area. Something was off. The hair on the nape of her neck was rising.

I'm being hunted.

And if there was one thing a werewolf understood, it was the hunt.

Once more, she let her stare sweep around the street. Only no one stood out to her as threatening. Not the elderly man walking his dog. Not the two teen girls posing for selfies in front of the beignet shop. Not the young boy break dancing for tip money near the souvenir shop.

Where are you?

The threat was out there. Her nostrils flared and she pulled in the scents of the city. But...

The light changed. She took her time crossing the street. Tension had gathered in her body and it took all of Vivian's self-control not to let her claws burst out. But instead of using her claws, she reached inside her jacket. Her fingers curled around her gun and she slipped it from her holster.

You'll find that I'm not easy prey. She knew these streets so very well. Knew how to hide. And how to hunt.

Vivian slipped into a small space between two buildings. Not an alley. Far too small for that. She flattened herself against the nearest wall. Then she waited.

Footsteps rushed toward her. Vivian's eyes turned to slits. She barely breathed as the unknown assailant rushed into that little space after her...

Vivian attacked. She grabbed her prey, shoved the would-be attacker against the brick wall, and Vivian put her weapon underneath the chin of the —

Reporter?

Vivian froze. She was staring straight into the terrified eyes of news anchor Sarah Steele. She had her *gun* aimed right between those terrified blue eyes.

"Please," Sarah barely breathed the word. Her blond hair fluttered over her shoulders. "Don't shoot me. I just...I just wanted to ask you a few questions."

Dammit. "You don't sneak up on someone like that! Got it?" Vivian started to lower her weapon. This was going to be a PR nightmare. "You want an interview, you ask like a normal person. You —"

Sarah's eyes seemed to bulge from her head. A high, desperate squeak burst from her lips.

"What is it now?" Vivian demanded, disgusted.

Then she realized...Sarah was looking over her shoulder.

But I didn't hear anyone else coming behind me. I didn't smell anyone. I didn't —

She spun around, trying to lift up her gun, but there was no time.

Claws sliced across her wrist and the weapon flew to the ground.

***

Two bitches for the price of one.

He carried them, one at a time, and dumped them in his ride. The captain had thought she was so smart when she'd taken shelter between the two buildings. He was smarter. He'd let the reporter distract Vivian, then he'd moved in.

And he'd made sure to use his vehicle to block the small space between those two old buildings. With his vehicle positioned there, no one could see what he was doing. No one saw the blood or the unconscious women.

It was his lucky day. To get both of them. Just like this...

Perfect.

Vivian Harris was out cold. He'd carved her up a little too much. But the reporter...

Her eyes were already fluttering open. He leaned over her and smiled. "Hello, Sarah Steele." He made sure to flash his fangs at her. "Guess what? You just scored yourself an exclusive."

CHAPTER THIRTEEN

Aidan shoved open the door at Hell's Gate. It flew back, bouncing against the wall, and at the loud crash of sound, the human who'd been sitting at his bar jumped to his feet.

He looks like Jane.

The dark hair was the same. The dark eyes were the same, though Jane's gaze had more gold flecks. Aidan cocked his head as he closed in on the shorter man.

Her brother was average height, average build. His jaw was a little soft and stubble covered the lower part of his face. His hands were clenched at his sides. "Look, fellow," Drew Hart blasted. "I don't know who you think you are or what the hell is happening here, but I was told my sister needed me. And I want to see her. *Now.*"

Ah...so he had a bit of Jane's give-'em-hell attitude. Good. "Jane isn't available at the moment." *She's walking into more danger and I'm about to rush after her sweet ass.* "So you have to settle for me."

"She's not available?" Drew's voice rose. "Listen, you," Drew said as his hand lifted and he jabbed his finger into Aidan's chest. "You don't *tell* me she's not available."

"Oh, bad move," Garrison muttered from his position behind the bar. "Shouldn't touch him, not even if you are her brother."

"What?" Drew cast a confused glance Garrison's way, then looked back at Aidan. "You need to—"

Aidan had just noticed the tattoo on the guy's forearm. Swirling, black...Aidan grabbed that arm and twisted it around for a better view.

Drew screamed—a little in pain and a whole lot in shock. Aidan shoved the guy back against the bar and studied the tattoo. "Omega." The guy had gotten a tattoo to match Jane's scar? *What. In. The. Hell?*

"Who are you?" Drew asked, voice breaking. He tried to shove Aidan back, but Aidan wasn't in the mood to move.

"I'm the man Jane loves."

"He's Aidan Locke." Garrison offered helpfully.

Aidan snarled at him. He didn't need Garrison's help right then.

"Wait—what? My sister loves you? She actually...she let you get close to her?" Then Drew shook his head. "No. Bullshit. *Bullshit.*

Mary Jane doesn't let anyone close. Not even me."

"Why do you have that tattoo?"

"Because I like Greek letters."

Aidan tightened his hold on the guy's wrist. "I could break this with less effort than it would take me to breathe."

Drew's eyes widened. He paled a little, then he laughed. "You actually think my sister loves you? *You?* Mary Jane is a cop! She helps people! There is no way — no flipping way — she'd fall for some psychopath like you. You want to break my wrist? Do it. Go ahead. But I am not going to tell you another damn thing about my family."

Don't kick her brother's ass. Don't. "I know all about Jane's burn. A burn that looks just like this scar."

Drew's cheeks weren't just pale any longer. They'd totally bleached of color.

"I know Jane saw her mother and stepfather die right in front of her. I know she called out to you, begging for help."

"No." The one word was hoarse as it broke from Drew. "She didn't. Mary Jane never called out. I was there the whole time and she never said a word."

What? Anger turned to rage as Aidan stared down at Drew Hart. The beast was close and Aidan used his power.

Let's see if he really is like Jane. "Tell me everything."

Drew's gaze seemed to turn foggy.

"Tell me where you were when Jane was attacked. Tell me what you did."

"Uh, boss..." Garrison began nervously.

"Tell me..." Aidan shoved all of his power into that order.

Sweat dripped down Drew's temples. "I hid. In the basement."

"Now I call bullshit. The vamp would have smelled you."

"Mom...mom always gave me this special lotion. Said I had to put it on every day. Me and Mary Jane. When we were kids, she told us it would keep the monsters away."

What?

"She was a fanatic. Always made Mary Jane and I use it. Realized later that it blocked our scents. Figured it was so our father couldn't find us."

Sonofabitch.

"I hid in the basement." No emotion was in Drew's voice. "I watched. They killed mom. They killed our stepfather. And they...they tied Mary Jane to that table. She was screaming and I-I smelled...smelled them burning her."

"Oh, fucking hell," Garrison whispered. He grabbed a bottle of whiskey and just started downing it. "And I thought I had it bad."

"I watched," Drew admitted as his head sagged. "I watched them hurt her. I didn't make a sound."

"You didn't try to save her?" But Jane cried out for her brother at night. Dammit. His Jane cried for help.

"The vamp...he left her, just for a moment. Went upstairs." Drew licked his lips and his unfocused gaze seemed to sharpen. "Wait — what's happening? Why am I — "

"*Tell me the rest. Tell me how Jane got out of that basement.*" Drew wasn't a vamp-in-waiting, but the guy's mind was strong. So strong that Aidan had to work hard to control him.

"I rushed to Mary Jane." The words came stiltedly. "Untied her. We ran to the window. There was one small window in that basement. I went through first. I turned around and put my hands back through the opening. I was going to get Mary Jane out. But...but the vamp grabbed her legs."

Garrison had frozen, the whiskey bottle inches from his mouth.

Aidan could hear the hard drumming of his own heartbeat.

"But...our father appeared. Our real father, the one I'd feared for so long."

"What?"

"He...he grabbed the other vamp from behind. Held him back so Mary Jane could get out." Drew's voice went ragged. "I don't think Mary Jane remembers that part. And it's good because...our father...that vamp attacked him. With fangs and claws and there was so much blood and our dad...despite everything, I swear, he was still good because he screamed for me to take Mary Jane and...to run."

Impossible.

But...

Drew is under my power. He has to tell me the truth. Aidan tapped Drew's arm. "Why the fuck do you have this tattoo?"

"To remind me that my sister suffered to protect me. To remind me every single day that there is good in the world. Because even though she won't let me near her, even though Mary Jane says something about her is too dangerous...Mary Jane *is* the good in my world. Wearing her mark is the least I can do."

Aidan let him go.

Drew exhaled on a ragged breath and shook his head. "Where is my sister?"

"Walking into danger. Isn't that her usual way of operating?" Aidan turned away. "And I'm going with her. Because I have her back." *Just as I know she'd have mine.* "You can stay —"

"If Mary Jane's in trouble, then I'm coming, too."

Hell. I know I have to be more careful with my words. I let that "can" slip out. I should've just said...You stay here.

Drew grabbed his arm and spun Aidan back around. "If my sister needs me, I'm there."

"No—"

"Some crazy ass goons of yours who just showed up at my house in the middle of the night. They said Mary Jane was in trouble, and I hauled ass here, no questions. Because I love her. Because I will not let her down again."

"You don't know what you're stepping into," Aidan warned him.

"One night, when I was about four years old, I saw my real father come home. He wasn't the happy, smiling guy I'd known. The guy who made me feel safe my whole freaking life. His skin was too pale, his body was shaking. And he had *fangs*. He came at me, and I ran." Shame burned in Drew's voice. "Years later, I saw my mother and my stepfather get murdered by vamps. And the father that I'd tried to forget— the father I'd been hiding from for so long? He was there. Fighting with fangs and claws. Fighting to save me and my sister." His breath huffed out. "So don't tell me I don't know what I'm stepping into, okay? I get it—monsters are real."

Yes, they were.

Drew's voice shook as he said, "My sister is fighting a vamp, isn't she? That's what's going on, and I won't let her be alone."

The guy still didn't get it. "It's not just vamps you have to deal with. This time, the killer is one of us."

"Us?"

Garrison cleared his throat and put down the whiskey. "Well, not you. He's like me. Like Aidan."

Drew dropped his hold on Aidan and backed up — fast. "You're vampires?"

"No," Aidan told him as he let his claws spring out. "We're werewolves." If this went poorly, he'd just make the guy forget.

What. The. Fuck? Werewolves?" Drew swayed. "Werewolves are real?"

"Plenty of things are real in this world." He held Drew's gaze.

"Are you...evil?"

"Only some days."

"No, he's not!" Garrison fired back. Like Aidan needed the guy defending him, but it was a nice gesture. "Aidan takes care of this pack. He protects this town. He's our law!"

Drew's hand clenched around the back of a nearby chair. "*Werewolves.*"

Yes, he obviously needed processing time, and that was time Aidan didn't intend to waste.

"Keep him close," he ordered Garrison. "Only, no handcuffs this time, got it?"

Garrison nodded. "Got it."

Aidan headed for the door, but quick footsteps thudded behind him. Without looking back, he threw out his hand and his fingers fisted in Drew's shirt. "Don't be a liability to me," he said. "If you're screwed up in the head because of this, you'll just distract me."

"I-I want to help Mary Jane. I want to make everything right."

That he could understand. "Then you stay close and you do exactly what I say..."

***

When Jane arrived back at the college campus, she immediately went in to have a one-on-one talk with the Dean of Students. Only that little chat went freaking nowhere fast.

She'd wanted a list of students who were in classes with Alan Thatcher and Travis Maller — then, she'd wanted that list broken down so she could see which students were from out of state. A simple enough request.

Because I think the killer has to be an out-of-state student. Aidan knew all the local werewolves. So it stood to reason that this guy — this new alpha — was an unknown because he'd come from a different state.

The Dean of Students—a guy named Shawn Hastings, *Dr.* Hastings, who had a double chin, a thick head of a black hair, and very twitchy eyes—was sweating as he stared at her. "I-I can't give you that information," Shawn said for what had to be the fifth time. "I must protect the privacy of my students."

His assistant stood just behind him, looking nervous as all hell.

"Your students are dying." He shouldn't need that reminder. "And I strongly suspect the killer is on this campus."

Shawn blanched.

"I need that list."

"And I want to help you." He patted a cloth to his sweating forehead. "But unless you have a warrant, my hands are tied."

A warrant would take too long. The killer had dropped a body for the last two nights, and her money was on him striking again when the sun set. Before she could argue again, Jane's phone vibrated. Jane looked down and read the text from Aidan. *I'm here.*

She quickly typed back. *Dean of Students. Meet me.* "I've got something better than a warrant." And she couldn't believe she was going to do this. It was wrong. She *knew* it was wrong, and she felt like a total hypocrite, but Jane didn't have time to waste. Dammit. The killer was going to strike again. She knew it.

He had a taste for the blood now. Human, werewolf — the killers were the same. Once they got the rush and the power that came from taking another life, they didn't stop. It was like an addiction.

"Better than a warrant?" Shawn asked as he rose. "Why, I'd like to see that — "

The door to his office flew open. Fast, very fast — that was her Aidan.

"What is happening?" Shawn's voice was a shriek now.

His assistant — and Jane was pretty sure the assistant and the dean might be involved because the woman's bright red lipstick matched the smudge on the dean's fancy white dress collar — immediately grabbed for the phone on his desk. *Probably calling security.*

"This is my partner," Jane murmured. "And you're going to provide him with a list of the students from out of state, students who were in classes with Travis Maller and Alan Thatcher."

The dean gaped at her.

The assistant's gaze flew around the room.

Jane tapped her chin. "You know what? Give me a list of the out-of-state students who were in Alan's dorm, too."

"No," the dean snapped. "Absolutely not. I told you, I need a warrant. Now it's time for you and your *partner* to leave, immediately."

Jane sighed. *I am breaking my own rules.* What did that say about her? Was her moral compass bent or totally broken? Her stare slid to Aidan, and she knew he'd get her message. "Told you," Jane murmured. "I have something better than a warrant." *I have my own personal alpha werewolf.*

Aidan stalked toward the dean's desk. She could practically feel the power swirling in the room. Aidan looked first at the young assistant. "Hang up the phone."

She did.

Then Aidan focused on the dean. "About that list…"

***

"Thank you, Aidan," Jane said quickly as they hurried out of the dean's office. "I wasn't exactly running high on charm today, and you totally saved my ass."

There were a lot of names on the list. More names than she'd hoped to see. And Jane knew the list might not even lead to the killer. After all, Travis and Alan could have met the guy at a campus party — or an *off* campus party. The guy might not even be a student, but at least it was a starting point for her.

It was *something*.

She began skimming over the list.

"Glad I could be of use," Aidan said, his voice oddly careful. "Jane, there's something I need to tell you."

But her gaze had just zeroed in on one name. A name that was familiar to her. "Quint Laurel," Jane whispered. "Sonofabitch."

"Jane?"

She looked up. "The day after Alan Thatcher died, I went to his dorm room. Quint Laurel was there. He strode inside and acted all torn up when I had to break the news to him that Alan Thatcher was dead."

"Maybe he *was* torn up."

"And maybe he was playing me. Maybe he was the killer and he wanted to find out just what I knew." She hurried toward the stairwell door.

But Aidan did that too-fast thing of his and stepped into her path. "Slow down."

"I can't! Time is running out." The sun was already sliding low in the sky. "I'm afraid he's going to kill again tonight, Aidan. That there will be another body found savaged in a cemetery."

"Then we put guards at the cemeteries," he said with a nod. "I'll send my men—"

"Up against another alpha?"

His jaw hardened.

"He'd be able to take down your men, just as easily as you would. And there's no way I can put human cops out there against him." That would be a serious blood bath. "No, we need to find him. You and I. We can catch him unaware. *Stop* the bastard."

"It might not even be this Quint Laurel —"

"No, but you talk to him for two seconds, and we'll know if it is or not." She stepped around him and shoved open the door that led to the stairwell. She rushed down the stairs, her thudding footsteps echoing around her. Aidan was close behind.

"Your brother is here."

She grabbed onto the railing so she wouldn't fall. Jane whipped her head back to face Aidan. "What?"

"When you were hurt, you called out for him. I…I wanted to help you, so I got my wolves to find him. Werewolves are good at tracking."

Her cheeks felt numb. "I didn't need to track him. I knew where he was all along. Safely *away* from me."

"Jane, he wants to help you."

Tears burned her eyes. "Aidan, what have you done?"

"He's outside. He's here to help," Aidan said again. His voice was halting, more hesitant than she'd ever heard him before. "Jane, I want you happy. I did this…so you'd be happy."

She swiped at the tears on her cheeks. Dammit, she cried way too much lately. That shit had to stop. "You ever think there's a reason I haven't seen him in so long? Aidan, jeez, look at me! I'm a magnet for monsters!"

He flinched.

"That's not what I meant. You're not what I meant."

"You sure about that?"

She swallowed. "Vampires. Werewolves. That's my life now. It isn't his. He's normal. You saw that, right?" Now her voice was hopeful. Because...

I don't know. Maybe he is like me. Maybe I'm about to ruin my brother's life, too.

"He's normal," Aidan said softly.

Her shoulders fell. Aidan's words were both a relief and a condemnation. *I was the different one. It was because of me that Drew lost his whole family. I brought the vampires. They wanted me.*

Because I'm the end.

"He loves you."

She started hurrying down the stairs again. "I want him safe."

"He wants to pay back his debt to you. He didn't help you when you were kids, and he wants the chance now."

What? She didn't stop, though adrenaline pumped through her body. "He's the one who got me out of that basement. Drew owes me nothing."

When she reached the bottom floor, Jane shoved open the stairwell door and raced outside. The sky was cloudy. Too dark. And there, just a few feet away, with his arms crossed over his chest and his eyes on her...

There was her brother.

"Drew?" Jane stared at him, absolutely lost. For a moment, she was a child again, huddled with her brother as they waited for police to arrive at their house. Her hand had gripped his so tightly. He'd been her whole world.

"Mary Jane." He smiled at her and looked so freaking happy to see her.

"You shouldn't be here," Jane whispered. "I'm working a case."

Drew took a step toward her. "You look good."

You shouldn't be here.

"I-I know, Mary Jane," Drew said, his words stammering. "About the vampires. About the werewolves. About everything."

Her gaze swung to Aidan. "What did you do?"

"I know," Drew said doggedly. "And I'm not scared."

Liar. She could practically smell his fear. Her desperate stare flew back to her brother.

"We can stop them, Mary Jane," Drew said. "We can stop them all..."

And that was when she knew that things were very, very bad.

I stayed away from Drew for a reason. He stopped being the man I knew...he was fanatical. I thought I was making him worse, that by leaving he'd get better, that it was me...

But maybe it had been him. All along...

Drew reached into his jacket and pulled out a gun.

"What in the hell is happening?" Aidan snarled. "He was under my control."

"No, I wasn't." Drew's chin lifted. "And I won't let my sister be, either. She'd never choose a monster. *Never.* I won't let you do this to her!"

He fired the gun, blasting it right at Aidan.

Jane didn't think. Didn't even pause. She just threw her body in front of his.

The bullet slammed into her chest. She heard Aidan scream. She heard Drew scream.

Blood soaked her shirt and pain tore her world apart.

In the next instant, Jane was on the ground, gasping, trying to take in a breath but something was wrong with her lungs. Aidan's hands grabbed her. He held her tight. "Jane! *Jane!*"

Her gaze slid to Drew. He was going to shoot again. "No," Jane whispered because she couldn't protect Aidan. Not now. She was too weak. And he was too focused on her to protect himself.

The thunder of the gun came once more. In the distance, she heard someone screaming. The kids on campus? Panicking because there was an active shooter. *Run. Everyone needs to run.*

Aidan jerked and she knew the bullet had hit him, but he didn't let her go. He rose with her in his arms.

"Leave my sister alone!" Drew roared.

Aidan took a step away from him.

Bam! Bam! Bam!

Three shots. One had burned across her arm before it sank into Aidan's chest. Aidan stared down at her. She wanted to speak but a rough whistle was the only sound coming from her lips.

I can't breathe. I can't get any air.

"Love...you..." Aidan whispered.

And then he fell. Her strong, big, bad, fierce wolf fell, and she tumbled from his arms. Jane barely felt the impact when she slammed into the concrete. Her body rolled down the few steps there and when she stopped, she was staring up at her brother.

He still had the gun in his hands. "Don't worry, Mary Jane. I'll make sure he stays down."

A shadow moved behind Drew. Fast. One that hadn't been there before. It just—appeared.

Stop him. She couldn't say the words. She tried. Tried so hard.

Stop. Him! Stop my brother!

And then the shadow took shape. Vincent stood behind her brother. His hand lifted and he grabbed her brother. His fangs flashed as he ripped into Drew's throat. Drew fired but the bullet seemed to go wild.

It didn't hit Aidan.

My werewolf guards. They have to be somewhere close on campus. Aidan had been making sure she had extra security since the last attack. The guards were there — they would come running soon.

She just had to hold on a bit longer.

But she felt so cold.

"This is how it ends," Vincent's voice wasn't smug. Not happy. Just flat. He was standing over her now. "Are you ready?"

Ready to die? No. No, she wasn't. Jane's hands flew out to grab the steps around her, and she tried to haul her body toward Aidan. If she got his blood, everything would be all right. She'd be strong again. She'd dig the bullets out of his body — they had to be silver because she'd seen the smoke coming from him when he'd first been hit — and he'd be okay, too. They'd both make it.

They'd live to fight and love another day.

She pulled her body a few desperate inches.

"No, Jane." Vincent crouched in front of her. Now his voice was sad. "That isn't your end."

Aidan. She couldn't even say his name. And black dots were dancing before her eyes.

"You won't get his blood this time. He won't save you." Vincent's hand feathered over her face. "Be content knowing that you saved him."

That terrible whistle came from her again as she fought so hard to say Aidan's name.

"The bullet went into your lungs. You're drowning in your own blood. It's a terrible way to go, Jane. Needless suffering." His hand slid down her throat in a soothing caress. "I don't like to watch anyone suffer."

No, no, he couldn't—

"After the end," Vincent murmured, "the beginning comes."

What?

He snapped her neck.

The whistling stopped. The black dots vanished.

Everything vanished.

CHAPTER FOURTEEN

It was a blood bath. Paris rushed toward the steps of the college, his beast raging inside of him. He'd gotten to the scene just moments ago because when he'd gone to Hell's Gate, Garrison had told him that Aidan had gone to the campus in order to help Jane. That they had a lead on the werewolf killer in town.

I wanted to give Aidan back-up. I was supposed to always watch his back.

Paris saw the two werewolves who'd been assigned to guard Jane, only they weren't guarding her. They were crouched over Aidan's prone body.

No. A roar broke from him. College kids had scattered, probably at the first blast of gunfire — smart freaking kids. So no one was watching as he leapt up the steps and bounded to Aidan's side.

I can smell the silver in him.

No one was watching when his claws burst from his fingertips and Paris drove them into Aidan's chest. Paris knew he had to get the bullets out. If Aidan was going to live...*I have to get them out.*

The silver bullets burned his fingers, but he didn't care. He got one bullet. Another. The third...*fuck, it was close to his heart.* "Get Dr. Bob on stand-by," he ordered the guards. *Guards who'd been fucking useless from the look of things.* But they desperately needed the doctor because even with Aidan's healing powers, the guy would still need help.

One of the werewolf guards immediately backed away and yanked out his phone.

"Where the hell were you two?" Paris demanded. "You were supposed to protect them." He pulled out another bullet, only this one had splintered. *Fucking pieces of silver are in him.*

"H-he said he had this," one of the guards mumbled. "When Aidan arrived, he told us to — to back off a bit. He was with her brother. It was supposed to be safe."

And for an instant, the red haze of fear that had nearly blinded Paris cleared. He'd been focused just on Aidan. He'd seen his friend, his alpha, lying so motionless. *I was afraid I was too late.* But the red haze had cleared a bit and now he saw...

Jane.

Not moving.

Not...breathing?

Oh, fuck.

"H-help m-me…" A desperate cry. Paris's gaze jerked toward the man who'd given that cry. A man with dark hair. With Jane's dark eyes. Blood pumped from wounds on his throat. "Vamp…attacked me," he gasped. "K-Killed my sister…"

Paris's nostrils flared. "*You* fired the gun. I can smell the gun powder on you. *You* shot Aidan."

His claws were still in Aidan's chest. He pulled out another shard of silver.

"I'm…h-her…brother…m-my M-Mary J-Jane…" More blood pumped from those wounds on the guy's throat.

Paris touched another tiny piece of silver. He yanked it from Aidan's chest.

And then Aidan's hand flew up in a flash. His fingers locked tightly around Paris's wrist. "Jane." The name was guttural.

I can't tell him.

Sirens screamed in the distance. "We have to get out of here," Paris said. "Human cops are going to be on the scene any minute." Because what the fuck else would happen when someone started shooting on a college campus? *The SWAT team will be coming. It will be a war scene.*

"Jane." Aidan's breathing was labored, the lines on his face deeper, and he was so pale — like death. "Need...Jane...give her...blood...save...h-her..."

There is no saving her now, my friend.

Aidan's hold tightened on Paris's wrist. The bones were grinding together. "Get...me...to Jane..."

"You can't help her, Aidan." It hurt to say the words. "She's..."

Aidan shoved him back. The alpha had been barely breathing moments before, but Aidan's shove sent Paris flying through the air. Aidan dragged his body to Jane. He stared down at her a moment, his expression utterly lost and broken.

Then he reached out to her. He touched her face. "Jane?"

Paris pushed to his feet. "We have to get out of here." He motioned to the two guards. "We *have* to take the alpha." They would understand what he meant. The alpha was going to fight them like hell.

His world is about to implode. If they didn't get him away from the humans, Paris wasn't sure what would happen. He could already hear the pop and snap of Aidan's bones. The alpha's wolf wanted out.

Paris shoved his hand into his pocket. His fingers closed over the syringe that he'd been carrying, just in case.

Because Annette isn't usually wrong.

"Jane?" Now her name was louder, more demanding as it burst from Aidan. The alpha used his teeth to slice open his wrist and then he put that bleeding wrist to her mouth. "Drink, Jane. Drink."

It was ripping his heart out to watch his friend suffer. Paris eased toward Aidan. "The cops are coming." Cops who weren't in on the whole paranormal secret. "We have to go."

"Drink, Jane." Aidan kept his wrist at her mouth. "Please."

Jane's chest was bloody and her neck was tilted at an...unnatural angle. Her eyes were closed. Her body totally still. It was obvious she was dead. It was also obvious that Aidan wasn't going to let her go.

"Jane." Aidan pulled her against him, holding her tight. "No, Jane, no. Don't do this to me."

The two werewolf guards closed in on Aidan. They reached out to him.

"Stay the fuck away!" Aidan's roar echoed around them.

The werewolves froze. They looked at Paris. The sirens were louder.

"Jane." Aidan began to rock her in his arms. Tears slid down his face. Paris had never seen the alpha cry before that moment. "Don't leave me. I don't...I don't want to be without you. Please, Jane, please..."

She'd already left. The alpha had to see that.

But how long will she stay gone? Unease slithered through Paris.

"I love you, Mary Jane," Aidan whispered. "You are my world. The person who always makes me smile. You bring me so much happiness...why, Jane, why? *Why did you take that fucking bullet?*"

Paris didn't know what Aidan was talking about. "We have to leave." They had only moments before the cops were there. And he could see a few of the college kids peeking out at them now.

"*Help m-me!*" That pain-filled bellow came from Jane's brother.

Still alive.

Still—

Aidan's head slowly turned toward the human.

Goosebumps rose on Paris's arms.

"You're dead," Aidan told the younger man. "Dead. And it will be a long, slow, terrible death. I will peel the skin from your body. I will make you scream. I will ensure that you leave this world in more agony than anyone else can imagine."

Oh, shit. This scene was getting bad.

Paris slowly pulled the syringe from his pocket. He didn't want to do this. "Aidan...we have to leave."

But Aidan was still rocking Jane in his arms and his gaze still promised death to her brother. "Are you ready to see my hell?"

Paris couldn't let that happen. The police were almost there. "I'm sorry," he whispered. Then he lunged toward his alpha, the syringe gripped tightly in his hand. He sank the needle into Aidan's back. The alpha roared. His claws flew out and slashed across Paris's stomach and then—

Then Aidan collapsed, falling down so that his body was over Jane's, and their faces were just inches apart.

Paris's breath heaved out and his chest jerked as he stared down at his alpha...and at Jane. She looked almost peaceful right then. Hardly like some terrible, sinister threat.

She will be.

Paris grabbed Aidan. He slung the alpha over his shoulder. And he gave Jane one last look. *I will remember you as you were.*

And not as she'd become.

"What about him?" One of the werewolves jerked his hand toward Jane's brother. The guy wasn't calling out any longer. He barely seemed to be breathing.

"Leave him." There was enough blood already on the ground. And too many witnesses lurking nearby. Eyes were on them now. "Let the cops deal with him."

Or maybe Jane's brother would die from his injuries in the next few moments. Save them all the effort.

Maybe...

Paris rushed toward his vehicle, Aidan was still slung over his shoulder. He jumped inside, the others helping him to secure Aidan. Moments later, he was gunning the engine and racing away.

He didn't let himself look back at Jane. What was the point? The woman he'd known was gone. Soon enough, Aidan would understand that.

Just as...soon enough...the alpha would have to stop the beast that Jane would become.

***

"I've never seen the alpha like this." Dr. Bob Heider was obviously hesitant as he studied Aidan's prone form.

They were inside Aidan's office at Hell's Gate. Paris had gotten them to the nearest safe place so that Heider could examine the alpha's wounds.

But the wounds are already closing.

"He's out cold," Heider continued. "But his vitals are good. The wounds are healing rapidly and—"

"I drugged him," Paris said. "So don't focus on him being unconscious. Just…just check everything else, okay?"

"You drugged your alpha?" Heider's mouth formed an "O" of surprise.

"Yes, well, it was either drug him or watch the guy peel skin from a human's body in front of who the hell knows how many college kids." It was already going to be a bitch handling the situation from the campus. When Aidan was back to normal — *when, not if, when* — then the alpha could do some serious damage control. Aidan would need to make sure plenty of people forgot all about the events of that day.

Paris raked his hand over his face. "Look, right now, priority one is making sure Aidan is all right. So finish examining him, okay?"

"He's fine. You got the silver out. You saved him."

No, I didn't. Sure, he'd gotten out the silver, but Paris thought Jane may have saved the alpha long before he'd arrived on scene. But Paris hadn't gotten the full story about what happened. Not yet. He figured Jane's brother was the one who knew that particular tale. "Finish his exam," Paris ordered once more, then he turned and marched from the room. He wasn't the least bit surprised to find Garrison pacing just outside of Aidan's office.

"Is it...true?" Garrison asked, his hand moving to yank on his shirt collar as if it had been choking him. "Is Jane dead?"

He hadn't felt for a pulse, but then, there hadn't been a need. "Her neck was broken and she was covered in blood when I left her."

"But...but was she *dead?*"

"Yes." He was certain of this. "She's gone, Garrison. I'm sorry." Because Garrison and Jane had formed a friendship. An odd one considering that Garrison had shot her the first time they met but...

Garrison's family had been killed by vampires, the same as Jane's. They'd shared that pain.

"I...I think I'm going to visit some friends out of town for a while."

Paris didn't comment on the tears he saw gathering in Garrison's eyes.

"I don't..." Garrison pressed his lips together then continued, "I don't want to be here when she rises. I can't turn on her." His hands fisted. "I swore to protect her, and I won't lift my claws against Jane, no matter what."

Even when she comes to rip out your heart? "You know it won't be her. She's gone."

"I'm going to visit some friends," Garrison said as he turned away. "Call me when...call me." Garrison hurried toward the stairs.

Paris didn't stop him, even though he straight-up knew the guy was lying. Garrison's *friends?* Those would be...

Me.

Aidan.

Jane.

Tension gathered at the base of Paris's neck. This situation was such a severe clusterfuck, and as far as he was concerned, there was only one way out of it. He pulled out his phone and then realized it had blood on it — Aidan's blood. *I touched the phone after I dug the bullets from my alpha.* He swallowed back his rage and his fear, and he called the one person who could help him.

Annette Benoit answered on the first ring. Her voice was soft and sad as she said, "Jane's dead."

"Yes." *Fucking hell, yes.* "And I need to make sure she stays that way."

"Then you want the fire."

Yes, dammit, that was what he'd wanted. A special batch of fire that would burn hell hot...hot enough to stop a vampire-in-waiting from ever rising. Hot enough to turn Jane into ash. And that batch of fire could only be created by a special voodoo queen — after all, she'd made it in the past. A guaranteed way to stop a vampire. Permanently. "Hurry."

***

"Your alpha is fine." Dr. Bob Heider marched out of Aidan's office thirty minutes later. "Fine except for the drugs *you* gave to him." Bob sure wouldn't like to be around when Aidan unleashed his fury on Paris. "Good luck handling him."

Paris never changed expression. "Someone will be waiting on your exam table."

What the hell? "Another kill? You need to get that rogue werewolf under control!" He marched for the stairs.

But...Bob stopped.

A woman was there. A gorgeous African American woman he'd seen before. *At Aidan's place in the swamp.* Her long, black hair skimmed her shoulders and power seemed to shine from her eyes. *Oh, shit. They called in the voodoo queen.* She made her way toward him and offered Bob the bottle in her hands.

He frowned. "What is this? Some kind of wine?" Like he'd take a drink she gave him. His mama hadn't raised a fool.

"It's fire."

"Uh, no, it isn't."

"When you break the bottle," she said, her voice oddly soothing, "the fire will rage. It will destroy completely. The beast won't have a chance to be born."

He glanced at Paris. "Is she making sense to you?"

"Jane was there when Aidan was attacked."

Bob's heartbeat suddenly seemed very, very fast in his chest. "She's okay?" She had to be okay or else Paris would've had him treat her, too. She must be—

"She'll be on your table."

Bob's knees nearly buckled. *Jane?*

"Use the fire on her," Paris ordered quietly. "You'll have access. You can do it before she changes. You can save lives by making sure Jane won't rise."

This was bull. "You're asking me to kill her? Kill Jane?"

Annette Benoit shook her head. "Jane is already dead. We're asking you to stop the monster before it can be born."

Jane wasn't a monster. She was...Jane.

"She'll be too powerful when she rises," Paris continued as he stepped closer to Bob. "This is our chance. When questioned later, you can just say a fire broke out in your office. We can explain it all away..."

Bob moved quickly away from Paris. "Screw that. I'm not *burning* Jane."

"She's not Jane anymore," Annette said, her expression grave. "How long will it take you to realize that?"

His chin jerked up. "I'm leaving."

Paris was in his way. The guy needed to take a freaking hint—

"Five hundred thousand dollars," Paris said.
He's offering to pay me to kill Jane?

"I want this done by the time Aidan wakes up," Paris continued in a dark, emotionless voice. "He shouldn't have to be the one to face her. He shouldn't have to go through that hell again."

"Take the fire, Dr. Heider," Annette urged.

He grabbed the bottle. "You're both nuts."

"You've seen what vampires do." Paris's eyes reflected his pain. "Do you think Jane would *want* to be that way?"

No, no, he didn't but...
Jane can't be dead.

He shoved past them, nearly running down the stairs so that he could get to the lower level of Hell's Gate. And, yes, the bottle was gripped tightly in his hand, but he wasn't going to use it. He wouldn't burn Jane.

But Paris's voice seemed to whisper through his mind once more. *Do you think Jane would want to be that way?*

CHAPTER FIFTEEN

Jane was on his table.

Bob stared at her face. So pale. So…peaceful.

Jane had rarely had much peace when she was alive. She'd always been rushing off to another crime scene. Always so desperate to stop a killer. To save a life.

And now she was on his table.

He had to blink a few times. This was wrong. Someone else should be doing the exam on her but…

I'm the only one who can handle the paranormal cases.

His gaze slid toward the bottle Annette had given him. It sat a few feet away, on a nearby counter. Was he really supposed to douse Jane with that liquid and walk away while she burned?

His hands were shaking when he turned away from her. He hurried over to his microscope. He'd taken a few samples from her earlier, and he wanted to see what was happening to her cells.

Maybe Jane won't turn. Maybe…

But he looked at her blood under the microscope. The blood of a dead woman. And the cells…they were already changing.

Evolving.

Something is coming back to life in Jane.

Breathing was hard. He stumbled and his shaking hands knocked over the microscope. He wasn't the one who usually handled the vampires. When he had a corpse on his table that showed signs of change — Bob always looked at the cells under his microscope — he put in a call to the werewolves. They were the clean-up team. Aidan and his crew came in. They stopped the monsters from going on a bloodlust fueled rampage.

But…

Can Aidan stop Jane?

Could Aidan kill the woman he loved?

"Jane, I am so sorry." Bob grabbed the bottle of liquid fire. His breath heaved out in heavy rasps. "You didn't deserve this." He could almost hear her laughter in his mind. He could see the way her eyes would narrow while she listened to him talk about a case. A faint furrow would appear between her brows.

I was her friend. I owe her peace.

He took a shuffling step toward the table.

"I'm sorry," Bob said again.

***

Aidan's eyes flew open. He stared up at the ceiling above him. His ceiling. His office. His club.

His...*Jane?*

A howl broke from him, one of pain and rage. One of grief—a grief that was already ripping him apart. Because when he stared at that ceiling, Aidan saw Jane.

Jane...covered in blood.

Jane...with her neck broken.

Jane...*gone.*

He leapt up from the couch, his claws out and his muscles stretching as the transformation burned like fire in his blood.

The door to his office flew open. Paris was there, his eyes wide, his face haggard. "Aidan..."

"*Where is she?*" Aidan was half-man, half-beast. All rage and pain and fear.

"You have to calm down."

In less than a second's time, he had Paris against the wall and Aidan's claws were at his friend's throat. "Where is my Jane?" Speaking was so fucking hard.

"D-dead," Paris gasped out. "But you...know that. She was dead—"

"She jumped in front of me." Each word was a growl. "Took the bullet...meant for me."

Dammit. He could have survived. As long as the bullet hadn't hit his heart…

"I-I'm sorry," Paris whispered.

Razor sharp teeth filled his mouth. Aidan wanted to rip and tear and claw. "You took…me away…from her." He dropped his hold on Paris. If he touched the other wolf a moment longer…*I'll kill him. My own friend…and I want to kill him.*

The pain in his chest wasn't lessening. It grew, burning hotter and harder every moment. And in his mind, Aidan just kept screaming Jane's name. He could feel his sanity slipping away. Moment by moment, breath by breath.

Need her. Can't…can't be without her.

"She was gone, Aidan." Paris slowly straightened. Blood dripped from the claw marks on his neck. "You kept trying to give Jane your blood, but she was already dead. Her…her neck was broken."

Aidan remembered that but… "Wrong." Drew had shot her. He hadn't gotten close enough to touch Jane.

So how did her neck get broken? I could have gotten to her, given her my blood…

But her neck was broken.

"I've taken steps," Paris said, his voice hesitant. "You…you won't have to deal with the repercussions."

His wolf clawed at his insides. "What have…you done?" His words were an animal's roar.

Paris flinched. "I couldn't let you go through it again…I…I didn't want you to be the one…"

To kill her.

Aidan howled again and he drove his fist into the wall right next to his best friend's head.

"No! *Aidan!*"

That scream was Annette's — she was rushing inside his office.

"She's going to burn, Aidan. It will all be over. Jane won't rise. She'll just go…" Annette put her body in front of Paris's. "He won't fight you, but I will."

She's going to burn. "Where is my Jane?"

"She's dead, Aidan," Annette said flatly. "Where do you think the dead go?"

To the ME. The fucking ME.

Without another word, he ran away from them.

"You're too late!" Annette yelled after him. "And, please, just let her go!"

Impossible.

"I told Jane…I warned her…she had to stop being the hero! It was only going to get her killed!"

And it had. She'd taken the bullet meant for him and lost her life.

***

Bob held the bottle of fire in his hands. "What am I supposed to do here? Open it? Pour it on you?" He lowered the bottle. "Smash it on you and watch you burn?"

Jane's expression was still so peaceful.

He couldn't do it. If the werewolves wanted her gone—then the werewolves could come and handle this shit themselves. He wasn't burning Jane. He wasn't—

"Just what the fuck…" A low, sinister voice demanded. "Do you think you're doing with *that?*"

Bob whirled around. A man was there—big, tall, with a face carved of granite and eyes that burned with hate.

And fangs. I can see his fangs.

"You thought to kill her while she couldn't even fight back? When she had no chance to defend herself?"

"No!" Bob shook his head, frantic. "I-I wasn't!" Who the hell was that guy? And why hadn't Bob heard him enter the exam area?

The vampire snatched the bottle from Bob's hands. Then he threw the bottle against the wall. It shattered and flames—hot, insanely, magically hot and blazing too fast—immediately began to roll up the wall.

"Jane will rise and you will not stop her." The vampire grabbed Bob and jerked him close. "*You would kill her while she slept.*"

"No!" That had been the plan the werewolves wanted, not him. "No, I —"

Fangs tore into his throat. Bob screamed. The bite was like being stabbed with an ice pick. The pain had nausea rising in his throat, and he struggled against the bastard, knowing that he'd be vomiting all over the vamp any second.

But the vamp tossed him aside. The vamp threw him so hard that Bob's back dented his filing cabinet. He crumpled onto the floor, struggling to see the vamp through the rising smoke and flames.

And the vamp…

He scooped Jane into his arms. The sheet that had covered her body fell to the floor.

"Y-you can't take her," Bob cried out.

"Like I'd leave her here for you to kill. Fucking bastard, why don't *you* burn?" Then the vamp was leaping toward the door, with Jane in his arms. Bob pushed to his feet and stumbled after him.

The fire is on the walls. On the ceiling. It was raging so fast and hard. Paris hadn't told him it would be this fast. It was unnatural. It was —

Voodoo. *What the hell did I expect?*

He had to get out of there.

Or he would be burning.

***

Aidan smelled the smoke and the acrid scent just made him run faster. It fueled the terrible fear and rage within him. *Jane can't burn.*

He needed to see her again. Needed to touch her. Needed to tell her how fucking sorry he was.

She'd given her life for him. That hadn't been the plan. Things *shouldn't* have ended that way. A burst of speed had him near the ME's building. Humans were rushing outside of that place, some coughing on smoke. Choking.

Where is Jane?

He didn't see her. Firefighters weren't even on the scene yet. They wouldn't make it there in time, not with a blaze like that, one that had magical aid. The smoke was thickening, the flames crackling, and Aidan ran right inside the burning building.

He knew his way to the ME's office — he could get there in the dark. So getting past the smoke and the flames wasn't hard for him. He held his breath as best he could and moved fucking fast. There were no prying eyes to see him.

He kicked in the door to the ME's lab. He heard coughing. And a weak... "H-help..."

But that voice wasn't Jane's.

It was Dr. Bob.

Aidan grabbed the ME and hoisted him over his shoulder.

"F-fire...spread t-too fast...g-got asthma..." The guy was wheezing. "C-can't breathe...s-smoke..."

"Where is Jane?" He didn't see her. Didn't smell her. But...

Maybe she's in one of the storage lockers. The lockers for the dead. His stomach clenched at the thought. Jane didn't belong there. She should be outside, running, laughing, *happy.*

"H-he took her. The vamp...they're g-gone —"

Aidan spun away from the flames. He raced through the building, but didn't go out the front exit, not with that freaking crowd out there. He went to the back of the place and hurtled through a big picture window on the first floor. Glass flew all around him.

The ME screamed.

Dr. Bob should be grateful. He was going to be able to breathe one hell of a lot better now that they were outside. Aidan ran with him, moving away from the flames. Then he lowered the doc and propped him up against a street lamp. "Breathe," Aidan ordered him. "Nice and fucking slow, got it?"

The doctor nodded, but he was wheezing hard.

The same way Jane was wheezing at the college. I remember that...

"I-I wasn't — wasn't b-burning — "

"Get your breath back first," Aidan growled at him. "Then talk to me." *Jane didn't burn. She made it out of the lab. She's —*

Dead?

Alive?

Aidan didn't know for sure.

"Don't listen to the sniveling bastard," a low, rumbling voice said.

Aidan stiffened. *Vincent.* He didn't spin around to confront the vamp, but he did let his claws slide out. *The better to cut off his head.*

"When I got to him," Vincent blasted, "the not-so-good doctor had a bottle of liquid fire in his hands. He was standing right over Jane. She was helpless. *Helpless.* And he was going to burn her to ash."

Bob's eyes were wild. Desperate. His wheezes had gotten worse. "N-not J-Jane — "

"I saved her." A hard pause came from Vincent, then he said, "You should be grateful to me."

"You saved her." Aidan's canines had lengthened in his mouth. The better to tear into the vampire. *I won't control my instincts this time. My wolf wants Vincent dead, and so the fuck do I.* "Is that the same way you saved her when you broke Jane's neck?" Because it was the only thing that made sense to him. She'd been shot—but her neck had been fine. One moment, she'd been wheezing. He'd been trying to get to her and then...

Jane was gone.

"Would you rather I let her suffer? Let her drown and choke on her own blood?" The vampire demanded and his words were all the confession Aidan needed. *He'd killed her.*

"*Would you?*" Vincent yelled at him. "Because that was happening. She'd taken *your* bullet. Risked her life for you, and I wasn't going to let her suffer needlessly."

"I could have given her my blood! Saved her!"

He heard the rustle of footsteps as Vincent rushed toward him. "*Jane wasn't meant to be saved! She was meant to be transformed!*"

Bastard. Aidan whirled, slicing out with his claws. His claws ripped into the vampire's stomach, cut deep, and then Aidan drew back, ready to take Vincent's head.

"Aidan?"

That was...Jane's voice. Jane's beautiful, sweet voice.

His head whipped to the right and then Aidan stilled. He didn't take the bastard's head. He couldn't move at all because Jane was stumbling toward him, walking out of a narrow alley. She was naked, and her hair trailed over her shoulders.

"She transformed quickly," Vincent whispered. "She's going to be so powerful. Probably even stronger than I am."

She didn't look powerful right then. She looked fragile, delicate, beautiful, and so very lost.

"Aidan?" Jane said his name again, almost desperately. "What's happening? How did I get here?"

He ran to her. Her scent had changed — grown deeper, richer. Even more lush. She didn't smell like a vampire. No death and blood clung to her. She was just his Jane.

He looked at her and didn't see fangs.

Her eyes were wide. Scared.

Jane shouldn't be afraid.

His wolf was oddly silent as Aidan grabbed Jane and pulled her into his arms. "It's okay," Aidan told her, knowing his hold was too tight but not able to ease his grip. He wanted to hold her and never let go. "You're safe. I've got you. Everything will be all right."

She shuddered against him.

"You…you need to have a care there, wolf," Vincent softly warned him.

Fuck that vampire. Vincent would be headless soon enough. Smoke drifted in the air around them, and Aidan still heard the crackle of flames.

Jane shuddered once more.

She's naked. She's probably cold. He finally eased his hold on her, yanked off his jacket, and looped it around her shoulders. "I'll take care of you," he promised her.

Again, his wolf was dead silent.

It was just the man talking. The man who was so desperate for her he couldn't see straight.

Jane. Not dead. Not gone. She was still right there with him.

Her head had tilted forward and her long hair covered her face. His hand — shaking — brushed back that hair. "Jane?"

"I don't...feel right, Aidan." She wasn't looking at him. Her head was still tilted forward.

You've been dead, sweetheart. Of course, you don't feel right. "You need to rest. We'll go back to our home." *Our* home. "You'll be fine. You'll — "

Slowly, her head slid back so that Jane was looking up at him. "I feel...hungry." And he saw the flash of her sharp teeth — right before she lunged at him and sank her fangs into his throat.

The pain was fast, white-hot, and shock held Aidan immobile.

Not Jane. Not Jane...I don't want to hurt her...

But the wolf that had been so quiet and still inside of him wasn't quiet any longer. He was howling, raking Aidan with his claws, and demanding to be set free.

The wolf's thoughts were basic.

Vampire. Kill. Destroy.

An instinct as old as time. Primitive.

But the man was still in control and the man just thought…

Jane is mine.

Her tongue snaked over his skin. A tremble shook him. He shouldn't be finding pleasure in her bite. It was so fucking wrong. Everything was *wrong* and —

"Aidan?" Jane said, her voice husky. "Wh-what am I doing?" And she was suddenly pushing against him. Horror flashed on her face even as drops of his blood dripped down her chin. "*No! No! Stop me!*" She was screaming now, terrified, anguished. "*Stop me!*"

That was just what the wolf wanted. To stop her. His bones snapped. He —

Vincent yanked Jane out of Aidan's arms and shoved her behind him. "It was way too soon for this little meeting. She isn't strong enough yet, and you —" His gaze raked over Aidan. "You are totally fucked up."

Aidan couldn't stop the transformation now. It was coming too fast. Fur burst from his skin, and he slammed down to the ground, landing on all fours.

"You have better things to worry about than us," Vincent said, his voice rough and fast. "Things like say, the other alpha in town. You know, the one that has been *killing* humans. Why don't you go after him? Take out all this aggression on *him?*"

Aidan's rage was focused on the vampire before him. Vincent. Vincent had done this. He'd changed Jane. He'd ruined everything. A growl broke from Aidan as razor sharp teeth filled his mouth. *Not a man's mouth, a beast's.*

"Jane, we have to go," Vincent said. "Right *now.*"

Aidan looked up, still seeing through the eyes of a man, for the moment. Jane was struggling in Vincent's arms, and her wide gaze was...

On me.

She stared at him with anguish and fear and — and love. Even then, after everything, he could still see her love for him.

"Stop me," Jane begged him softly.

"Stop saying that shit!" Vincent yelled back. Then he locked his arms around her stomach and started running with her down the tight alley. "Stop it — or he will!"

The last of the shift burned through Aidan's blood.

"Oh, my God." Dr. Bob's voice. Still breathless and now absolutely terrified. "*Don't kill me. Don't kill me. Don't...*"

The doctor wasn't the beast's prey.

The vampires were.

Aidan howled as the shift finished, the man now gone and only the wolf in his place. He bounded down the alley, steps behind the vampires. So close.

"Aidan..." Jane's voice.

The wolf stumbled.

My mate.

And then both vampires vanished.

CHAPTER SIXTEEN

It was hard to think straight. Jane's body was too hot. Her skin too tight. And her mind...

Hunger. Need. Blood.

She could taste blood on her tongue. The flavor was rich and oddly sweet. And...and Jane feared it was...*his.*

Everything was cloudy. Her thoughts were in chaos. She'd been in an alley. She thought she had, anyway. Aidan had been there. She'd...bit him?

Had she killed him?

"Jane." It was that voice again. The annoying one that kept bossing her around.

"Jane, you need to feed."

The fangs in her mouth—the ones that were fully extended and *burning* – told her that he was right. But... "Leave me alone." Her voice was a rasp. So weak and broken. That was how she felt.

Every part of her seemed broken.

Did I kill Aidan? Her—her fangs had been in his throat. But...he'd shifted, hadn't he?

"Stop moping." The annoying voice came once more. The vampire's voice. "Your werewolf is still alive, though I think he'd like nothing more than to tear us both apart."

At those words, Jane's lashes lifted. The vampire—Vincent—stood just a few feet in front of her. It was dim all around them, and the place smelled a bit dank. Mildew hung in the air, the scent had her nose twitching.

"Are you in control?" Vincent asked her.

"Fuck off."

He nodded. "That sounds relatively in control." His gaze slid over her and he winced. "Sorry about all the manacles. I'm totally not into bondage, but until I see how you're going to react to this whole new vamp life you've got going on, they seem like a good idea."

Because the bastard had her chained up. Both of her wrists were locked in heavy, metal cuffs above her head. Her feet were chained up, too. She stood against a wall, trapped. At his mercy.

Her day was truly shit. Or was it night now? She had no clue.

"I think this place used to be an old BDSM club," Vincent explained to her, as if they were having a friendly little chat. "When I came to town, I bought it and made a few quick modifications."

"Because you knew...you were going...to change...me..." Speaking was so hard. Each word left her throat feeling raw.

Vincent shook his head. "I knew *you* would change. It was meant to be. Even your voodoo queen saw it, didn't she?"

Don't be the hero. Just...don't be. Annette's words played through her mind, like a song stuck on repeat.

"She saw it," Vincent continued, "but even the famed Annette Benoit couldn't change anything."

"You...did...this..." Her voice didn't even sound human. More like an animal's. Her stomach was knotted and her whole body *hurt*.

"You were choking on your own blood, Jane. You were dead, your body was just still suffering. I ended your pain."

You broke my neck. I remember that part, you asshole.

"I am not the enemy." Vincent took a step closer to her. His eyes drifted over her face. "You need to realize that. I am your one friend in this world. I can help you."

She closed her eyes. The bloodlust was building inside of her again. Nearly uncontrollable. Her fangs shoved against her lips. Her throat was parched.

Want. I need...

"You attacked Aidan. Do you remember that?" Vincent asked her.

Shame twisted around her heart.

"And he tried to kill you."

A tear leaked from her eye. She felt it slide down her cheek.

Vincent sighed. "You have to stay away from him, or he *will* kill you. You and I need to leave town. As soon as you're strong enough, we'll be out of here. Hell, we'll leave the freaking country, just to be safe. He won't get you. I'll keep you safe."

She didn't want to be safe. She wanted her old life back. She wanted Aidan.

"Jane." Her name came from him, hard and demanding. "Jane, I am not the enemy. I came here to help you because I knew the change was coming. You don't have to be a monster. You have vampires all wrong. You don't *have* to be evil."

Tell that to the vampire who killed my family. Tell it to my father, tell —

"Even your father eventually regained his humanity. How do you think you escaped that vampire attack when you were eleven? When your worthless excuse for a brother saved himself first and you were struggling to get out of that little window in the basement?"

How did Vincent know about that?

"Your father came to your rescue. He gave his life so that you could escape, not that I expect you to remember that, of course. You probably didn't even look back. I don't blame you. You just wanted to run, right? To escape?"

Her eyes squeezed closed even tighter. *Stop talking.*

"After the initial change, I won't lie...being a vampire is brutal. Especially for humans who are made into vamps, the ones that needed the transfusion for the change to occur in their bodies. The bloodlust overwhelms them. It's all they know. But for you and me...we were born to be this way. We were never really human — *that* is the part that was the lie about us. We were always meant to be vampires."

Don't look at him. Don't.

Her body jerked because the hunger was twisting through her.

"Some vampires go mad with their power. They exist to torture. To kill. To destroy."

She didn't want to be like that. But already, Jane could feel her humanity sliding away. *Need blood. Need it.*

"You won't be this way," Vincent said, as if he were making a promise to her. "I won't let you make the same mistakes I did." His voice was grim. "You will be the end. Just like you were supposed to be...only they're wrong about how that end will come. You'll change everything for the vampires. I know you can do it. *I know it.*"

He knew nothing.

Her lashes slowly lifted. "Blood." It was all she could manage. So guttural. So…desperate.

He nodded. Then he…he lifted up what looked like a plastic bag, one that was filled with red liquid. "I've got all the blood you need, right here."

Bagged. Not from a person. Somewhere deep inside, joy burst through Jane. She wasn't going to feed from a person. She could just take the blood bags! She wouldn't be a monster! She wouldn't!

He ripped open the bag. "Open wide, Jane." Vincent was smiling. Looking happy…or as happy as a vamp could look.

She opened her mouth. He lifted up the bag and blood poured past her lips, over her tongue, down her throat. That terrible, twisted need she had felt moments before began to lessen as she gorged herself and then—

Jane vomited. The blood all came back up— and landed right on Vincent.

And in a very dim part of her mind, Jane thought…*Serves you right, asshole. That's what you get for killing me.*

Vincent wiped the blood vomit from his eyes. "We may need to try something else."

The bloodlust grew again, even stronger than before. She snapped at him with her teeth because his throat suddenly looked way too appealing.

Vincent hurriedly stepped back. "We *definitely* need to try something else."

***

"Where is Jane?" Aidan asked Annette as he stood in her shop, in the private back room. Paris was right behind him. Garrison lurked in the shadows, poking at the objects on her shelf. Garrison had been trying to sneak his little ass out of town, but Aidan had stopped him. Pack didn't run. Pack stayed together.

No matter what.

He knew Garrison was afraid of having to hurt Jane...*Join the fucking club.* That was why they were all there with Annette. *Because there has to be another option. We can't kill Jane.*

Annette sat at the small table she used for her scrying work, and her gaze was on the mirror before her. To Aidan, the mirror looked completely black, but he knew that Annette saw...things...in that dark surface.

See Jane.

Annette smoothed back her hair. "How did your beast react to her?"

"Can't you see for yourself?" He snapped. "Isn't it all right there in that fucking glass?"

She looked up at him.

Paris put his hand on Aidan's shoulder. "Easy."

Aidan's lip curled in a snarl. "There is nothing *easy* about this situation." It was a fucking nightmare. "I lost my Jane."

"And now…" Annette murmured, her face sad. "You think she will attack you…turn on you…the same way that your mother did."

His teeth ground together. "Isn't that what vampires do?"

Her gaze searched his. "Jane is not your mother. You are not your father."

That wasn't an answer to his question.

"How did your beast react to her?" Annette asked again. Aidan just stared at her. Annette's fist slammed down on the table, making the scrying mirror bounce. "Dammit, I don't *see* what happened, Aidan! That's why I'm asking! Now stop being a dick and tell me!"

Silence.

Garrison cleared his throat. "You shouldn't call the alpha a dick."

"Then he shouldn't be one," Annette snapped right back. "Look, I get this is hard."

Aidan laughed. "Hard doesn't cover it." She wanted to know? Fine. "Jane went for my throat and my beast went for her. I shifted before I could stop myself and if Vincent hadn't vanished with her." *Fucking parlor trick that I still don't understand.* "If he hadn't vanished, I would have killed them both." It was a truth that made him sick.

Killed…Jane.

His hands fisted. "I don't want this."

"Guilt can be a terrible monster to carry," she said, her voice softening. "I'm sorry."

"I did this to her. If I'd moved faster, if I hadn't brought in her bastard of a brother…"

Annette shook her head. "Fate can't be changed. Jane was born to be a vampire."

"Fuck fate. Jane was born to be mine."

Her brow furrowed at his words, and Annette leaned over her mirror once more. "Yes," she said, voice a bit dazed. "I think she was."

And her brother is a dead man. I've already got a call in to Vivian's office…I want access to that prisoner. Drew Hart was in intensive care at the local hospital, under constant police protection. Once Aidan spoke with Vivian, that protection would vanish. Drew *would* die.

A life for a life.

Why the hell hasn't Vivian called me back already? He'd put her in that position as police captain for two reasons. One — Vivian was fucking fantastic at the job. And two — she was a werewolf who'd always been loyal to the pack.

He could always count on her to do what he needed.

Only Vivian hasn't called me…

"There are other threats out there," Annette said and her words were way too close to Vincent's for Aidan's comfort. "Others you need to face before you see Jane."

He knew where this was going. "The other alpha." The sonofabitch who was killing in Aidan's territory.

Annette nodded. "You think he won't have the same urge that you do? When confronted by not one, but two vampires, his primal instincts will overwhelm him. He'll attack. He'll destroy Jane."

Aidan's chest was ice cold.

"But I suppose that's what you want," Annette mused silkily. "For her to just be…gone."

Aidan shot to his feet. "I want her back. I want my Jane back." His throat seemed to throb where she'd bit him. "I want her in my arms. In my bed. In my life." Then he had to say the truth that tore him apart. *"But my beast wants her dead."*

Annette turned her hand so that it faced him, palm up. "Give me your blood so I can see…"

He gave her his hand. She sliced across his palm with her knife and as the blood dripped onto her mirror, he saw Jane.

Jane and blood. The two would always be bound together in his mind.

***

"Jane."

She hung limply in her chains. Every part of her body hurt. Her lips and tongue were so swollen. The thirst *wouldn't* end. It was ripping her apart. She wanted to feed so badly. So. Badly. She'd do anything to stop that terrible hunger. *Anything.*

Then a smell hit her. Light. Sweet. Intoxicating.

Her eyes flew open.

Vincent stood a few feet away. A woman with dark red hair was before him and…blood trickled down the woman's throat.

"I think the problem," Vincent said, "is that you need live prey."

Jane shook her head. *No. No. Stay away.*

The woman's eyes were dazed, unfocused. Was she drugged?

Vincent pushed his victim — no, *my victim* — forward. "Does her blood smell good, Jane?"

Damn him. *Yes.*

"Are you hurting, Jane?"

I'm being ripped apart. But I deserve the pain. I —

"Take a few sips of her blood and the pain will stop."

Jane shook her head. "S-stay away…" It was all she could manage. Barely a whisper.

Vincent's face tightened. "The longer you delay, the more powerful the bloodlust becomes. Soon you won't be able to control yourself at all. You'll attack everyone in your path. You'll be beyond thought. Beyond control. That's why so many new vampires go on their bloody rampages. That's why Aidan's mother couldn't be stopped."

Aidan's…mother?

"She tried not to feed. She held out too long. She'd starved herself, refusing to eat at all, going weeks…until she was only a shell. She lost herself completely. She turned on the ones closest to her. She destroyed them. Took all of her family in that bloodlust, and only Aidan escaped."

Tears were pouring down her cheeks now. Aidan hadn't told her. He hadn't said…

Paris tried to warn me. He'd told her to ask Aidan about his family, but she hadn't. All that time, Aidan had been with her, and he'd known…he'd realized just what would happen to her in the end.

Because I am like his mother.

But…but he'd loved Jane anyway. Despite the hell he knew would come.

"Drink from her, Jane," Vincent urged. His voice was a dark temptation. "You don't have to be a monster. If you get the bloodlust under

control, you'll be okay. I will help you. Guide
you."

Her tongue swiped over the tip of one fang
and...

Bam.

Bam.

Bam.

What was that sound? That terrible banging?
Jane's gaze darted to the woman's neck and she
saw the pulse racing at the base of her throat.

Bam.

Bam.

Bam.

Oh, sweet Jesus, she could hear the woman's
heart beating. And that beat called to Jane.

"I won't let you kill her, Jane. I promise, I
won't. I'll stop you after just a few sips."

Jane's hands jerked in the restraints. Her
wrists were already raw and bloody. She was
wearing just a coat—Aidan's coat. His scent was
all around her.

I need him.

Just thinking of him made her bloodlust
grow even stronger. Her mouth opened.

"I won't let you kill her," Vincent promised.
"But I *will* make you drink from her." And he
lunged forward. One hand grabbed Jane's head
and he shoved it against the woman's bloody
throat. And his other hand held the woman there,
trapped against Jane.

No, no, she didn't want to do this!

But the woman's blood touched her lips.

There was no going back. Jane opened her mouth wide. Her fangs sank into the woman's throat even as Jane mentally shouted...*No! Run away! Run away! I'm so sorry! I can't stop! I can't!*

The blood flowed over Jane's tongue. Unlike the bagged blood, this was warm. Hot. Seeming to burst with life and flavor and—

Jane shoved the woman back. "Wrong," she rasped.

"No!" Vincent shouted. "It's not wrong!" He tossed the woman aside and grabbed Jane by her shoulders. "It's your nature! It's—"

She vomited the fresh blood on him.

He stiffened.

Her stomach cramped. The hunger nearly tore her apart but...

I can't keep the blood down! Didn't he see? Something was very, very *wrong.*

Once more, Vincent wiped the blood vomit from his eyes. His expression had turned pensive. The woman sobbed behind him.

"You're right," Vincent finally said. "Something *is* wrong."

***

"Before she..." Aidan stopped and cleared his throat. Annette was swirling his blood over the surface of her mirror. And he was still breaking apart on the inside.

I have to keep it together a little longer. My pack needs me.

"Before she was killed, Jane...Jane had just discovered a lead on the other alpha." He rubbed his neck, then stopped when he felt the tender skin that had been left from Jane's bite. "She suspected a college student, some punk named Quint Laurel."

When he said the name, Annette nodded, as if something had just been confirmed for her. Then she told Aidan, "He has one of your pack."

"What?" The sharp question came from Paris. "Who? Who does the bastard have?"

Annette's fingers stilled on the mirror. "The woman of power. The captain. He has her, and he's going to kill her soon."

Fucking hell. Aidan had been so caught up in Jane—

That I let down my pack.

"He doesn't even understand what he is. A lost boy...turned into a savage beast. Without guidance, that's what happens. An orphan, he came to this town, not knowing, not understanding...and then changing."

Garrison whistled. "Alphas change at twenty-one. If the guy didn't understand what he was...and all of a sudden he shifted...it's a wonder that he didn't lose his mind."

"Maybe he did lose it," Paris said as he paced nearby. "That would explain his kills."

Annette's head lifted and her eyes seemed to stare right through Aidan. "He had no guidance. It can make all the difference."

Did she think he was going to *guide* the punk? "Screw guidance. It's too little, too late for that. The guy is a killer, and I'm stopping him." His wolf was eager for the battle. All the rage and fear that Aidan had inside…it was going to burst free. He'd shift and give his beast full reign.

A blood battle. To the death. It was the only way for alphas to fight.

"Do you see him?" Aidan asked Annette.

She nodded. "I see him now because he wants to be seen. He wants the whole world to know what he is. That desire is practically pouring from his cells. It's why he's killed. Why he hunts. The world should know his power."

"Where." Not a question, a demand.

"With the dead, of course."

So the killer had gone back to his playground in the cemetery. Aidan whirled away.

"Aidan…will you kill her?" Annette called after him, her question hesitant.

"I'm not going after Jane right now," he said, not looking back at her. *One crisis at a time.*

"No…" Annette's voice was sad.

Paris hurried to follow behind him. Garrison closed in, too.

I'm not going after Jane. I'm going to kill a werewolf bastard who made the mistake of killing in my town.

As for my Jane…I need her to stay away from my wolf.

Far away.

***

The door closed behind the werewolves as they rushed out of her shop. Annette's shoulders fell. "No," she said softly, pained to her core, "you aren't going after her…but Jane will find you."

She could see it in the blood.

So much blood.

***

"Aidan, stop!" Paris yelled.

Aidan swung around, snarling. "I don't have time to waste—"

"No, but I have something…something that might help us. It caught my eye when I saw Garrison nosing around Annette's shelves." His hand opened, revealing a vial. "I figured if this was strong enough to knock you out…then maybe—"

"I'm not interested in knocking out the other alpha. I'm interested in kicking his ass." He spun around. His prey waited.

"Wasn't talking about him," Paris mused. "I was thinking of someone else that you may not want to kill."

Now Aidan did pause.

"I've got a few extra syringes. I picked them up, when, you know, I was planning to knock your ass out."

Aidan growled.

"Better to be safe, right?" Paris pushed. "You want the vial or not?"

Aidan considered it. He knew what Paris meant…his friend was giving him the option of knocking out Jane if their paths crossed. Knocking her out and *not* killing her. His jaw locked as he said, "You keep it."

"Aidan—"

"*You*, Paris." He looked back. "And when the time is right, you'll know what to do." *Maybe you'll use it on Jane. Maybe you'll use it on me.*

Or maybe…maybe you'll just watch us destroy each other.

CHAPTER SEVENTEEN

Annette stared down into her mirror once again. Aidan would find the other alpha, of that, she had no doubt. And Aidan was strong enough to win the battle, but…

But that isn't how I see it ending.

Her breath caught in her throat as she gazed into the mirror. *No, no, no!*

The images tore through her mind and she jumped to her feet. She had to get to Aidan. Had to stop him. Annette grabbed her car keys and raced outside.

And she slammed straight into the vampire who'd been waiting for her. Not that he *looked* like a vampire. He was tall, handsome, dressed expensively. His hair was perfectly styled, his body strong and —

And when I look at him, I know exactly what he is…because I saw him in my visions. I saw him die on a Viking ship.

"Annette Benoit," he murmured, his voice smooth and rich and deep. He gave her a little bow. "I have to say, I'm honored to meet you."

Annette jerked out the wooden stake that she kept in her bag, for emergencies just like this one. "I'm not so honored." She shoved the stake against his chest.

He...didn't stop her.

The stake cut through his skin. Blood soaked his shirt.

But she didn't drive the stake down into his heart. He wasn't fighting her, and that was just...*wrong.*

"Wrong," Annette whispered, the word settling deep within her. *Something was wrong.*

"I like my heart, old and battered though it may be," the vampire said. "So how about we just leave it where it is?" Carefully, his fingers closed around her wrist and he eased the stake out of his chest. "Thank you."

Her temples were pounding. "What's happening?"

"I don't know. And since my witch isn't close enough to help me figure things out...I thought you might be able to take her place."

Annette's eyes narrowed on him.

"Jane can't take blood. When she tries, she just vomits it up." His voice roughened, belying his controlled appearance. "And every moment that passes without her getting blood, well, it's a moment that drives her closer to the edge. Soon, there won't be any sane thought for her. She'd slip over that thin line that separates good and evil, and Jane *will* be lost, just like so many other vamps have lost themselves to the bloodlust."

Annette shivered.

"Jane has to take blood. It is a simple matter of survival for her. But she has to be *controlled* when she does it. Taking a life when you first drink...that's the tipping point for vampires. The darkness grows within them after that act, and there is no stopping it from consuming their souls."

Her breath heaved out. "But Jane can't take blood."

"No...no, she's starving and we have to find a way to help her." The faint lines near his mouth tightened. "This wasn't the way it was supposed to work. But Jane...something is different."

Wrong. Her heart stuttered in her chest. "Where is Jane now?"

"She's safe. Don't worry. I left her chained up."

She flinched.

"She's in an old building near the St. Louis Cemetery. She won't hurt anyone, not as long as she stays chained up."

St. Louis Cemetery.

Aidan was going to that cemetery. *Oh, hell.*

"She won't stay chained up long," Annette announced. "She'll break loose." She grabbed the vampire. "You've been using your witch's magic to vanish?"

He nodded.

"Good. Then use it now. Get us to Jane, as fast as you can." Before it was too late.

***

Quint Laurel smiled at his prey. The police captain was spread out, her blood still seeping from her wounds, as she lay before the old crypt. The blond reporter — Sarah Steele was sobbing, too terrified of him to move.

Soon, the whole world would be terrified.

"You're going to film me," he told the reporter. Then there would be no denying what he was. The humans would all understand. He motioned to the phone in her hands. The woman was so far gone, a freaking wreck, that she hadn't even thought to call for help. Not that he would have let her but...still, her fear was incredibly gratifying. It was like she was his puppet on a string. *Pull that string, pull it.* "You'll record every moment. Then you'll show it on the news. You'll show the world."

"Please," the news anchor whispered as heavy tracks of mascara bled down her cheeks. "Let us go. Just let us go."

"No." Then he turned back to the cop. The bitch who'd dared to call him a coward. He let his claws out as he closed in on her. She gave a low moan when he approached, and Quint smiled. A moan meant she was conscious. A moan meant she was about to feel all the pain he would give to her. "I think I'll start with your face," he decided. "Women can be so vain. Let's take that pretty face away first." He lifted his claws.

But...but she moved. She was bleeding heavily, but she lunged up at him and she sliced into his stomach. His blood pumped out. "What the—"

"Did you think..." she panted, "you were...the only one?" Her hand lifted and he saw claws sprouting from her fingertips. "Think...fucking...again..."

Quint stumbled back. "No." He put his hand to his stomach. "*No.*" Thatch had tried to tell him some bullshit about there being other werewolves in town, when Quint had made the mistake of flashing his claws at the guy one drunk night. Thatch had heard tales...tales about wolves going into Hell's Gate, but Quint had gone there and seen *nothing.*

No one else is like me. I'm the power. I'm special. I am everything.

"Yes." Vivian Harris dragged her body upright. "There are more...and you...you broke our laws. Werewolf laws. Human laws." Her eyes seemed to glow. "You will *die.* The alpha is coming. He will come...for me."

"The who? The fucking what?" Quint surged toward her but she slashed him again—right across the face. He howled in pain.

Vivian laughed, the sound pain-filled and mocking. "Now…who's the vain bitch?"

Rage nearly blinded Quint as he jumped on her.

And—

He heard another howl split the night.

***

She was so hungry. Thirsty. Pain burned through her constantly, and Jane just wanted that savagery to end.

This wasn't living. This was hell.

Her mind was trapped in chaos. The need to feed controlled her. Her lips were swollen, raw, and—

A howl.

Jane stiffened. She'd just heard a howl. Aidan's howl. She knew the sound of his wolf. Her nostrils flared and she caught the scent of blood in the air. Only…it wasn't human blood.

Werewolf blood.

Jane began to salivate. She yanked at the chains that bound her. Jerked again and again. The scent of that blood grew stronger. Her need burned hotter.

Her wrist broke — the right wrist. She kept jerking against her bonds. Harder. *Harder.*

The chain snapped free from the wall. Her broken right wrist slipped from the manacle and she shattered the manacle that had bound her left wrist. Then Jane looked at the chains around her ankles.

I need that blood.

Snarling, she locked her fingers around those chains. She pulled and pulled and pulled —

Free. The chains broke. Jane stood there, breath heaving, fingers broken. Blood covered her ankles and her hands.

Her nostrils twitched. *The werewolves are close.*

And she liked the way they smelled.

Jane straightened. She was still wearing his coat. Aidan's coat. His scent was on her. She pulled the coat closer. Zipped it up her body. The jacket fell to the top of her thighs, shielding her nakedness. Her bare toes slid across the dirty floor as she crept forward.

I'm free now.
Get the blood.
Get the werewolves.
Free.

Jane started running.

***

"Get the fuck away from her," Aidan roared.

The young alpha froze, his body crouched over Vivian's. Then, in the next instant, he whipped around, staring at Aidan in shock.

"You've got my pack member there." Rage pumped through Aidan's body. "You *dared* to hurt her?"

The soon-to-be-dead bastard laughed. "Who the hell are you?"

Aidan rushed toward him. He slammed his body into the younger wolf's — had to be freaking Quint Laurel — and Aidan put his claws to the guy's throat. "I'm the alpha of this town, and you're the bastard I'm here to put down."

But Quint was strong. He laughed up at Aidan...and began to shift beneath him.

Like that's supposed to impress me. "Get Vivian to safety!" Aidan bellowed, knowing Paris would obey. Aidan hadn't come to that cemetery alone. "And get the human out of here!" The blond woman just stood there, watching them, a phone in her hands as she filmed the scene. Quint had probably put her under his control, using his power to manipulate her. "Erase that fucking video!"

Paris scooped Vivian into his arms.

Garrison curled his hand around the blond woman's shoulder. "Why don't you give me that...?" He took the phone from her.

And Aidan...he let his own beast take control. *I want to kill. I want to destroy. I want to rip this bastard apart.* Because Aidan was being torn apart. Ripped apart by his own emotions. The needs that just wouldn't stop.

Jane.

His claws burst out and his wolf took over.

***

"That was…" Annette drew in a steadying breath as the world stopped spinning around her. "Not a way I ever want to travel again." She jerked away from the vampire. "Which building?"

He pointed straight ahead. She ran inside the old BDSM club. Maybe she'd been there a time or two before, back in the place's heyday.

"In the back," Vincent said, "last room on the right."

"Jane!" Annette called. "Jane, I want to help you!"

But…when she rushed into that last room on the right, Jane wasn't there. Bloody manacles were on the floor, but Jane was gone. Annette staggered to a stop. The vampire thudded into her back.

"Go find her," Annette whispered. "Hurry. Find her." *Before Aidan does.*

***

Jane's bare feet pounded over the pavement. That powerful blood was in the air, calling to her. A heavy, stone fence waited just feet away — Jane ran forward and leapt right over the fence. When she landed, she crouched and looked around the cemetery. Her nostrils twitched.

To the left. Go. Left. Jane bounded forward, darting around crypts and then — then she came face to face with her prey.

Paris held Vivian in his arms. Vivian was bleeding. So much blood. So much sweet blood.

Jane's teeth snapped together.

"Oh, hell, no," Garrison muttered from behind Paris. "Tell me she's not all vamped up."

Jane wanted to talk to them. To tell them all to run but...

There's so much blood. And it smells incredible.

She crept toward her prey. Paris had gone statue-still. "Jane," he said, "I don't want to hurt you."

I don't think you can.

Her hand reached for Vivian. She licked her lips.

"Jane..." Vivian's weak voice. "Jane...h-help me..."

She doesn't know what I am.

Vivian thought Jane was still just her friend. *I'm about to feed on my friend. No, no, no.*

"Get...her away..." Jane rasped, then she turned and fled even deeper into the heart of that

cemetery. *This is the city of the dead. This is where I belong. I can't attack. I can't drink. I should be dead.*
   Dead.

She ran faster, aware that she was crying, her chest shuddering. She pounded on her chest, wanting to stop the terrible pain that she felt, wanting it all to end. As she should have ended when her brother shot her.

She darted around another crypt.

Howls penetrated the chaos of her thoughts. Terrible, frenzied howls.

Jane saw two beasts. One was a big, black wolf...with blue eyes that were forever burned into her memory.

The other beast...it was smaller, a white wolf with pale green eyes. As she stared at it, the white wolf slowly turned toward her. It sniffed the air, as if confused, and then its eyes lit with a killing fury.

Aidan always said...a werewolf has a primal instinct to kill a vampire.

That wolf coming toward her...it was going to kill her.

He's the other alpha. She was having moments of sanity—desperate moments pushing through that wild, driving bloodlust that twisted her mind. *The other alpha will kill me...that way, Aidan doesn't have to do the dark deed. He won't have my death on his conscience. He won't carry that guilt forever.*

She stretched her hands out at her sides. The white wolf was bounding toward her. Its heavy jaws were hanging open, and saliva dripped from his razor sharp teeth. This was the beast she'd been hunting. This was the beast who would kill her.

She could welcome her end. Her death would stop Aidan's pain. It would stop her own pain.

Jane started to close her eyes.

But...

Screw this. I'm not ready. The wolf leapt for her and Jane caught him around the neck. Her strength surprised her. She held that wolf easily. She lifted him up—

And Jane drove her fangs past his fur and into his neck. The wolf let out a terrible cry—a scream of pain, a howl of fury—and he thrashed in her hold, but Jane held him fast. And she drank.

His blood is hot and rich. I like it.

And she wasn't vomiting it up. His blood was flowing over her tongue and she just wanted to keep taking. *Taking and taking and taking until nothing is left.*

Jane shoved the wolf away from her, throwing him into the stone wall of a nearby crypt. "But I'm...not...a...killer." Her breath heaved out. Each word was a struggle but she did it. She spoke. She fought the bloodlust. She *won*. "You're...under...arrest..."

The white wolf leapt back to his feet. He shook his head. His blood had darkened his white coat. He pushed back onto his hind legs and hurtled into the air, coming right at her.

Because obviously, you want some more, huh, bastard?

But Aidan collided with him. The two wolves hit in a tangle of limbs. They rolled, clawing and biting and fighting with a savagery that she'd never witnessed before. They were strong. They were powerful. They were—

Aidan sank his teeth into the other wolf's throat, right in the same spot she'd attacked. Only Aidan hadn't gone for some little bite.

Jane sucked in a sharp breath as she stared at the scene before her.

Aidan ripped out the other wolf's throat.

The heavy, coppery scent of blood flooded her nose again. And this time...*I can smell death. It's coming.* Jane watched as the black wolf backed away from his prey. The white wolf slowly shifted, his fur melting away from his body. Soon a man was on the ground where the wolf had been. A man struggling to take a breath. Wheezing on the ground.

I was like that. So desperate to live.

Jane took a step toward him.

The black wolf spun to confront her, snarling.

Jane lifted her hands. "Easy."

The black wolf stalked toward her — no, *Aidan* stalked toward her. Jane didn't retreat. She locked her knees and stood before him.

Behind him, Quint Laurel wasn't struggling to breathe any longer. He was sprawled on the ground, his body spread before a crypt, slashed and broken, just as he'd left his victims.

"Jane, get away from him!"

Her head jerked to the right. She saw Vincent running toward her. Annette was right behind him. Jane blinked. How had those two gotten together? "I kept the blood down," she whispered. She should be revolted. She *was* but…

But I'm in control now. I can think semi-clearly. And I don't want to hurt Aidan.

So she didn't run…running would have just made his hunting instincts even stronger. If she ran, he'd attack. He was moving toward her so slowly. His head was low to the ground, his body tense.

"Aidan." Jane said his name with longing. "Aidan, I'm so sorry."

He stilled.

"I didn't want it to be this way. I wanted to stay with you, always." She couldn't look away from his eyes. A man's eyes in the face of a beast. "I don't want to hurt you."

Do you want to hurt me? Are you thinking about ripping out my throat, just as you did to Quint Laurel?

"Jane." Annette called her name sharply. "Jane, are you in control?"

She nodded.

"How is she in control?" Annette demanded. "Vincent, what is happening?"

"She fed." He'd stopped a few feet away. Aidan's head swung between Jane and Vincent. "But you didn't kill, did you, Jane?" Vincent sounded proud. "You pulled back. You didn't let the darkness out."

She felt full of darkness right then. Darkness and pain and…power. It pulsed just beneath her skin.

"Her eyes glow like a wolf's," Annette said. "How is that possible?"

A low growl shook Aidan's body. His focus was now completely on Vincent. *Uh, oh.* "He's going to kill you," Jane said softly. "You need to take Annette and you need to get out of here."

"I won't leave you," Vincent yelled back. "I can take you both away from here. He won't hurt you—"

"I don't want to leave him." That truth went straight to her soul. "I always just wanted…to be with Aidan." And she would be with him, until the end. "I'm sorry," she said to Aidan once more. They both knew how this story would end.

Monsters didn't get happy endings, no matter what they wanted to pretend. It just wasn't in the cards for them. "Go," Jane said to

Vincent and Annette. The mark on her side—that stupid burn she'd carried for so long—seemed to ache.

Vincent looped his arms around Annette. They vanished. And Aidan...he turned his glowing eyes back on Jane. She sagged to her knees. A tired smile curved her lips. Aidan crept closer to her. She lifted her arms. "Can I see you as a man? Just once more?"

The wolf stilled.

"While I enjoy your beast," Jane murmured, "it's the man I love. I want to see him again. Can I see him again? Please? Just once more?"

And...the wolf lowered its head. The beast's body shuddered. He gave a pain-filled, desperate cry, one that chilled her already cold skin. The fur slid away from him, seemed to melt. Strong, muscled flesh appeared. Claws vanished and Aidan's hands were pressed to the ground. She saw his wonderful, thick hair. And when he tilted back his head to look at her...a trembling smile curved Jane's lips. "Hello, Aidan."

He rose, not speaking.

Probably because he was trying not to kill her and battling his primal instincts took all of his energy.

"I have control right now," Jane said. "I-I don't know how long it will last, but...but I feel in control. Do you?"

He still didn't speak, but he did take a step toward her.

"I remember trying to breathe at Tulane. Gasping. Vincent..." She remembered his hand on her throat. Jane swallowed. "One minute, I was on that campus, then suddenly, I was in that alley outside of the ME's building. Smoke was all around. You were there. I-I bit you, and I'm sorry."

"Don't be sorry." He was back in the body of a man, but his voice was definitely still beast-like.

He reached out to her. Jane didn't flinch. She didn't try to run. She just...knelt there. Waiting. She'd had a choice to make.

Now he had to make a choice, too. *Kill me. Or love me.*

"You...*still smell like you're mine,*" Aidan rasped.

She wouldn't cry. "And you still look like you're mine. My werewolf. My Aidan." She rose to her feet and stood on her toes. When he didn't attack, Jane pressed her lips to his. "I wish we'd had forever."

"I do, too." He pulled her against him and held her tight.

She heard the rustle of footsteps behind her. Too late.

Aidan...he was distracting me. He was —

"I'm sorry, my Jane."

She tried to yank out of his arms, but he held her too tightly. She caught a fast glimpse of Paris. He had something in his hand. Something—

He injected her.

"Told you that would come in handy," Paris muttered.

Jane's veins began to feel cold. Her knees buckled, but Aidan scooped her into his arms.

"I love you, Jane," Aidan said. And it was the man talking, not the beast.

The man killed me?

Her lashes slipped closed. At least there was no pain this time. If she was dying again...

At least there is no pain.

CHAPTER EIGHTEEN

Jane looked so helpless.

Aidan swallowed the thick lump in his throat as he stared at her. She was strapped down to an exam table, heavily sedated—sedated enough to knock out a damn elephant. *Or an alpha werewolf.* The vial Paris had taken from Annette had certainly come in handy.

After they'd drugged Jane, he'd brought her back to his home, the estate deep in the swamp. Aidan had only kept his most trusted wolves with him...and a few other *needed* individuals.

Dr. Bob Heider was currently curled over his microscope.

Annette was staring into her scrying mirror.

Paris was staring at Annette.

And the bastard vampire Vincent...well...Garrison had a gun pointed dead-center at the vamp's heart. A gun that was loaded with wooden bullets.

"The gun isn't necessary," Vincent stated for what had to be the twentieth time. "I'm not here to hurt anyone. As I told you from the beginning, I want to help Jane."

Something inside of Aidan just broke at the guy's words. He flew toward him, caught the vamp's neck in his hands and snarled, "The way you helped her when you broke her neck?"

Vincent blanched. "She was already dying. Did you want me to prolong her suffering? You couldn't get to her, you were barely breathing yourself! And your blood kept...changing her. I was afraid of what she'd become if she took more. I didn't want her in agony, I didn't want—"

Snap.

It was too easy to break Vincent's neck.

Aidan released a long, hard breath.

"Did that make you feel better?" Paris asked him, voice curious.

He considered it. "A little bit." Aidan motioned to Garrison. "He'll wake up again in a few minutes. That broken neck will heal all too soon, so keep the gun on him."

Garrison nodded. His hold was tight on the weapon. A little too tight. "Don't get trigger happy on me yet," Aidan warned him. "The vamp came to us willingly. And he's provided us with a lot of information about Jane."

Like the fact that Jane hadn't been able to keep down bagged blood or human blood that had come straight from the source. She'd only been able to take werewolf blood.

And...according to Vincent...the fact that Jane hadn't killed when she'd taken that blood meant her humanity remained. At least some of it. Jane wasn't a killing machine.

Neither am I.

Because while the beast had raged, while the wolf had snapped and snarled, it hadn't gone for Jane's throat. *Even my beast didn't want to kill her.* The wolf had gone against its natural instincts because Jane...

She still smelled like she was mine. I looked at her and thought...Mine.

Was that how it had been for his father? Was that why he hadn't been able to stop Aidan's mother?

Am I just fucking fooling myself? Prolonging all of our pain? He raked his hand through his hair. "Fuck me. What the hell does 'the end' even mean?" Aidan demanded. "Why was it branded on her?"

Garrison pointed toward Vincent's slumped form. "That's probably something you should've asked him."

"Yes, well, I will." He paced back to Jane's side. Her cheeks had a little color in them. Her hair had been washed, her body washed—all of the blood cleaned away. *I did that. I knew she'd want to be clean.* He'd dressed her, too. Carefully. Tenderly. Because she was still his Jane.

She always would be.

"Her blood has mutated," Bob said as he straightened away from the microscope Aidan had brought in for the doctor to use. "But it's…it's not like other vamp blood that I've seen."

Aidan curled his fingers around Jane's hand. "What does that mean?"

"It means…shit, it means her cells actually look like—like *yours*."

Aidan kept his hold on Jane, but his gaze zeroed in on the ME. "Explain."

"It's like a weird mix. Half vamp, half werewolf. I'm seeing traits of both when I examine her cells. It makes no sense to me. I mean, she has to be one or the other right?" Dr. Bob yanked off his glasses and pinched the bridge of his nose. "I am so working above my pay grade here."

Annette gave a low gasp, and the mirror she'd been holding slipped from her fingers. It hit the floor and splintered, heavy, dark chunks flying in every direction. "You did this."

Aidan blinked.

Vincent moaned. "Fucking bastard…"

Annette hurried toward Aidan, carefully stepping around the chunks of broken glass. She pointed at him. "You changed Jane."

"No, that would be the jerk-off vampire—"

"He was right," Annette cut in, shaking her head. Her finger jabbed into his chest. "You had given Jane your blood. But Jane wasn't a werewolf when you did that, and she wasn't human, either. I saw…in the mirror…*you* changed her."

Aidan's muscled tensed.

"Ripped sheets," Annette whispered. "In my mirror, I saw Jane's hands become claws as she gripped the sheets and gave herself to you."

Aidan felt heat sting his cheeks. "That would be damn personal, Annette. Do you always see people having sex in that mirror?"

"Jane was already different then. A wolf had started to rise within her. You suspected…that was why you came to me."

Aidan glanced back at Jane. "She'd been injured so badly. I was just happy to have her with me. She…she seemed a little different." He winced at that. "Her senses were sharper. She was stronger, but I…I thought it was just temporary."

"You can't fuck with nature," Vincent snarled. The vamp was back in fighting form. The broken neck hadn't slowed him down nearly long enough. "When you do…bad things happen. Why do you think most vamps are so screwed up? They aren't supposed to be *made*. Humans can't handle the transformation. They go wild with the feelings and the needs exploding in them. Vamps are supposed to be born. Like me. Like Jane. Born and then *guided* so that we can keep our control. I'm Jane's guide. I'm here to help her."

A born vampire had a guide? "Where the hell was my mother's guide?" The question ripped out of him, the bitterness and pain never far from the surface. "When she was killing my family, where was her guide, huh? *Where?*"

Sadness flashed on Vincent's face. "I don't know. There...there aren't many born left. Until Jane, I was worried there wouldn't be more. Vampires aren't all evil, despite what you think. I've tried hard all these years to fight my own darkness. To help others. That's why I'm here now. I will do *anything* to see that Jane makes it through this change."

"That's why we're all here," Aidan muttered, his fingers still holding tight to Jane. "To make sure..." He cleared his throat and focused on Bob Heider. "I knew when I pulled you out of that fire that you'd come in handy."

Bob's eyes narrowed as he slipped his glasses back into place. "Are you saying you didn't just save me because it was the *right* thing to do?"

Aidan stared back at him.

"*Liar...*" It was a soft whisper, so faint that, even with Aidan's enhanced hearing, he almost missed it. But—

His gaze whipped down to Jane.

Her lips moved again, the smallest of motions.

"*Liar...*" Her voice was louder. "You saved...him...because it was...right."

"She shouldn't be awake." Paris grabbed another drug-filled syringe and hurried toward them. "She shouldn't be —"

Jane's lashes lifted. She stared up at Aidan and said, "If he knocks me out again, we're going to...have issues."

"Stop, Paris." Aidan couldn't look away from her eyes. His beautiful Jane. "Are you...in control?"

"Are...you?"

"Yes."

Her lips curved. "Then so am I."

Without thought, he bent and pressed his lips to hers. "I missed you," he whispered against her mouth.

Missed her so much that his entire word had gone dark.

"Uh, excuse me." Dr. Bob's voice — though not as pompous as normal — filled the room. "About these tests..."

"The tests aren't needed now," Annette announced, as if giving a decree. "Aidan changed her. He didn't know it at the time but giving Jane his blood...it made her different."

Aidan was trying to figure all of this shit out. Staring into Jane's dark eyes, he said, "You can only feed from werewolves."

A furrow appeared between her brows.

Annette stepped toward the exam table. She smoothed back Jane's hair. "You can only feed on them because you need the blood of your own kind to survive. To give you power."

But Jane was shaking her head. "Werewolves aren't just going to let me drink from them..."

"Not them," Aidan stated. "Me. You drink from me."

Fear filled her eyes. "I don't want to hurt you. If I lose control...I-I will."

I won't let you lose control. "That's why when you have your first drink, we'll do it with these straps in place." His hand moved to the metal strap that slid over her chest. "Just as a precaution."

"But your wolf..."

"I will keep him controlled." And if he didn't, well, he'd make sure Paris was close with his drugs. Still, there was something else Aidan needed to test out before he was sure they were in safe waters. "Paris, come closer to Jane."

Paris inched closer.

Jane tensed.

"Smell her," Aidan ordered.

Jane's nose scrunched. "That is so—"

Paris leaned in close to Jane and inhaled.

"Do you want to kill her?" Aidan asked, then held his breath. Just because his beast was in control around Jane, it didn't mean that other werewolves would react the same way. In the cemetery, Quint Laurel had certainly been desperate to get at her...but the young alpha had already been in a killing fury. Had he attacked because Jane was in his way? Because he recognized her and wanted her dead? Or had it been something else entirely?

If her vamp scent was going to send his wolves into attack mode, then Aidan would have to leave the city with Jane. There would be no other choice.

"I don't want to kill her." Paris seemed surprised. "Didn't want to kill her at the cemetery, either. She...kind of smells like apples."

"And lavender," Garrison blurted.

Aidan's gaze shot to the younger wolf.

"That's...how Jane has always smelled," Garrison's cheeks flushed. "Apples and lavender. She's still the same."

No, she wasn't. She'd changed, and there was no going back. *Just as my mother changed.* But this time, things were different. Aidan was using science and magic and even his own blood to ensure that he didn't lose Jane to the darkness. He wasn't his father. She wasn't his mother.

Their ending didn't have to be the same.

"Everyone...get the fuck out," Aidan ordered.

People got the fuck out—fast. And they sealed the door shut behind them. Aidan stayed at the side of that exam table, unable to take his eyes off Jane. He'd had the exam room put in because he'd needed a place to patch up injured wolves. He'd never realized Jane would be in that little room.

"Am I really...some half wolf, half vampire thing?"

He put his hands on either side of her head and leaned closer to her. "You are Mary Jane Hart. The woman I love. Always. The most beautiful person I have ever seen."

Some of the pain vanished from her eyes.

"I want you to drink from me, Mary Jane."

He could see the tips of her fangs peeking out behind her lips. Earlier, Vincent had warned him that when Jane woke up, she'd be hungry. He'd said that her hunger would be the strongest during the first few weeks as her body fully adjusted to her new state.

But Vincent doesn't know anything about werewolf blood.

"Don't let me hurt you," Jane said, voice trembling.

"That's why we have the straps, remember?" He gave her a smile. Then Aidan lifted his right wrist and put it at Jane's mouth. Her eyes were on him. She licked his inner wrist, just over his pulse point, then she bit him.

There wasn't pain from her bite. A hot lancing seemed to pierce his skin and then pleasure flooded Aidan's veins. Thick and wild and consuming, the pleasure had his body stiffening, his cock hardening, his heartbeat racing—

Jane pushed his hand away. "I hurt you."

Hurt sure wasn't the word.

"Aidan, I'm so sorry."

He grabbed the bar across her chest and yanked it away. The heavy steel broke with a hard groan. Then he tore away the bar that covered her hips. "I want more."

"You…what?"

He pulled her up. Stared into her eyes. "I like your bite, Mary Jane."

"That's…that's not possible."

He was pretty sure that anything was possible, with her.

She swung her legs around to dangle off the table, and he stepped between her spread thighs. He curled his hands around her hips, bringing her closer to him, and then he offered her his neck. It was a move that an alpha werewolf was never supposed to make to another. It was submissive. It was…

Me, offering myself to her.

Her mouth pressed to his throat. She licked him again and then she bit him.

The pleasure was even more intense this time. Firing his blood, making him shudder and quake. His cock jerked toward her, wanting inside her body, and he wasn't about to stop. Perhaps, after everything that had happened between them, he should have used finesse. Charm.

But, no, *because* of everything, the moment was too elemental. The desire too fierce. He needed to take her, to claim her, to know that Jane—his Jane—was still with him. Always.

Forever.

His claws shredded the pajama pants he'd put on her so carefully. He ripped away her panties. And he shoved down his jeans so his cock could be free.

She kept drinking from him.

He kept needing her.

He positioned his cock at the entrance to her body. She was wet, eager for him. He tightened his hold on Jane, and then Aidan thrust deep.

She pulled her mouth away from his throat, gasping.

"More, Jane," Aidan said. He didn't know if he was talking about her bite or the pleasure they were giving each other. He just knew it couldn't end. They couldn't end.

This wasn't the end.

He thrust into her, faster, harder, and when he couldn't get deep enough, he picked her up off that table and held her easily in his arms. He lifted her up and down, working her along the length of his cock.

He stepped on something sharp — probably a chunk of that fucking mirror — and just ignored the quick flash of pain. Again and again, he thrust into Jane.

She came for him. He felt the contractions of her sex around him. She cried out with her climax, and he was right behind her. Aidan emptied himself into Jane, coming hard and strong, coming until he could barely breathe because his need for her was so powerful.

And in the aftermath, his heartbeat slowly returned to normal. His shaking hands lowered Jane back to the exam table.

"You didn't kill me," Jane said.

"The pleasure almost killed me," Aidan confessed.

She smiled at him. A smile that lit her gorgeous eyes and made his chest ache. They'd done it. They'd survived the storm. Survived the hell that came for them.

And they were stronger now. They'd stay stronger.

"I love you, Jane." He would fight with every breath in his body to protect her.

Today. Tomorrow. *Forever.*

***

It was hours later when Annette slipped into the lab room in the depths of the alpha's house. Jane and Aidan were upstairs, no doubt lost in each other's arms. They thought the danger had passed.

She wasn't so sure.

"I think this is a really bad idea," Bob Heider muttered from behind her. "The last thing I want to do is piss off Aidan Locke."

Her gaze slid over the floor — the broken pieces of her mirror. And...

Aidan's blood. She knew it. Just the way she'd always known certain things. Annette picked up that bloody chunk of glass. The instant she touched it, her hand chilled.

It's not over. Not yet.

"You need to run tests on this blood," she said, giving the chunk of glass to Bob. "Run the tests and then tell me what you find — "

"*No.*" Not Bob's voice. The growled word had been far too dark and deep for Bob. *Paris.* Shit. She peeked to the left and saw that Paris was standing in the shadows of the room. He'd been watching them the whole time, and now his gaze was on the glass. Very slowly, his golden stare rose until he was looking straight at Bob. "You tell *me* what you find."

Oh, no. This wasn't going to be good.

Because Annette strongly suspected that Jane wasn't the only one changing. Aidan had given his blood to a vampire. He'd bonded with her. His wolf…it hadn't attacked Jane. An alpha *should* have attacked her. The difference in her blood — that mix of wolf — might be enough to confuse the others in the pack so that they wouldn't attack, but an alpha wolf should have still felt the primal urge to kill her.

Only…he hadn't. And he hadn't killed Vincent, either.

Because Aidan is changing, too.

The rules of the paranormal world were changing. And she was very, very afraid of what might come next…

The end.

For them all.

***

Jane rolled over in bed and smiled up at Aidan. She'd thought her chance with him was over — that her life was over.

And, well, her human life was gone. She was still getting used to her fangs — if she wasn't careful, she'd bite her own lip. And the heightened senses made things a little confusing but…

I have Aidan.

For her, having Aidan was what mattered. He was at her side. He had her back. Just as she had his. Their bond was so deep. Deeper than blood.

Deeper than family.

"Why do you look sad?" Aidan asked her.

Jane blinked quickly. She'd thought he was sleeping. "I was...thinking about my brother."

"Don't."

She gave a bitter laugh. "Not that easy." And this was the hard part. "Aidan, I know you plan to kill him."

"Because he fucking shot you, yes, I—"

"Don't."

He drew in a deep breath.

"Let me handle him. He's my family. My responsibility." Even though she didn't know what the hell she was going to do about Drew. Not yet.

Kill him?

No. Because while she might be a vampire, while she might not have total control of her new self yet, Jane knew she wasn't a murderer.

She was still a cop. And her job was to uphold the law.

To protect.

"He won't hurt you again, Jane," Aidan promised.

"No, he won't." She'd make sure of that. She leaned forward and pressed a kiss to Aidan's lips. "You know...things can be easier now."

"Easier?" Doubt was heavy in his voice.

"Just think...with all of this extra strength and power, I'll be able to track down criminals twice as fast as I did before."

He groaned.

"And I pity the dumbass who tries to resist arrest with me," she added.

"Jane..."

"What? The world doesn't have to be all doom and gloom." It *wasn't*. She'd survived her change, she was with Aidan and, for the most part, she still felt like her old self. "I will use this change to help me. To help others."

Because despite Annette's orders, Jane didn't intend to stop playing hero. Not now...maybe not ever.

Aidan stared at her, silent.

"There are some things that you just can't change," she said.

His expression softened. "No, I guess you can't." His fingers slid into her hair and he pulled her down for a kiss. "I love you."

And she would always love him.

Her werewolf.

Her partner.

Her mate.

The End

###

The final book in the Blood and Moonlight trilogy, BITTER BLOOD, will be available in spring of 2016! Aidan and Jane will be back one last time...and the changes coming will blow their world apart.

A NOTE FROM THE AUTHOR

Thank you so much for taking the time to read BETTER OFF UNDEAD. I hope that you enjoyed the story.

If you'd like to stay updated on my releases and sales, please join my newsletter list www.cynthiaeden.com/newsletter/. You can also check out my Facebook page www.facebook.com/cynthiaedenfanpage. I love to post giveaways over at Facebook!

Again, thank you for reading BETTER OFF UNDEAD.

Best,

Cynthia Eden
www.cynthiaeden.com

ABOUT THE AUTHOR

Award-winning author Cynthia Eden writes dark tales of paranormal romance and romantic suspense. She is a *New York Times, USA Today, Digital Book World,* and *IndieReader* best-seller. Cynthia is also a three-time finalist for the RITA® award. Since she began writing full-time in 2005, Cynthia has written over fifty novels and novellas.

Cynthia is a southern girl who loves horror movies, chocolate, and happy endings. More information about Cynthia and her books may be found at: http://www.cynthiaeden.com or on her Facebook page at: http://www.facebook.com/cynthiaedenfanpage. Cynthia is also on Twitter at http://www.twitter.com/cynthiaeden.

HER WORKS

Paranormal romances by Cynthia Eden:
- BOUND BY BLOOD (Bound, Book 1)
- BOUND IN DARKNESS (Bound, Book 2)
- BOUND IN SIN (Bound, Book 3)
- BOUND BY THE NIGHT (Bound, Book 4)
- BOUND IN DEATH (Bound, Book 5)
- THE WOLF WITHIN (Purgatory, Book 1)
- MARKED BY THE VAMPIRE (Purgatory, Book 2)
- CHARMING THE BEAST (Purgatory, Book 3)
- DEAL WITH THE DEVIL (Purgatory, Book 4)

Other paranormal romances by Cynthia Eden:
- A VAMPIRE'S CHRISTMAS CAROL
- BLEED FOR ME
- BURN FOR ME (Phoenix Fire, Book 1)
- ONCE BITTEN, TWICE BURNED (Phoenix Fire, Book 2)
- PLAYING WITH FIRE (Phoenix Fire, Book 3)

- ANGEL OF DARKNESS (Fallen, Book 1)
- ANGEL BETRAYED (Fallen, Book 2)
- ANGEL IN CHAINS (Fallen, Book 3)
- AVENGING ANGEL (Fallen, Book 4)
- IMMORTAL DANGER
- NEVER CRY WOLF
- A BIT OF BITE (Free Read!!)
- ETERNAL HUNTER (Night Watch, Book 1)
- I'LL BE SLAYING YOU (Night Watch, Book 2)
- ETERNAL FLAME (Night Watch, Book 3)
- HOTTER AFTER MIDNIGHT (Midnight, Book 1)
- MIDNIGHT SINS (Midnight, Book 2)
- MIDNIGHT'S MASTER (Midnight, Book 3)
- WHEN HE WAS BAD (anthology)
- EVERLASTING BAD BOYS (anthology)
- BELONG TO THE NIGHT (anthology)

List of Cynthia Eden's romantic suspense titles:
- WATCH ME (Dark Obsession, Book 1)
- WANT ME (Dark Obsession, Book 2)
- NEED ME (Dark Obsession, Book 3)
- BEWARE OF ME (Dark Obsession, Book 4)
- MINE TO TAKE (Mine, Book 1)
- MINE TO KEEP (Mine, Book 2)
- MINE TO HOLD (Mine, Book 3)

- MINE TO CRAVE (Mine, Book 4)
- MINE TO HAVE (Mine, Book 5)
- FIRST TASTE OF DARKNESS
- SINFUL SECRETS
- DIE FOR ME (For Me, Book 1)
- FEAR FOR ME (For Me, Book 2)
- SCREAM FOR ME (For Me, Book 3)
- DEADLY FEAR (Deadly, Book 1)
- DEADLY HEAT (Deadly, Book 2)
- DEADLY LIES (Deadly, Book 3)
- ALPHA ONE (Shadow Agents, Book 1)
- GUARDIAN RANGER (Shadow Agents, Book 2)
- SHARPSHOOTER (Shadow Agents, Book 3)
- GLITTER AND GUNFIRE (Shadow Agents, Book 4)
- UNDERCOVER CAPTOR (Shadow Agents, Book 5)
- THE GIRL NEXT DOOR (Shadow Agents, Book 6)
- EVIDENCE OF PASSION (Shadow Agents, Book 7)
- WAY OF THE SHADOWS (Shadow Agents, Book 8)

Made in the USA
Las Vegas, NV
19 January 2022